ALL YOUR FAULT

JEWEL LAKES SERIES BOOK FIVE

CLAIRE WILDER

ALSO BY CLAIRE WILDER
clairewilder.com/books

MAILING LIST
clairewilder.com/subscribe

READER GROUP
facebook.com/groups/wilderwomenreaders

SOCIAL MEDIA LINKS

ABOUT THIS BOOK

He's everything I shouldn't want.

When my husband got sick, he made me promise to find someone else when he was gone. On my first attempt, I crashed and burned. So I swore never to try again, focusing only on my foodie blog and my girls. But when pictures of me on an accidental non-date with my friend's brother—serious curmudgeon and yes, seriously hot single dad Will Archer—explode my blog hits, I have to rethink my strategy.

Getting sexy, surly Will to pose as my fake boyfriend could be the thing to course correct my struggling blog. But how can I ask him when our shaky friendship is clearly hiding something much deeper? Something neither one of us wants to admit is even there?

All Your Fault is the conclusion to the Jewel Lakes Series: a single parent, age-gap romance with a guaranteed HEA.

PROLOGUE
MICHELLE

This prologue appears as the epilogue at the conclusion of Twice Burned (Jewel Lakes Book Four)

"Mom! Push!"

I looked up from my phone. My eight-old, Macy, had slowed nearly to a stop on her swing. She'd asked me for a push a full minute ago. *Shit*.

"Sorry, sweetie," I said.

But my sister Reese was already striding over. "I got it."

"Thanks," I said, guilt running through me. I shoved my phone in my pocket, cursing that little rectangle once again for having such a hold on me. I needed to be on it to run my foodie blog, Bella Eats, but I didn't need to be on it 24/7, especially not here.

I was at Millerville Central Park with my two daughters and older sister while we waited for an appointment for Emma, my ten-year-old. The park was huge, occupying a whole block of downtown, and even though office buildings lined all four sides, the park—with its grassy, lightly treed landscaping, water feature, and elaborate play equipment—felt more like the rest of the county than a spot in the middle of its biggest town.

We came here a lot, even when we weren't waiting for appointments. But no matter how many times I came, every time I stepped into this place, I was still reminded of the first time we came, almost exactly one year ago.

We'd been here for our first appointment with this same neurologist, to get test results for Emma. She'd been having headaches and I'd been in a panic; sure it was a sign she'd inherited Frayne's Syndrome—the fatal illness that Joe had been diagnosed with and would have passed from if he hadn't died on the job. Our family doctor had explained it was unlikely Emma had the condition, as she wasn't also experiencing seizures. But tests were required to be sure, and to ensure that the fatal component of the syndrome, a deterioration of the lining of the brain, wasn't present.

Reese was still in New York then, and I'd asked my friend Hank—Joe's best friend, who'd been with him when he died—to meet me at the park at the last minute. I framed it as a catch-up—we hadn't seen each other in a while. Though really, I was looking for moral support. But Hank hadn't come alone. He'd brought his older brother, Will.

A spread of heat ran through me even now, a year later, thinking of that chance encounter.

We'd been early, just like today, and after a while, Hank had to go. Will Archer—a total stranger, and kind of a surly, grumpy one at that—must have sensed my nerves, because he'd offered to stay with me and the girls.

Will was a natural with them—he had two girls of his

own, he'd told me. Teenagers. He chased Emma and Macy around, completely ignoring his constantly buzzing phone while he made them shriek with laughter. And he'd talked to me about everything and nothing all at once—tussling with me over things so ridiculous I'd had to laugh. I never would have thought I could laugh that day, but he'd somehow completely distracted me from one of the most terrifying appointments of my life.

He'd stayed right up until it was time for us to go in.

"Thank you," I'd said to him at the door of the office building when it was time to leave. I'd been overwhelmed with gratitude at this stranger's kindness.

He'd nodded, suddenly serious. I never told him the specifics of why we were there, but he'd said, "I hope you get the answers you're looking for," as if he knew.

I had gotten the answers I'd been looking for—Emma's tests were all negative. Though we wouldn't know for sure until she turned thirteen, when we could test for certain genetic markers to tell us for certain, it looked like we were out of the woods. As I drove back home, sobbing grateful tears over the results with the girls asking why I was smiling and crying at the same time, I couldn't help but think Will had been our lucky charm.

When I told Reese about him later, she'd asked me why I hadn't gotten his number—or at least reached out to him through Hank.

I'd shaken my head, shocked. "Why would I ruin that perfect day?"

Besides, she knew all about the relationship I'd attempted after Joe and what a disaster that had been. And she knew about my intentions to never wade in those waters again.

And I'd never seen Will again, anyway.

I scanned the green space now for Emma, spotting her over by the water feature. She was pulling her mittens off, just what I'd asked her not to do.

I sighed, but couldn't help smiling. Emma was definitely the more defiant of my two girls; the one more like me. She even had my olive skin and brown curls. Would she ever do something as ludicrous as trying to make a living out of a food blog when she grew up, I wondered?

At the reminder, I pulled my phone out once more, checking the notifications on my most recent post, which I'd very cleverly called *APPLE PIE IN THE SKY*. Nothing new in the past two minutes.

"That high enough?" Reese asked Macy, who squealed in approval.

Reese jogged back to where I stood. "You okay?" she asked.

"Totally," I said, shoving my phone back in my pocket. And I was, all things considered. Just fine. Especially since Reese had moved out here this summer.

I felt a surge of gratitude for my older sister. We'd been close as kids, but our lives had diverged after high school when I met my husband Joe, and started a family. There were several years where we only saw each other a few times a year. But when Joe died in a blaze six years ago, Reese had come right back to my side, as if nothing had changed. She never once mentioned the fact that over all those years I'd gotten absorbed in my own life. She was just there for me when I'd needed her. A shoulder to cry on—a rock when I was still tumbling around in a river of grief.

"What time do you have to go in again?" she asked.

"Not for a little while." Our appointment wasn't actually

for another hour. I always built in a buffer when we came here, as the kids always begged to come to the park, which was right next door. But I didn't want Reese to feel obliged to wait.

"Reese," I said, "Seriously, you don't have to wait for us."

"It's fine!" she exclaimed. "I'll run some errands in a few."

"Promise I'll get my car in shape soon," I said. It had been making weird noises, and I hadn't wanted to risk it conking out on the way to this appointment. But I also didn't exactly have ample room in the budget to get it looked at.

"I said it's fine," Reese said, elbowing me. I knew she meant it. Back when the girls were young and Reese would visit, helping out with everything from babysitting to housecleaning, Joe used to ask me how anyone survived without a big sister. "I honestly don't know," I'd told him. Reese was everything to me, even if at that time we didn't see much of each other.

"Anyway, if you don't mind, I think I'll go tell Emma to put her mittens back on," Reese said now.

I followed her gaze. Even from here I could see Emma's hands were now bright pink with cold. Guilt shot through me for the second time in as many minutes—I should have told her to put them back on right away. The water was only a few inches deep, and Emma was old enough to know not to go in, but I should have said something, instead of staring at my damn phone, anxious to see how my latest blog post was doing.

Reese must have seen it on my face, because she said, "Hey, I'm sure she's fine, it's just the perfect excuse to check out those hot dads next to her."

"Oh my God, Reese," I said, laughing.

A few feet from Emma there were a couple of guys watching a toddler by the smaller climbing structure. The one facing in our direction was good-looking: tall, well-built, dark hair, dark scruff—exactly Reese's type.

But my eyes fell on the one with his back to me. I couldn't see his face, but he was just as nicely built as the other guy, with broad shoulders, salt and pepper hair, and a well-tailored wool coat over dark slacks. He bent over just at that moment to right the toddler, who'd fallen over.

It hit me like a rush of air—that guy reminded me of Will Archer. I would have kept staring if I didn't see Emma, waving wildly at me, her hands now in mittens. Her expression was an exaggerated *are you happy now?*

I gave her a thumbs up and she ran off with Macy, who'd followed Reese over there. The mittens would be off again in no time, I knew, but it was the effort that counted.

When I looked back toward where the men had been standing I saw they'd separated—the dark haired one was now chatting with Reese while the girls threw pebbles in the canal next to them. Reese tossed her sandy blonde hair over her shoulder as she laughed at something the guy said. My older sister couldn't have looked more different than me—she'd inherited Mom's Irish coloring while Dad's full-blooded Italian features went to me.

But the other guy was gone, along with his son.

My heart sank a little, which was ridiculous. I'd only been curious about him because he'd reminded me of someone else. A man I didn't even know.

My phone buzzed in my hand, startling me. I'd been lost in thought and the screen had locked. But the banner that popped up said *One new comment*. I tapped it open, holding my breath.

. . .

BellaEatsFan7: OMG I'm so sorry. My heart just breaks for you.

The air exploded out of me like a popped balloon, my stomach sinking with it.

How? How had this person taken this happy little post and found something to feel sorry for me in it? I scanned the words I'd published, looking for anything I might have let slip. I hadn't said a word about going to an appointment with the pediatric neurologist like I normally would have. I didn't mention Joe's birthday having passed last week.

Then I saw it. It was the tiniest thing, something only my longtime readers would pick up on. I'd mentioned how I'd probably take this pie to Thanksgiving dinner next month and had written, 'For most people, Thanksgiving is a special time for being with the people closest to you.'

Any reader of my blog would know that in my case, I wasn't most people. My girls and I had a gaping hole in our family where Joe had been. With all my previous posts as evidence, it was as good as stitched into every word I'd written.

Angry now—not at the reader, but at myself—I got up and walked over to my girls, who'd migrated to the play equipment.

"Is it time yet, Mom?" Emma asked when I reached them.

"Not yet," I said, getting down and pulling both girls into a hug.

This was what mattered. That both girls were healthy and happy.

Emma was the worrier. My chest twanged as I pulled back and looked at her. "Are you okay?"

I nodded. "Never better."

"Does that mean we still have time to play?" Macy asked.

"Yes."

"Come on Emma!" she yelled at her sister, who after one last curious look at me, followed Macy in a dash over to the climbing dome.

When I stood I saw Reese was on her way back to me, her face lit up. Her chat with that guy must have gone well.

"I'm going to go," she said as she approached.

I pasted on a smile. I didn't need to ruin her good mood. "On your own?"

"Yes," she laughed." Then she quirked a brow, inspecting me. Sisters always knew. "You okay?"

"Totally," I said.

She folded her arms.

"It's nothing. Just another pity comment. It's fine though, not that bad." I waved it off as if it was nothing, even though it was one more kick in my side. Besides, saying it sounded ungrateful. The commenter had cared enough to say something nice. I should take it that way.

"Okay," said Reese. She glanced over her shoulder at the guy she'd been talking to. He was on his phone now. She was distracted. Happy.

"Did you have a nice chat with Mr. Hot Dad?"

"Yes I did, thank you very much. That was his nephew, actually. And I may or may not have given him my number."

I smiled, ruefully. "Maybe I should put a hot guy on my blog; maybe that would make my readers happy."

I hadn't meant to say that out loud, but Reese's eyebrows went up. "That's not a bad idea, Mich."

"What? I was kidding, Reese. That's a terrible idea!"

"No, really. Didn't that engagement ring Steve gave you get you a spike in page views?"

She was right. I'd only worn the ring for a couple of weeks before I knew there was no way I could go through with marrying the man I'd tried to be with after Joe. I'd vowed then never to wear another one. Who could ever live up to Joe? But in the short frame of time I'd worn the ring, one of my hawk-eyed readers had spotted it on my hand in a photo of me chopping red peppers.

"Your readers really went for it, as I recall," Reese said.

They really had—the comments had been endless.

OMG are you ENGAGED!?!

I spy future happiness, finally!

I harrumphed. "I never meant to show it to them. I didn't want anyone to see it. It's how I knew I had to call it off."

"Yeah, but think of how your readers would react if they saw you dating again?"

"But Reese," I said now, unable to hide the disappointment in my voice. "I want people excited about the food, not my personal life." It had been a problem I'd been chewing on for a long time now—that people seemed to care more about my life than the food I shared.

But after saying it, I immediately felt ungrateful. I should be happy to have readers, period. To make any kind of money off my blog, no matter how meagre.

Maybe I'd never be known for the food posts on my foodie blog. Maybe they weren't good enough, and I should just lean into the personal stuff. But I wasn't the same person who started that blog. I wasn't even the same person who kept it going after Joe's death. My girls and I had a good life together now. Sure, I still stressed about money, and the girls not having a dad, and all the million other things people stress out about. But I wasn't the tragic figure I'd become on Bella Eats. Moreover, I didn't want to be known that way. I wanted only to share my love of food with my readers. My quest for the perfect pancetta. The most melt-in-your-mouth eggplant parmesan.

I didn't want to continue to feel like I was monetizing my grief.

"Well then... what about starting fresh?" Reese said now. "Maybe you should think about some of those other things you used to talk about. Selling grandma's tomato sauce. Starting a restaurant!"

I looked at my sister, my heart hurting. "Those were just fantasies, Reese," I said. "I need to build on the base I already have."

"I could get you a job at Gastronomique..."

Reese was a server at the fanciest restaurant in the county. I smiled, trying to make it reach my eyes. "I love you, Reese. I do. But I'll be okay."

I would be too. I'd figure this out like I always did.

"Anyway, you should go," I said. "We're going to go upstairs in a minute." We weren't, but I could tell she was sticking around for me.

"Okay."

After we hugged and said our goodbyes, I stood there a moment, looking out at the girls, reassuring myself things would be just fine.

Then I heard a strange noise behind me. A deep voice, going, "Vrrrrrooom!"

I turned. Salt-and-pepper hot dad was still here, flying his toddler around only a few yards away.

But now I could see his face.

My stomach dropped.

He looked up, and our eyes locked. He slowed to a stop, looking as surprised as I felt.

"Michelle?"

This wasn't just a guy who looked like Will Archer.
It *was* Will Archer.

1

WILL

Well, holy shit.

Only a moment ago, talking with my friend Eli, I'd been thinking about the last time I spent any time in this park.

"Buddy—you okay?" Eli had eyed me with active concern.

Eli was my divorce buddy. As in, we'd met in the waiting room of our shared lawyer's office last year and spent our time griping about our respective marriage breakdowns.

"Yeah. Fine. Just got all this work stuff on my mind," I said. It wasn't a lie. I was at this all-day symposium here in Millerville when I had a shit-ton to do back at my office in Barkley Falls town hall.

It wasn't the whole truth. But what was I supposed to say?

Whenever I go by this damn park I look for a woman I met here one time.

It was a ridiculous thought. I'd been to this park a dozen times before meeting her. I'd written a boring-ass report about its irrigation systems for my work as Town Manager where we were thinking about implementing something similar.

Not only that, but it wasn't my habit to be thinking of women at all—at least not more than as friends or in passing.

I made sure of that.

And yet, like a mirage in a goddamn desert, here she was, Michelle Franco.

A breeze blew between us and the maple tree behind her came alive, its orange leaves whirling. The same breeze lifted a strand of that thick, curly dark hair that spilled over her shoulder like a waterfall.

"Hi," was all she said. She blinked, her lashes flashing ink-black against her cheek.

Suddenly, I had the horrifying thought that maybe this wasn't Michelle Franco. Maybe Michelle Franco was some messed-up figment of my imagination. Maybe that day in the park with my brother a year ago had been my head messing with me, showing me a picture of what I once would have thought was the perfect woman. It made sense—that was right around the time I'd inked my long-overdue divorce papers and swore I'd never go near another woman.

She still hadn't said anything else. A strange squeaking sound came from somewhere nearby. I hoped to hell it wasn't me.

Finally, she spoke. "Nice to see you, Will."

I let out a breath. "Yeah," I said. "You too."

Damn, I wasn't sure I could be any more awkward.

"Who's your friend?" she asked.

For a long moment I was confused. I turned to look toward where Eli stood talking on the phone, gesticulating angrily. By the way his face had turned stormy when he'd looked at his phone, I'd assumed the call was from his ex. I'd taken his nephew Jack—the whole reason we'd met at this park on my work break—to give him some space.

Jack.

I looked down. I was still holding Jack. Sideways. "Oh, shit."

So that's where those noises were coming from.

I turned Jack upright, setting him on his feet. "Sorry, guy."

The toddler giggled. Except for being a little red in the face, he looked okay. I hoped.

"Do you often forget you're carrying your child?" Michelle asked.

"He's not—" I began, but her mouth—those soft, plush lips—twisted.

She knew he wasn't mine. We'd talked at length last time about us both having two girls.

With great difficulty, I tore my eyes from her lips. "This is Jack, my buddy Eli's nephew. My girls are a little big for airplane rides."

A lot big actually.

Jack, probably a little disoriented from hanging sideways, tried to take a step, but fell on his butt, giggling. I reached down and helped him to his feet. He made his way over to the sandbox next to us.

"Teenagers, as I remember," she said.

"Almost adults, terrifyingly. Hannah's 18, Remy's 16. And yours are Emma and Macy."

Her eyebrows went up. "Good memory."

"Kids are easy."

"Unlike full-grown people?"

"Exactly."

She was smiling. God I loved her smile.

But I was serious about that—kids *were* easy. They were innocent. Funny. Didn't let you down the way adults did.

"Your girls here with you?" I asked.

"No. I like coming to the playground on my own. Slides are my favorite." She smiled again, and something inside of me unfurled. Fuck again.

"You're funny," I said.

Michelle tipped her chin toward the play equipment. "They're over there." Her smile dipped slightly. "We have another appointment."

That was why she'd been here last time, for an appointment for her daughter.

The laughter that had been rising in me died away as quickly as it had come.

"How's Emma?"

Michelle took a moment to answer. Maybe she was surprised I'd remembered. "She's going to be okay. She doesn't have the illness my husband had."

Her husband. Why the fuck did a spike of jealousy run through me at that word coming from her? For a dead man?

Then I registered what she said. "I didn't know that's what you were looking into," I said, truthfully.

My brother Hank had only recently discovered that his best friend Joe had been sick before he died in that fire. Joe hadn't told him.

"He knew he was going to die anyway," Hank had said over beers last summer. "It's why he went into that burning building so many times. He sacrificed himself to save all those people."

"Would you have done the same thing?" I asked.

"Probably," he'd said. "Would you?"

Years ago, before I was a dad, I would have said yes, no question. But leaving my girls behind like Joe had? Even if they only had a few months left together? I couldn't help thinking about how that had made Michelle feel. Like she'd had no say in it.

"I don't know," I said, feeling shitty about either decision.

I definitely didn't know Michelle had been worried about Emma having the same condition as Joe. I had no idea she'd been going through that that day, just that she looked like she shouldn't be alone, and I'd been more than happy to ignore every obligation I had to make sure she wasn't. I don't know what had come over me that day—I should have left with my brother. But I didn't, and somehow it had been the best couple hours I could remember in years.

A fluke that I obviously couldn't replicate because this time I was being all kinds of awkward.

"Well, she's fine. A little prone to headaches but otherwise okay," Michelle said.

"I'm glad," I said. I really was. I wanted to say something more—it seemed like there was more to that—but it was none of my business.

I checked my phone for the time. I should bring Jack back to Eli and get back upstairs. Half of me was desperate to get the hell out, back to safer territory. Work. More work. Remy for the week, now that Hannah was away at college, and more work.

But the other half wanted to stay exactly on this spot, knowing this time might for sure be the last time I'd see Michelle. It was the same part of me—this stupid, hopeful, naive part I thought I'd buried long ago that squeaked out the thought—*it doesn't have to be.*

I could have stayed here, and asked her more questions. Just like I could have asked my brother for Michelle's number when we'd first met. But I didn't. It was attraction, that was what I told myself last time, and I didn't want to be around anyone I was remotely attracted to unless I could be sure it'd be a one-time thing. And I couldn't be sure of that with Michelle. I sure as hell didn't want to get involved with anyone. Not since my twenty-year marriage had tanked. Painfully.

Just then Jack shrieked. He'd poured sand from a bucket onto his head and was of course trying to get it off his face with sandy hands. I grabbed him, grateful for the distraction, and brushed the sand off his face before he could make it worse. Once he'd calmed down, I hoisted him up on my shoulders.

"Can't get any trouble up there," I said.

Michelle was looking at me curiously.

What the hell was I doing? "I... better get Jack back to his uncle," I said, suddenly wanting to bolt. "I have to get back to work." I looked up to the building where the symposium was happening. A petite blonde woman stood by the front door, tapping into her phone. She looked up and waved, smiling.

"Shit," I said, under my breath, giving a non-committal wave back.

The woman was a staffer at Millerville Town Hall. Something in the planning department. Earlier that morning, when I'd made a dry joke about hyping up ice fishing to keep tourists here over the winter, she'd laughed a little too exuberantly. I'd given her a discrete once-over before reminding myself I restricted soulless flings to out-of-towners. Living in a small town, it was the only way of assuring things wouldn't get complicated.

"You work there?"

"No, I'm the Barkley Falls town manager. I have a... thing here today."

"Thing?" Michelle glanced over at the woman, who chose that minute to flip her weirdly shiny blonde hair over her shoulder.

Shit again.

"I'm at a tourism conference. Symposium. For attracting more tourists."

Good one.

Michelle raised an eyebrow. "Is she a tourist?"

"I almost forgot how funny you were," I said. She'd done this last time, too. Teased me. No, jousted with me. I'd fucking loved it.

This time Michelle laughed. It was a throaty, gorgeous, sound that sent something hot shooting down south.

Luckily, just then, two little girls came running over, shrieking. Michelle's girls. "Mom!" the bigger one—Emma—said. "Macy is *not* letting me tag her every time—"

She stopped talking, staring at me.

"Girls, do you remember Will?" Michelle asked. "He's here with his friend's nephew, Jack. Will, this is Emma. And that's Macy."

I'd forgotten how Emma looked so shockingly like Michelle, with her brown curls and intense, thickly lashed eyes. She had an attitude to match her mom's too, as I remembered.

Emma folded her arms, inspecting me.

Yep.

The younger one, clinging to her mom's leg, was just plain adorable. Big eyes, caramel hair, and an upturned nose. "Hi," Macy said shyly.

"Of course I remember Gemma and Lacey," I said.

Emma smiled but tried to hide it, but Macy laughed exuberantly. "Noooo, *Emma* and *Macy*," she corrected, letting go of her mom and standing with her little hands on her hips.

"That's what I said, Cagney and Lacey!"

Now all three of them laughed, Michelle throwing back her head as she did so. That warmth came back.

Look away. Look anywhere else.

But before I could, Michelle's eyes met mine. My mouth went dry. Her laughter died off, the smile falling off her face once more too. The sensation was so foreign, so alarmingly full-bodied, I froze. Luckily Jack chose that moment to yank a fistful of my hair.

"Ow," I said.

The girls snickered.

"I... should get this guy back before he—ow!" I said again as Jack yanked at another handful of my hair.

"Are you going to swear again?" Emma asked.

"Pardon?" I swung the grabby toddler off my shoulders, holding him against my chest where his arms couldn't reach the top of my head.

"You swore last time we saw you."

"No, I didn't."

"Yes, you did. We got a swear jar when we moved here cause Mom swore so much when she was moving all the boxes in. So if you swear, you have to pay us a dollar."

"Emma!" Michelle said.

"It's alright," I said, still digesting the fact that they'd moved to the area. I glanced at Michelle. I knew last time they'd had to drive from out of town to get to their appointment. I remembered Michelle saying something about traveling to Millerville so they could see the best pediatric neurological specialist in upstate New York.

"Moving sucks," I said. "But it's no excuse for swearing." I shot an exaggeratedly admonishing look at Michelle.

Michelle gawped. I could tell she was trying to keep from laughing.

"Having a swear jar sounds fair," I said. "Damn fair."

Emma and Macy shrieked while I scowled and made a show of pulling out my wallet with my free hand. The girls spent the next few minutes trying to get me to swear again while Michelle watched, lips pinched between her teeth.

Over by the building, the woman tapped at her watch. Shit.

"Girls, Will has to go back to work now," Michelle said. "It'll be our turn to go any second too."

"Bye, Will!" Macy said, running off. Emma only gave me a curt little nod.

"You better go," Michelle said once they'd gone. "She's waiting for you. It was nice to see you again. Say hi to Hank?"

I wanted to say something more, but Jack was making another grab for my hair and Michelle was already walking away.

My stomach sank. "Bye, Michelle."

She turned and gave me a little wave that made my chest clench.

That was it? Would it be the last time I saw her? Or would we run into each other in the grocery store? Make small talk? I had the sudden absurd image of running a hand through her hair. Getting up close and whispering something—what?—in her ear.

I headed over to where Eli was still on the phone on the bench. When he saw me approach, he mumbled something into the phone and ended the call.

"I gotta run," I said, thrusting Jack at him.

Eli took the boy awkwardly, setting him on the bench next to him like he was a backpack or something. The dude had no idea how to handle kids. Luckily Jack seemed unphased.

Then I saw Eli's face. He looked pained. "You okay?"

"Who was that?" he asked, not answering my question.

We both looked over at Michelle, who'd joined her girls on the swings. Her hair flowed out behind her like she was some kind of mermaid.

My stomach did a little lurch. Who was she to me anyway? Not a friend. An acquaintance? That sounded so... distant.

"Friend of my brother's," I landed on. I didn't like that either. It took me out of it.

"You look at all your brother's friends like that? What happened to our pact?"

Heat rose up my neck as I jerked my eyes from Michelle. "It's intact."

The night after Eli had made his first appearance for his divorce hearing, we'd made a half-drunken oath at a bar here in Millerville that we'd rescue each other if we saw the other getting sucked into anything resembling a relationship.

I should have just taken off then—I was going to be late for the session upstairs, and I sure as hell didn't want to talk about Michelle. But Eli looked so stricken, and so thoroughly unsure of what to do with Jack, who was stuffing something in his mouth, that I hung back, gently extracting what turned out to be a stick from Jack's pudgy fingers. "You have anything for him to eat?"

Eli nodded, patting his coat pocket and pulling out a string cheese that looked a little worse for wear.

All Your Fault 23

"Talking to the ex is always rough," I said. Maybe he needed to talk about it.

"It wasn't her," he said, unwrapping the snack.

"What?"

"It was my sister. Our parents' business is going down the tubes."

"I didn't know your parents had a business. I thought your mom—" I cut myself off, but Eli nodded.

"Yeah, she passed, this year," he said, the words slightly choked in his throat. "But she left some weird stuff in her will, apparently. Related to the business."

Then he waved a hand, clearly not wanting to talk after all. "Anyway. Thanks for helping with Jack. You're the only person I know who's any good with kids. Sorry the meet-up was kind of a bust. Family shit, you know?"

I knew about family shit. But I glanced over at Michelle and her girls, still over by the play equipment. "Not a bust," I said before I realized I'd spoken.

After saying goodbye to Eli, who said he was going to camp out at the park specifically to avoid having to head back to his family, I began heading toward the office. The blonde woman was still standing there. It had been a half-hour coffee break, but still, she was clearly willing to be late waiting for me.

Shit. The thought of having to head upstairs with her, be in an elevator, maybe having her sit next to me at the conference...

I veered in the opposite direction, my legs carrying me before I knew what I was doing.

"Hey," I said.

Michelle turned, her gorgeous curls swinging around her shoulder.

I cleared my throat, reached into the breast pocket of my

coat, and pulled out a card and the pen I always kept there. My eyes darted to the woman by the office to make sure she was watching. Then I bent over the card, scribbling a note on the back. "Remy—my youngest—is always bugging me for new babysitting clients. I don't know if you're ever in need, but here's her number. Just in case."

"Oh," she said.

"Also... I'm hoping you don't mind me handing you this card kind of... suggestively."

She blinked. "What?"

I held the card in two fingers, tipped toward her.

"The woman at the door."

She turned to see.

"Don't look!" I said sharply. "It's the same woman from before. I need her to see me interested in someone else."

Michelle's eyes met mine. Some invisible thing crackled between us.

"Just for show," I clarified.

It's nothing. Just nerves.

Something flashed behind Michelle's eyes. Could it be disappointment? Before I could analyze it too much, it was gone. She gave me a smile and took the card. "Alright," she said. "Give me your hand."

I extended my hand to meet hers. When our fingers touched, that warmth from before ignited, sending a tingling down my arm. God fucking help me.

Michelle kept hold of my hand, leaning in toward me, her lips at my ear. "Kiss me," she said.

A strip of heat ripped down my neck, curling in my stomach. "What?"

"On the cheek."

I hesitated, then slid my hand up, gripping her jaw. I

leaned in, pressing my lips to her cheek, as requested. She smelled like... Sweetness. Caramel. Vanilla.

"Will?" Michelle asked, our faces still close.

"Yeah?"

She whispered in my ear: "You owe me."

Even as the sensation of her breath there did dangerous things to my nerve endings, I had to grin. When I looked back at the office building's entrance, the woman was gone, the glass door swishing shut.

"Okay," I said. "I'll ask Remy to give you a discount."

She laughed, and this time, the sound curled down to my goddamned toes.

2

MICHELLE

It may have taken two whole weeks, but I think it was safe to say I'd put Will Archer completely out of my mind.

Mostly.

Sure, it had taken a little effort. And some deliberately applied focus on my blog. It didn't hurt that the girls and I went home to Long Island for a weekend visit, either. My parents were the only thing I missed about New York City. Reese and I were close to them, and we mostly got along swimmingly.

That is if you left out the questions from Mom. Which happened fast this time. We were in the kitchen working on dinner, and the moment I'd finished getting Mom up to date on how the girls were doing, we quickly slid into dangerous conversational territory: me.

She started with the classic Mom questions: *Are you doing okay? Are you eating properly? You look skinny.* I'd laughed at that one. Maybe to Mom I did. But once she was through those, she slipped into what my older brother Pietro used to call CEO mode. Mom had worked at a busy managerial job before she retired early to help me after Joe died. Her favorite question was "What do we need to figure out?" If you answered honestly—and needed the help—she was like a machine, drawing up lists and action items and timelines. I liked figuring things out too, and, though I loved my mom to bits, I didn't always like doing it her way. I needed to do things on my own. My therapist told me it was because I was the baby of the family. It was probably why I'd been the first one out of the three of us to settle down and start a family. But no matter how much I knew it was there, I still wasn't always able to shake that need to do it all myself —even when it was clear I needed help. Even at the worst time of my life, pregnant and newly widowed, I tried to manage on my own. I pushed everyone away, needing to show them how strong I was. I knew it was because if I couldn't show them, how could I believe it myself?

Now, Mom knew better than to press on the issue of how our lives were going. She knew I was competent, and six years on, an experienced single mom.

But on the topic of relationships, she didn't exercise the same restraint.

Today, Mom's questions about my personal life weren't incessant, but they were insistent, and I knew she wouldn't give up this time. Steve and I had split last year, and I'd told Mom I was going to spend the year on my own, not jumping straight into something new. But that year was up, and any day now I'd have to tell her the truth—that the year on my own had galvanized my private decision that there would be no one after Steve. That I planned on raising the girls as a strong and single woman.

The only problem was, if I told her, that made it official. And that meant it was official that I was ignoring Joe's dying wish.

Guilt rolled hot and heavy in my chest. If only I could put this conversation on ice for life. But I could feel Mom's eyes on me. I could practically hear her rolling the questions around to find the best way to crack me open.

"How's the internet thing going, honey?" Dad said, peering up from his newspaper over in the attached living room. I didn't know he'd been paying attention. When Mom turned to grab something from the fridge, he gave me a wink. He was rescuing me.

I smiled gratefully. "The blog?"

"Blog. Such a weird word."

I laughed. "I guess it is." I told them a bit about my latest posts—how I'd made what felt like a hundred practice pies before nailing the apple pie recipe. How I was trying to sprinkle in new foods in amongst Nonna's staples, which Mom, Nonna and I used to make together in Nonna's kitchen when she was still alive.

"Well, I just love hearing you talk about cooking," Mom said. "And I love having you here, too." She patted my hand, then sighed. "Shame Therese couldn't come home with you this time, though." Mom and Dad were the only ones Reese let call her by her proper name. "First Pietro can't make it home for any of the holidays. Now Therese is abandoning me, too?"

Pietro lived in London and had just informed Mom he wouldn't be making it home for Thanksgiving or Christmas this year. She still hadn't forgiven him. Reese not coming home for the weekend wasn't exactly the same thing. Still, Reese had moved to Jewel Lakes to be close to me and the girls, which meant it was really *my* fault Mom and Dad were on their own.

"Reese wanted to come," I said. "Her work just hasn't

been great about letting her have days off." Guilt ran through me. I knew I was shifting the onus on her work as the reason she wasn't here. It was technically the truth, though. Reese had told me that Gastronomique's original owners, who'd hired her, had recently retired. The new owners were New York City transplants, but unlike most people who moved to the area, they hadn't relaxed into the new, slower, pace of life in Jewel Lakes. They weren't the most pleasant people either, Reese said, in less than pleasant terms.

"She should work somewhere else!" Mom said. "Time off is important, I should know."

I lowered my phone from where I was taking photos of Nonna's famous tomato sauce bubbling on the stove.

Mom had managed a huge staff of people at her office. When Joe died, she'd tried to switch to part-time hours to look after me. When they wouldn't let her, she'd quit, even though she'd loved her job and was too young for retirement. I couldn't exactly push her away after that. She's helped me as much as Reese through those early, raw years of grief. I still felt guilty about her retiring, even though Mom assured me she'd adjusted just fine.

"You're right," I said. But I also knew Reese didn't necessarily want to keep working as a server. She was good at it, but she had other dreams. Ones I wasn't quite sure Mom would understand.

Then Mom said, "Does she still sing?"

I was surprised by the question. I shook my head. "I don't think so."

"Damn that man."

That was even more surprising—that Mom knew it had something to do with Simon.

"I didn't know you knew," I said softly.

Mom raised an eyebrow as she sniffed at the sauce. Of course she knew.

Reese had once wanted to be a singer. Back when we were kids, she'd sing everything she heard. She'd make me laugh by holding up a wooden spoon in the kitchen when we were home alone, belting out the words to songs that required a range very few people had. As she grew, her love for music grew, too. And even though performing on stage was the one thing she was shy about, she used to go to open mic nights in New York.

But something had happened with her ex, Simon—something she hadn't even told me about. After they broke up, she didn't sing. And she'd never told me why.

"Did she tell you what happened?" I asked.

Now it was Mom's turn to shake her head. "I was hoping she'd told you."

I cleared my throat, pulling my phone up again to take pictures. Reese would be pissed if she knew we were talking about this. I may not know what had happened, but I knew she'd never forgive me for getting Mom involved—even in speculation.

"What do you think about this?" I asked Mom now, to change the subject.

I also did actually need to focus on these photos.

I'd spread an assortment of herbs and a perfectly crumpled tea towel on the old enamel worktable in the corner of the kitchen. The table was my grandmother's, and we'd rolled out cookies on it when Reese and I were girls, just like my girls would do with my mom.

"Let me see," Mom said, coming up behind me. She was totally mystified about what made a good food picture, but she put her arms around my shoulders, kissing me on the temple like she had when I'd been a teenager. "It looks beautiful, sweetie."

A memory hit me in the gut, so hard and sudden I almost made a sound. Mom, here at this table, with her hands on my shoulders, just like now.

Joe, me, and Emma, then only a year and a half old. It was Thanksgiving, and Joe's parents were here too. We'd sat all our parents down ahead of the rest of the family to tell them we were expecting Macy. All the grandparents had gushed. Mom had gotten up and stood behind me, kissing me on the head. Her reaction felt subdued, but I'd been distracted. It should have been the most joyful day. A new baby, sister, granddaughter. But as I looked over at Joe, he'd given me the most tragic smile. Only a week before we'd discovered we were expecting, we'd gotten Joe's diagnosis.

Frayne's Syndrome. Terminal. He had under a year to live.

We didn't tell them that day. We couldn't mar the happy news, the joy in all their faces. Joe had just pressed his foot against mine under the table and we'd both pretended the tears on our face were ones of joy.

When I told my parents later that we'd known, Mom had broken down. *I knew,* she'd said. *I knew something was wrong.* She had sensed it, I knew then.

Dad, meanwhile, had been angry. *You shouldn't have carried that burden, Bella. Not on your own.*

But it was Joe who'd had the burden, not me. After his diagnosis, he'd slipped into a deep depression. He said it was the headaches that kept him on a temporary leave from work, lying in bed all day with the curtains closed, but I knew it was much worse than that. He'd fallen into darkness. Not even his baby girl coming into the room and kissing him on the cheek before I had to usher her out again helped.

It was the blog, of all things that pulled him out of it. I told him I was going to tell them everything. I had no other outlet then. Joe was my only outlet, and I was going to lose him. It wasn't a threat, just a desperate need to help him, and to help me. We had months left together and I couldn't stand for this to be the way they went.

I started small, telling him I wrote about how we'd met. He'd been attending a false alarm at the restaurant I worked in, and he'd knocked my container of freshly chopped onions I'd been prepping onto the floor. Cutting onions was my least favorite kitchen task—I was particularly sensitive to them, and my eyes had burned for an hour doing the work. They were still red when the fire alarm went off. I'd yelled at him, this gregarious firefighter who'd given me a killer smile when he tromped into the kitchen in all his gear. The next day he'd come back to the restaurant in plainclothes, with a gift. A pair of work goggles.

"Do you remember that, Joe?" I'd asked him as I sat on the edge of his bed. He'd looked up at me, tears in his eyes.

"I'd never forget," he said. "I don't want to forget."

The next day I told him I'd written about how he was a hero. How he'd once saved his colleague in a warehouse fire. The next, how he loved going to schools, telling kids about firefighting. "You're an inspiration," I told him.

"What about the food?" he'd asked me after a week of this.

"What do you mean?"

"This is your food blog," he said from the darkness, holding my hand.

"It's a life preserver right now," I'd whispered.

The next day, I'd come home to find him in the kitchen,

making meatballs. I'd been so shocked, so filled with joy and heartbreak and love and sorrow I'd dropped the bag of groceries I'd been holding. Eggs cracked on the floor, and Emma had shrieked with delight.

Joe had been the one to comfort me then.

"I'll make it count," he said. "Whatever time we have left, I need to do that for us."

I swallowed down the lump in my throat now, blinking hard to keep the tears at bay. The last thing I needed was to go down that old road. Except for not following through with my promise to Joe about finding someone else, I was at peace now. I really was. The fire department had covered all that therapy for me.

My goal with my therapist was always to get to a place where I could think of Joe only with happiness. I wanted to be able to talk to the girls about their dad without breaking down. I wanted to minimize the impact of this tragic event on them. So I'd worked my ass off. I'd spent whole years in a sea of sorrow, working out as much of the pain as I possibly could. And it had worked, sort of. I'd been at the point for a while now where I could do that. It wasn't that I'd forgotten Joe—not in the least. But I got out the darkest of the grief with the help of my therapist and now kept him tucked safely in a little corner of my heart, pulling him out only when I was feeling particularly melancholy. Overall, because of my herculean effort, I got through most days just fine. Which was why I thought I could figure out being with Steve.

But now I knew the truth—I couldn't replace what I had with Joe. Or rather, I didn't want to. It felt much better to not be with anyone—not seriously anyway. Short term flings I could consider, but that was nearly impossible as a single mom.

And how was I supposed to tell my mother all of this?

Instead, I spent the rest of our time together—between photo arranging—telling Mom all about the blog and how I was busy trying to make it succeed. It was all Greek to her—followers and reposts, affiliate links and sponsors. But she nodded along dutifully.

Later, at dinner, Dad asked what a reblog was, practically scratching his chin as I tried to explain.

"I noticed all those people writing at the bottom," Mom said. Unlike Dad, who was lost on the computer, she did keep up with the blog, even if she didn't know all the terminology. "They're always asking you about your personal life."

And just like that, she'd deftly circled back around.

"Well, that's part of it, Mom," I said. "I need to strike a balance between letting them in to see the real me and the food part of it."

"But how can you show them your personal life when you don't have one?"

"Mom!" I laughed. "I have a personal life!"

"Do you, sweetie?"

"Yes," I huffed, irritation creeping in now. I jammed the meat thermometer into the roast with more force than was strictly necessary. "Reese lives nearby."

"She's your sister," Dad piped up.

"That's still a personal life!"

Mom gave me the side-eye.

For a moment, I thought of Will. *Well, there is someone, who somehow, in only two meetings, has made me feel things I never thought I'd feel again.*

I nearly laughed out loud.

My irritation bloomed hotter thinking about him. No matter how much I tried not to think about him, there he was. I saw right through that crabby exterior—he was a sweet, tender man. I knew he was, not only from the way he played with Emma and Macy but the way he looked at me when he asked me questions. Like he cared. Like he thought I was interesting and smart, and maybe even attractive. And yeah, he was flipping gorgeous, with those serious eyes and stiff jaw under his stubble.

"Well, I'm glad Therese is there for you," Mom said, as she began clearing the dishes. She'd already ushered Dad away to play with the girls. "At least you have someone to keep you from being too lonely."

I sighed. "Mom..." I turned so I could look her in the eye, ready to break it to her. But when I did, she was smiling at me with love and sadness.

"It's only because I know how happy you were with Joe," Mom said softly. "I'd love to see you like that again."

For the second time today, my throat went tight. "I'm happy, Mom," I said. "I promise."

I was. I was just fine.

I hugged my mom, fiercely. And I let the tears come, only a little.

∽

Now, pulling away from my parents' place in the falling light with Emma and Macy waving from the backseat and a stack of leftovers in aluminum foil on the seat next to me, I knew Mom was right. Not about finding happiness with someone else, but about needing more of a personal life. Right now, all I did was parent my girls and hyper-focus on Bella Eats. I also spent a lot of time worrying about bills, which didn't help anyone and was definitely not something I needed to share with my readers.

I needed to get out and give my readers—and my mom—more happy stuff to chew on. I knew from that one picture of the engagement ring I'd briefly worn that nothing would make them more engaged than a romance. But me having fun in a non-romantic way had to count for something.

"Mom?" Emma asked from the back seat a while later.

I peered in the rearview. Macy had her head tipped sideways, her mouth agape. She'd passed out soon after we left the city. But Emma always had trouble falling asleep, in the car and at home.

"Yeah sweetie?"

"Are you going to find us a new dad?"

The question sent my heart thudding. "What? Honey, why are you asking that?" We'd had lots of conversations—especially after Steve—about how we were sad about their dad being gone, but we didn't need to fill his shoes. How we could be perfectly happy with just us. Girl power.

"You and Aunty Reese have a dad," Emma said, almost as if she was embarrassed to point it out. "He's really nice. He doesn't have a nice couch we're not allowed to sit on, and he used to take you hiking and to little league, and… he did stuff with you guys, he said."

God, Steve and his precious designer couch—it was one more thing that landed in the no pile once I started evaluating things between us.

"Emma," I said, while my heart cracked a little, right down the middle. My therapist had warned me about how this kind of thing might come up, but that was years ago. Emma had always seemed so… *okay* about everything. But I couldn't keep pretending it hadn't affected Emma, too. Though she'd only been four when he died, she and him had been close.

Plus, she could see how it had affected me.

I swallowed. "You don't need a daddy to be happy, remember?"

"I know," she said, her voice soft. "But I want you to be happy."

Had she been talking to Grandma? "I am happy, sweetie," I said, for the second time that night. But now I wasn't sure who I was trying to convince.

It was just before ten when we got home, and the house was freezing. After I bundled the girls into bed, I lit a fire and went to the kitchen to uncork a bottle of wine. I was happy, damn it, and enjoying life. This was a nice bottle of wine—Reese had gotten it for me as a thank-you for helping her move. As I poured, my eyes went to the fridge, where a little white card sat under a magnet.

I should throw that out.

I almost had when I got home from the park the other week. Instead, I'd stuck it up on the fridge, just in case.

In case what? In case you decide you might want a roll in the hay with Will Archer?

For the briefest moment, I pictured him there, standing next to me. His hand took the bottle from me and set it aside. Then, he leaned down and kissed me, his tongue darting so quickly against mine I might have imagined it.

The thought was so jarring, so electric, my hand slipped on the bottle of wine. I nearly dropped it, splashing Bordeaux on the countertop as I set it upright.

I *did* imagine it. All of it.

After wiping up the spill, I moved to the living room, lowering myself uneasily onto my couch. I took a long sip of wine, enjoying the warmth that spread through me as it slid down my throat. It was relaxing, but it didn't purge the image of Will from my mind.

The imagined feel of him.

What did he look like under that wool coat he'd been wearing? Under the expensive suit I knew he wore?

Then I gave my head a shake. I didn't want my brain to equate happiness with hooking up with Will. I also didn't want my daughters thinking that I needed a man to feel fulfilled.

What I needed to be happy was to focus on my blog.

I snapped a photo of my Bordeaux next to the flickering fire. That was as close as I was getting to romance. Maybe it would suffice for my readers.

I knew it wouldn't.

No, what I really needed was to get a life, not imagine one with Will Archer. I'd show my readers how happy I was.

I texted my sister.

It was only a half-second before she responded with a phone call.

"An actual night out!" Reese squealed.

I laughed. "You sound pleased."

"Pleased? I'm over the flipping moon! There's a new coffee shop opening in Millerville and they're having their grand opening on Friday. Apparently, they're going to be a music venue too. I actually got the day off work."

I smiled at Reese's mention of the music. "Sounds awesome," I said. I was already envisioning posting a few photos of the opening to the blog. I could write up a special article on 'evening coffee shop fare'. Late-night cakes, tarts, and fancy coffees. And the readers would see me actually having fun.

"Okay well, let me just ask Hank and Casey if they're up for watching the girls on Friday," I said.

"Oh no," Reese said, her voice falling. "Sadie told me she and Chris are going out to this event too. It's' her and Chris's first date night since little Lucy was born. I'm pretty sure she said Casey is watching her this weekend?"

My stomach sank. I'd met Sadie only once—she was Casey's good friend, and she ran the vintage shop in town, which was how Reese knew her, from practically setting up camp in the shop since she'd arrived.

"So... I guess that means you can't go?" Reese asked. I could hear the disappointment in her voice.

My eyes went to the card on my fridge.

Hank and Casey weren't the only ones who could help. Nerves danced in my stomach even as I said the words.

"No. I have another babysitter I can ask."

3

WILL

Mayor Fred Billingsly had been talking about golf for five minutes straight. I know because I'd timed him.

Surreptitiously, of course, with the ostentatious gold clock he kept on his giant mahogany desk. I stifled a yawn, shifting in my seat and hearing my back crack.

There were a hundred things I needed to do. Listening to the mayor wax poetic about golf wasn't one of them. If I was mayor, I don't think I'd spend a day in this office. I'd be out there making Barkley Falls a better place.

I glanced at Fred's sweeping windows behind him. Outside, the sky was already darkening. Wind whipped orange leaves on the giant oak tree outside Barkley Falls' town hall.

For a moment I was taken back to the park last week. The way the leaves had blown around Michelle like she was some kind of autumnal angel.

My stomach flipped even at the thought of her.

Not good.

"I told Bill a five-iron was the way to go..." Fred droned on.

Anyone else and I would have cut that shit off immediately. I didn't have patience for long-windedness. But as town manager, I reported to the mayor, and if I wanted to keep my job which, if I was being honest with myself, no longer held quite the same thrill for me as it used to, especially right at this moment, I needed to let him go on at least a bit longer.

Maybe I should even pay attention. Maybe golf would help me keep Michelle Franco out of my damn head.

It had been years since I'd spent this much time thinking about a woman. Years. Hell, since I was a teenager with Jill if I was being honest. I wasn't even sure teenage Will tried not thinking about Jill this hard. At least back then I'd been busy with extracurriculars. Basketball, Yearbook Club, and one year, Class President. All the things Dad thought were too ambitious; things I specifically involved myself in probably half because I knew it would piss him off.

"What kind of father doesn't want his son to be class president?" I'd asked Mom after a particularly gnarly fight with him.

"He's proud of you," she'd assured me, "he's just not good at showing it."

Even back then I couldn't help but feel like that was bullshit. How hard was it to pat me on the back and say, 'good job'? Instead, when I brought him news about another one of my successes, he'd say things like, 'what does a yearbook have to do with the real world?'

Now, I had a real-world job. And all my efforts in high school *had* helped prepare me for it, thank you very fucking much.

Not that I was doing a good job of it this week.

I ran a hand over my chin as Fred carried on, my stubble prickly under my palm. I'd shaved this morning, hadn't I? I could swear I'd run a razor over my silvering beard in the bathroom, giving myself yet another pep talk.

You didn't want her to call anyway. Quit being such a baby.

One of Fred's furry caterpillar eyebrows jacked halfway up his forehead as he described a particularly grueling shot.

I pictured Michelle's eyebrow going up as I asked her something at the park. The way her lips parted when she laughed. The way her laughter had felt like it was dancing across my skin.

I could feel it now.

Damn it.

I wrapped my hand around my phone in my pocket, gripping it so tightly I had to tell myself to let go before I cracked the screen. Why was I so goddamned glum about Michelle not calling? It wasn't like I'd given her my number. It was Remy's number. For babysitting services only.

Maybe she just didn't need a babysitter.

"Will?"

"Yes?" I said. Shit, he'd asked me something.

There was a tense pause, then Fred nodded vigorously. "You're right. You're right, Archer, that's precisely what I mean."

He launched back into it.

I said a silent prayer I'd told my assistant Sheila to call me for something urgent if I wasn't out in twenty minutes.

Mainly because I knew Fred hadn't called me in here to talk golf. I knew he'd called me in to pitch me, once again, the idea that I ought to run for his seat next year.

There wasn't a chance that was happening. I may have often thought about all the things I'd do differently than Fred if I were mayor, but I would never actually run for the

All Your Fault

job. I knew exactly what it entailed—I'd met enough of them over the years—and I wasn't interested.

Fred was my least favorite of the three mayors of Barkley Falls I'd watched pass through the office since I'd been here. The first mayor I'd worked with had been a feisty Black septuagenarian named Barbara Chambers. She was all of five feet tall but had somehow had the biggest and angriest residents, developers, and business owners eating out of the palm of her hand. If she'd asked me to run, I might have actually said yes. I respected the hell out of that woman and a decade later still jumped whenever Barbara called, which was about once a year to demand to know what was happening at her beloved town hall. Of course, she always knew precisely what was happening, she just wanted someone to tussle with over what she thought should be done about it. If I ran into her on Main Street, usually with her purple-haired best friend Pearl Bradley, she'd harangue me in person. They'd tell me what they'd do, and I'd tell them what I'd do, then both women would give me a little wink or a grin and tell me they'd see me at the next quarterly Ladies' Auxiliary rummage sale, where I did all the lifting of donations too heavy for them to handle.

But Fred? Fred did more socializing than mayoring and cared less about the people of Barkley Falls than his cronies and their development projects. He was a self-centered blowhard whose every word of correspondence I needed to edit; whose ridiculous ideas for putting Barkley Falls on the tourist map usually benefitted his real estate investment firm, and who liked to go on and on and on about golf. And then on some more.

If I suspected there was anything intentionally unethical or illegal about his actions, I'd take action. But, for all his irritations, I didn't think there was. For now, I still worked for the guy, and I didn't need another headache at the moment.

I generally gave Fred a five-minute limit on golf talk, but today I'd been distracted by the scent of caramel and vanilla. By long, thick lashes and a sultry voice. By a woman whose flashes of pain I saw when she thought I wasn't looking. But a glance at the clock told me he'd been going on for fifteen minutes.

"Fred," I said, during a brief pause, "If you don't mind I should be getting back to it." I started getting up.

"Right you are," he said. Then, "Have you given any more thought to my offer?"

There it was.

"You know I'm flattered," I said, which wasn't exactly true. I knew Fred getting me in the mayor's seat wasn't because he loved my stickhandling of every single issue in this town. It was strictly for his own interests—he was planning on taking his real estate firm into private development after his term was up, and he wanted the ear of someone he knew in the mayor's seat. "But I'm perfectly happy where I am." It wasn't quite true, but Fred didn't need to know that. Besides, what else was I going to do? Starting a business wasn't really my jam, I liked the giving-back-ness of the public sector, and I'd reached the top where I was. Unless, of course, I accepted Fred's offer.

"Fine where you are, huh," Fred said. "Even the weddings?"

I gritted my teeth. People booked weddings on the village green all year round, even in the dead of winter. The gazebo backed by Opal Lake was stunning—I'd admit that. But somehow, without vocally complaining (who was I to ruin someone's foolish attempt at romance?) Fred knew the goddamn weddings were a thorn in my side. Which meant all of town hall knew, too.

"I don't mind the weddings," I said, working to unclench my jaw. "I don't even run them; I just like checking up on them to make sure things are going smoothly. No drunken nonsense."

"Sure, of course."

The truth was, weddings aside, I was fine with this job. I was good at it. I could get a lot done in this town and I didn't need to get elected to keep doing it. Sure as hell not under Fred's wing.

"Shame," he went on. "You'd make a fine candidate. Except for the family situation."

My hackles went up once more, this time even higher. "My personal life is none of anyone's concern," I said.

Fred had shaken his head like someone had died when I told him I needed some time off last year to deal with my divorce. Then, just a few weeks ago, Remy and I had run into him at Aubrey's, our local diner. We'd just come back from dropping Hannah off at college and were drowning our sorrows in burgers and milkshakes. That and arguing over Remy's mediocre boyfriend once again. The two of them kept getting together and breaking up again. "That's not how relationships are supposed to be," I'd told her.

"How would you know?" she'd shot back.

My stomach had dropped. She was right. What kind of role model was I?

Then Fred had walked through the door.

"Ah crap," I said. "Don't draw any attention to us," I'd whispered, as if we were trying to avoid one of the more annoying alpacas on Hank's farm. The last thing I needed was for the mayor to see me arguing with my daughter.

Both of us leaned over our milkshakes, making sure to

keep our eyes off the mayor, who was hobnobbing with half the restaurant.

Then he'd bellowed, "Archer!"

He'd spotted us in our corner booth, which wasn't nearly as concealed as I'd hoped. When he came over, he'd clapped me on the back before visibly recoiling at Remy. Specifically, at her newly shaved undercut, nose ring, and Ramones t-shirt.

"My, you've... grown since the last time I saw you!" he said to her as if she were six and not sixteen.

My daughter might dress a little avant-garde, but it didn't mean she wasn't a great kid. Or that she didn't have her shit perfectly together, except for the boyfriend situation. She worked summers at the theme park near Moriarty and had a thriving babysitting business the rest of the year. But Fred didn't need to know that.

"Sixteen now," I'd said stiffly. How dare he judge a teenage girl by her choice of outfits? "Her own person."

Remy had smiled at me, and I gave her a wink.

After he left, she'd given an olympic level eye roll. I didn't even call her out on it, either.

"I'm not going anywhere near public office," I said now, "so my family is not up for discussion." I'd restrained my voice, but I could tell he heard the note of warning.

"Listen, I just know you'd have a better chance of having the public warmed up to you if those pretty girls of yours looked a little more like—"

"Fred," I said, my restraint slipping.

"Alright, papa bear," he said. "Understood. For now. But listen, giving you the sales pitch wasn't the reason I asked you in here. It's to ask a favor."

I sat back in my chair, my shoulders relaxing slightly. Hopefully, the matter was done and dusted. And with any luck, I could get back to my desk soon. Even though that gold clock said it was nearly time to head home.

"What is it?" I asked.

"Ever heard of Rolling Hills Resort?"

"I don't think so," I said, unable to keep the suspicion out of my voice. The tiniest tickle of something not exactly pleasant—my spidey senses maybe—flickered in my gut.

"It's in Quince Valley. You familiar?"

Actually I was. Quince Valley was in Vermont, a good three hours northeast of Jewel Lakes County. Though I hadn't been there since I was a kid, I remember it being as beautiful as home, with rolling green hills, and a sparkling blue lake.

"My father took us fishing there when we were kids," I said.

More like he took us to watch him fish. I don't remember catching a single bass in that lake. Or if I did, he made me throw them all back for being too small. But suddenly I remembered—there had been a grand-looking hotel peeking from the trees when we were down on the lake. It had a dock, with rich-looking people in fancy clothes stepping off into paddle wheelers. When Dad saw we'd drifted too close one time he'd scowled and rowed us hard back to the quiet, weedy end of the lake.

"Fabulous fishing up there and the hotel's a real stunner. Apparently, it's going to be on the market soon, and Haverford Developments is thinking of putting in an offer."

Charles Haverford was a well-respected developer who did business all over Jewel Lakes County. And apparently across state lines too. But why was Fred interested? Unless he was planning on going into some kind of partnership with Charles? Which would be a conflict of interest given he led development approvals here at City Hall.

"I'd like you to go up and do a little reconnaissance at Rolling Hills. I have a standing reservation in the presidential suite."

"What, you want me to stay at the resort?" That twinge turned to something stronger. Never mind his conflict, if he was considering developing here and wanted me onside, it would be so I could sway the future Mayor.

Or better yet in his eyes, *be* the future mayor.

"Don't worry, it's the first room they renovated," he said. "Only the second wing is stalled."

"That's not the problem," I said. "Fred, I can't do recon for your business." It was ludicrous that he was even asking me.

Fred waved me away. "It's not about that. You're on the tourism portfolio, aren't you? We won't have any public investment into Haverford's application, naturally. But I know our town could desperately use a focal point for tourism."

"What about your company? Are you collaborating with Charles?"

Fred lifted his eyebrow once more. "Now Will, that wouldn't be permitted so long as I'm mayor."

It wasn't really an answer, but still, I relaxed just slightly. Recon for the tourism portfolio could be good. It was gorgeous here, but we saw a definite drop in tourism over the winter months.

"A resort like that could be the jewel in Jewel Lakes, if you will," Fred said, squinting as if peering at an imaginary tourism pamphlet before him.

I wondered if he'd come up with that on his own, or if Charles had mentioned it and he'd run with it.

"In any case, Charles has some land in mind. He'd like to put in an application the moment a sale closes. It's a bit of a controversial property, there's some conservation nonsense on a portion of it, so I want us to be ready with evidence that a resort of that nature would be a benefit to this community."

I lifted an eyebrow at 'conservation nonsense'. "Fred, preserving the natural elements of Jewel Lakes is important. Critical, really, not just for tourism. For the whole community. For wildlife. For the environment."

"Of course. We'll figure that all out when we come to it."

"When Charles comes to it, you mean."

"Precisely. Besides," he pointed a beefy finger at me, "as you've just demonstrated, you deserve a thank-you for your care of this community. You've been running the show here really. Our finance director told us we made a tidy sum in event sales this past summer, and that, along with whatever we make on the Christmas fair next month, should be enough to fund a couple of artsy-fartsy grants."

Classic Fred.

I wasn't convinced it was a thank-you so much as more buttering me up. I was about to say so when he said, "Besides, a man like you would appreciate the resort's finer appointments."

Once again, I had a vision of staying in a well-appointed hotel room, kicking back next to a roaring fire. A gorgeous, curly-haired woman patting the bed next to her. Naked.

"That's very kind of you," I said, cutting off those thoughts.

But the dark cloud that had been hanging around me lifted, just a little. It would be relaxing to go up there on one of the weekends when Remy was at her mother's.

Maybe that was the problem. Not that I was disappointed Michelle hadn't called, but that I needed a break. A solo getaway, with a good bottle of wine. A rare steak. I was warming up to the idea of the presidential suite, no matter what Fred's motives.

"When were you thinking?" I asked.

"How about seeing it in full swing? New Year's Eve?"

"Your standing reservation is still good over New Year's?"

"I would go myself but the missus has booked us flights to Hawaii. Speaking of which, you have a lady friend you might want to take?" Fred waggled his eyebrows. "A married man is more electable, they say."

Suddenly my mood nose-dived once more.

Thank god my phone buzzed in my pocket just then. Sheila, right on time.

"Sorry, Fred," I said, pulling it out.

I glanced at the screen, already tsking as if knowing the call would be important and I was sorry it would tear me away from this meeting.

But it wasn't Sheila. It was Remy. My heart jumped. My girls never called me at work, only texted. It was after school hours—four-thirty. Visions of Remy's car wrapped around a telephone pole danced in my eyes, sending adrenaline shooting through me. Or maybe she was calling to tell me something had happened to Hannah at school.

Panic wrapped around my throat. "It's my daughter..."

"Go on," he said.

I leaped up, heading to the back of the room while the mayor picked up his phone and began barking something at his assistant.

I stabbed my screen with my finger to take the call. "Remy! What's wrong?"

"Hey, Dad."

She didn't sound mortally wounded. She was speaking anyway.

"Are you okay? Are you hurt?"

"Dad, I'm fine."

"Oh thank god."

"Geez, overreact much?"

I gritted my teeth for the second time that afternoon. "Remy, if you're not hurt, why are you calling? I'm in a meeting with the mayor."

"You should be thanking me then."

I had to suppress the threat of laughter. I turned away from Fred.

"Seriously, why are you calling?"

"You told me to tell you right away when that lady called. For babysitting?"

Suddenly my heart went back into a full gallop.

Michelle.

I glanced over my shoulder at Fred, but he was guffawing into his phone now, probably talking to a golf buddy.

Michelle Franco had called my daughter. Which meant she hadn't torn up my business card.

Which meant I might see her again.

I wasn't quite sure how to feel about that. I was tightly coiled. "Oh, that's great. Great," I said.

"Dad... are *you* okay?"

"Of course. Why wouldn't I be okay? I'm okay. When did she want you to babysit?"

"Friday."

"Great. That's great."

"Dad, what is *wrong* with you?"

"Nothing. I'll drive you on Friday." With graduated licensing restrictions, she wasn't allowed to drive at night past 9pm—which, if Michelle was on a date or something, would probably be too early to come home.

Why did my stomach do a sick little drop at that

thought?

"Go do your homework," I said, gruffer than I meant to.

I hung up to what I swore was the sound of Remy rolling her eyes.

4

WILL

By the time Friday night rolled around, my brain had run through about ten thousand scenarios, both of what I would say to Michelle when I saw her (and what Remy would say when I insisted on walking her all the way to the door), and why she might need a babysitter.

The obvious answer was that she had a date. It shouldn't have mattered to me—not in the least. But for whatever reason it did. It mattered a lot.

"Ready?" I asked Remy, who was putting on her sneakers as slowly as I'd ever seen a kid put on sneakers. It was like she was a toddler again.

"Dad, why are you even grumpier than usual?" She asked. "You seem... anxious." Her voice was deeply suspicious, and her face was too when I looked over at her.

"I'm not anxious," I said, stiffly. "I just want to get going."

"So, who is this lady again?"

"I told you—just a friend of Uncle Hank's."

Remy's eyebrows scrunched together, then, as she

inspected my face, they flew up. Her mouth fell open too like a lightbulb had gone off. "Oh my god, you have a *crush* on this woman. Dad, is she married? Are you going to have an affair with—"

"Remy!" I barked. "Enough."

She put up her hands, but her lips still twisted like she was trying not to laugh.

"She's not married," I said, grabbing my coat and practically tearing off the hook while I was at it.

When she went to say something more, I shot her a look that had her snapping her mouth shut. But it quickly spread into a grin.

I grumbled and headed for the door.

"Oh, just one sec," she said. "Almost forgot my art stuff."

"I'll meet you in the car," I said. I couldn't help but be impressed that Remy was putting so much thought into this job.

I used to be excited about my job, too.

Not for the first time, as I climbed into the car, I considered my discussion with Fred. His dogged pressure to try to get me to run for his seat next year had been funny at first. How had he thought *I* would be interested in—or a good fit for—public office?

To be fair, as a fresh-faced college kid, being in public office had once been a goal of mine. Even if it was just to piss my dad off. Dad wanted me, the oldest of the three kids, to take over our family's mechanic shop. He barely talked to me when I said I wanted to go to college instead. We'd had a humdinger of a fight which centered on him believing I thought I was 'too good for honest work'. I ended up yelling that the reason I didn't want to take over the garage was because of him.

All Your Fault 55

To this day I felt a mix of guilt and fury when I thought about that.

But Dad and I had never gotten along. Still didn't—ever since my sister Stella moved away, only Hank kept up with the weekly visits to his care home.

I sighed. I may not want to run a garage, but I was pretty sure I didn't want to be a politician either.

Still, that hotel stay in Vermont sounded pretty sweet.

Hell, maybe I'd go and then put in my notice right after. Quit my job and take off. Sell my old, restored brick Victorian in Barkley Falls and take an early retirement. Very early—I was only 40.

When Remy moved out, I could leave Jewel Lakes altogether.

But the thought gave me a hollow feeling inside. I loved this town. I was involved in a ton of community organizations. I had friends here. Hank and I were close.

And Michelle was here.

I swallowed that thought down. Except it wouldn't stay down because I was about to see her.

Where the hell was Remy? I pulled down the visor mirror checking my hair as if I was a teenager heading to a date. Which was absurd because I was the adult here. This was just my daughter going for a job, and I was dropping her off because that's what dads did.

"Sorry," Remy said as she climbed into the car. "Couldn't find all the brushes."

I snapped the visor shut. "Hairbrushes?"

"God dad, that was a way weak dad joke, even for you."

I grinned, despite the jumble of shit running around my head. I'd never get tired of being a dad.

It was a short fifteen-minute drive to Amethyst Lake, where I'd just learned Michelle lived. In the summer, Remy could have ridden her bike—there was a direct trail from Opal Lake, which Barkley Falls edged, due north to Amethyst. That part of Jewel Lakes was mostly old farmland, and though the area was hilly, the path wound through the fairly flat parts. But now, in mid-November, it got dark before five. Jewel Lakes was as safe as they came, but there was no way in hell my teenage daughter was trail-riding in the dark. As we pulled off the highway, flurries began splattering against the windshield of my Highlander.

"It's only October," I griped.

Beside me, Remy made an exasperated sound. When I glanced over, her face was lit up with the glow of her phone.

"Let me guess, Draco problems?" I asked. Last week, her shaved undercut had apparently been a balm to their teenage friction because all I'd heard was swooning on the phone. But by the beginning of this week, they'd been back to bickering.

"Why do you want to know?" she asked.

"Because I care about you."

There was a long pause. I could tell she was debating how much to tell me. "Well, we're on a break. Again."

Dare I hope this one would be permanent? Draco wasn't a bad kid, but together they were way too much drama. "Oh yeah?"

"Dad, you don't know anything about relationships, okay? So don't try to dictate how mine should go."

That stung. I bit my tongue—literally, I had to clamp down on my tongue to not say something I might regret. Kids didn't know how harsh their words could be sometimes. Besides, maybe she was right. But like hell she knew what she was doing, either.

"Does Mom talk to you about any of this stuff?" I asked, my voice tight. I was already dreading the answer.

"Sometimes. But she's always telling me to have fun while I'm young."

My stomach churned as the old wound cracked open.

When the girls were in middle school, Jill had gone through something like an early mid-life crisis. She'd only been in her late twenties then, but she'd started worrying she'd missed her best years by staying with me and having kids early. She talked about how I'd left her behind while I went to school and launched my career. How I'd relied on her to look after the girls while I developed professionally. She was right, of course, but we had talked it out to death when it was going on, and she'd always insisted she didn't want to go to school, that she wanted to stay home.

I'd been blindsided—devastated, really. People were allowed to change their minds, I knew, but when she'd told me she wanted to go back to school in New York City—and not have us go with her—I knew this was more than that. I told her I'd give up my job and move the kids to the city with her, but she insisted we stay. She said we shouldn't disrupt our lives, and I supposed that ended up being a good idea, at least for the girls who got the continuity of staying in our house and at their schools.

From the outside, I could have said it was Jill's fear of missing out that had triggered things failing between us. But really, it had to have been fractured from the beginning. She thought I was what she wanted, but it turned out I'd only made her unhappy.

Hearing that Jill was still singing the song of 'don't waste your youth like I did' was like a blow. She'd been talking about me.

"Well, you'll have your whole life to have fun," I said, trying not to let Remy see. "Don't spend it all on Draco."

Was I saying what Jill wished someone had said to her about me?

A few minutes later, we reached Michelle's road.

"Where the hell is this place?" I asked, and though it had been an out-loud thought Remy answered.

"She said it was on the back of some old farm. Like an outbuilding or something?

If I didn't know Michelle, and this was some random new client of Remy's, I might have turned around right then. But I did know Michelle, and there wasn't a chance in hell I wasn't at least figuring this out. I couldn't say I wasn't a little worried about how remote it was though.

I told myself to calm the hell down. We had fantastic emergency services throughout Jewel Lakes County, including my own brother, Hank, who was a firefighter. I'd text him after I dropped Remy off to see if he was working, just for my own peace of mind. If he wasn't, I'd get him to get his buddies at the station to keep an ear out.

Finally, I spotted lights through the trees. Winding up an ambling path behind one of the older farmhouses, I found it —a ramshackle building that must have once been an outbuilding, now converted into a living space.

I parked my SUV and fought with Remy, but lost, about walking her up to the door.

"Dad, I'm not a child, I'm *babysitting* children."

Disappointment ran through me that I wouldn't get to see Michelle. But that wasn't what I was here for.

"Fine. But I'm waiting here until you go inside."

She gave me a quick hug. "Thanks for the ride."

I was surprised, and touched, that she'd think to do that. Maybe she was doing just fine without my worrying. "Text me when you're done," I called after her and she waved without turning around.

When the front door opened, I felt a little jolt in my stomach as Michelle's figure appeared, illuminated by the light behind her. She lifted a hand at me and I did the same. I fought the urge to get out and run up the path to casually ask her how it was going.

But I'd promised Remy.

I'd promised myself too.

~

I'D MADE it to the end of the driveway when my phone buzzed. It was Fred texting me for details of a deal that had been passed by Council this week.

"Seriously? On a Friday night?" I very much wanted to get back home and—well, I wanted to say I'd kick back with the glass of chardonnay I'd put in the fridge to chill, but I knew I'd head to my study and catch up on work myself.

I turned onto the main road, so I wasn't blocking the driveway, then pulled onto the shoulder. I began going through my phone, looking for the information the mayor was after.

"Given any thought to that resort stay?" he texted while I searched.

I swiped the text away, annoyed. I *had* given thought to it actually. Late at night fantasizing once again of lying in a giant hotel bed with Michelle, this time going so far as imagining her hand on my cock.

My crotch jumped right there.

Goddammit, Archer.

I was so distracted I didn't even think to register that the lights behind me had to be from Michelle's car. Or the sound of the engine.

I only looked up when I heard a soft thud behind me. In

my rearview, I saw the glowing red of taillights blurred behind falling snow.

My stomach dropped. I dropped my phone and leaped out of my car into the freezing night air.

Michelle's hatchback was in the ditch.

5

MICHELLE

I can quite honestly say I'd never been so embarrassed in all my life. Not even that time I discovered I'd worked the first hour at my waitressing job with my pants inside out because I'd overslept for my breakfast shift.

No, this was worse. I saw the taillights of Will's car out of the corner of my eye as I'd come down the slope of the drive. I didn't know why he was still on my road, but I was thankful it was dark out so I wouldn't have to do an awkward wave or roll-down-our-windows thing to chat.

But when I turned onto the road I'd been distracted by the strange rattling in my engine. And realized too late that my completely bald tires—which had managed okay on the gravel and dirt drive—were gliding across the asphalt like a pair of ice skates. I couldn't get enough traction to turn even slightly in the direction of Barkley falls.

"Shit!" I'd exclaimed, pumping the brakes desperately.

Thank god I was going at a snail's pace. Still, I shrieked as the car thudded into the soft embankment on the other side of the road.

Of course. On top of Reese canceling on me too late to

call off Remy—she'd gotten called into Gastronomique to cover a shift—my bold decision to go to the coffee shop opening on my own now seemed like the stupidest decision I'd ever made.

My readers were right—my life was tragic, and it was my own damn fault.

A few seconds after impact, the door of my car opened, a rush of freezing, flurry-filled air smacking me in the face.

"Michelle!" Will exclaimed, breathless. His face was a rictus of worry. "Are you okay?"

I let out a breath. "I'm fine," I said.

"You sure?" He looked significantly more panicked than I felt.

"Will, I'm fine," I said. "Seriously."

He obviously didn't hear the warning tone in my voice because he was still focused on how I'd gotten here.

"Don't you have snow tires?"

"I didn't think it was going to snow this early," I snapped. I could hear, as I said it, how bad that excuse was. That I was being defensive because he was right.

I knew my tires were shot. I knew half the car was shot, but two grand for both the regular and snow tires I needed had sent me into a spiral.

You always were stubborn as a mule.

I startled. I'd heard that in Joe's voice. For a moment, I glanced up, looking around as if I'd see him standing there, arms folded, laughing at me. He'd always teased me about being stubborn.

But only Will was standing there, his hair whipping in the wind, his stupid handsome face all sharp planes in the dark.

"I couldn't... I haven't gotten around to getting them," I said.

"My sister still owns our family's garage in town," Will said. "I can get you some at cost."

The irritation flooded back. It was nice of him—objectively, I could see that. But I didn't need my hand held. Not when I felt stupid enough for not having gotten the tires sorted sooner.

"It's fine, I'll take care of it," I said.

Always gotta do stuff yourself, eh Mich?

Joe was right, I was being obtuse, but I was in too deep now.

Will put his hands up. "Fine. Just—let me help you out of the ditch, at least?" I could hear the annoyance in his voice now too.

"I'm *fine*," I said, throwing the car into reverse. Will jumped out of the way of the door as I put my foot on the gas.

But the car didn't move. The tires screamed as they spun in place. Of course. Of *course*.

To my horror, I felt tears filling my eyes. I rubbed them away fast on my shoulder. The wool of my coat scratched at my face, doing nothing but smearing the tears around.

"Why are you still standing there?" I snapped at him.

"Because you can't get out of this without help, Michelle."

"You'd be surprised at what I can handle on my own," I said.

"I don't think I would," he said softly. "But I'll leave you to it."

Then he was gone, leaving the door open and wet blots of snow hitting my face like little slaps. I went too far—I know I did, and guilt unfurled in my stomach. But I slammed the door shut angrily. I didn't need Will Archer. I *could* figure this out on my own. I had to.

Why the hell hadn't I just turned Remy away at the door? I could have given her twenty bucks for her trouble. Twenty bucks I really couldn't spare but was half of what I'd intended to spend to go out to this stupid show in the first place.

But it was too late to worry about that now. I needed to get my car out of this ditch.

I picked up my phone and dialed the number for Triple-A. Then I remembered I hadn't renewed my membership.

I tried the gas one more time, gritting my teeth in frustration, hot tears running down my cheeks. Of course, the tires just spun, the car rocking in place.

I grabbed for the door handle, jumping out of the car, slamming the door behind me.

Will hadn't moved. He was leaning against his car, his arms folded against his chest, snow dotting his shoulders.

"You're still here," I said.

"Did you really think I was going to leave you like this?"

I should have been annoyed. I wasn't a damsel in distress. I was a single mom for god's sake. I knew how to handle myself. But as much as I tried to re-stoke my irritation, I just found myself oddly touched.

"Even after I was such a... a," *Jerk* was on the tip of my tongue.

"A stressed-out person who just slid off the road?"

I smiled, despite myself. "Yeah. That."

"It's okay. Apology accepted."

I frowned. I'd been working up to an apology, but I hadn't said it yet. "I didn't—"

But Will waved his hand at me as if I'd been about to lay it on thick. Then he grinned. He was teasing me.

Except I was too distracted. I don't think I'd ever seen him smile like that—open and happy and... alive. Even when he'd played with the girls at the park he'd given them more of a pretend scowl for laughs.

"I don't have Triple-A," I blurted out, turning away. I needed to move this along, not stand here in the sloppy snow staring googly-eyed at Will Archer. No matter how gorgeous he was, any time of day and in any weather, I still needed my car out of the ditch.

"Don't need it," he said, getting up from where he'd been leaning on his vehicle. He walked around the front of his car.

"You going to haul it out with your bare hands?"

His back was to me and he didn't say anything, but he began pulling on something. His elbow went out behind him, once, twice, and god help me if I didn't picture him shirtless as he turned around with a length of cable in his arms. Something twinged down low.

"You have a winch," I finally clued in.

He gave a curt nod and kneeled at my back bumper.

"You're going to get your nice pants dirty," I said.

"How do you know I'm wearing nice pants?" he asked, and I swallowed down a laugh. I couldn't believe I was out here in the dark getting my car hauled out of a ditch by a man in what was likely a designer suit.

My readers would love this.

Really, they would. One more piece of bad luck I could document. Even as I felt annoyed at myself for continuing to spin the narrative I was trying to avoid, I knew I'd get a boost in all the money-making parts of the blog.

"Do you mind if I take your picture?" I asked. "For posterity." But I couldn't fib, not about this. "Actually, for my blog."

"What kind of blog is it? Search and rescue?"

I pinched my lips to keep from laughing. "It's a food blog actually."

He paused, looking up at me with a confused face.

"My readers like personal updates too." That was putting it mildly.

He studied me a moment more then went back to searching under the bumper. "If you say so."

"That a yes?"

He grunted.

"I'm taking that as a yes."

I walked around snapping a few photos of my car with its nose pointing down into the ditch. Of Will, on his knees in the frosty mud. Of both him and the car when he stood up and pulled at the cable.

Then I tucked my phone away, already thinking about what kind of post I could tie into this latest debacle. Something about warm drinks for bad luck.

∽

Only ten minutes later both our cars were in my driveway. I hadn't been too badly stuck; my little front-wheel drive hatchback didn't exactly have much power. I got out of mine after parking it. We met out in the driveway. The snow was still coming down, still melting when it hit the ground, not quite cold enough to stick. I was freezing, and I pulled my coat tight around me.

I'd behaved badly. I opened my mouth to speak, but Will got there first.

"Do you want a ride?"

"A ride?"

"To your date."

I was so surprised, I laughed. "My date? Even if I had

been going on a date, I don't think it would look great having you drop me off for it." Then I cringed.

But he didn't even seem to notice that I'd basically called him hot. Thank god.

"I'm used to drop offs, especially ones where I need to park a block away so as not to embarrass anyone."

I tried not to laugh again. For some reason, I didn't want Will knowing I found him so entertaining. Or maybe I didn't want to find him so entertaining.

"It was a date with my sister, actually, and she stood me up."

Will's expression softened and he seemed to relax. Or had I imagined that? Then his brow furrowed. "So where were you going?"

The embarrassment came back, heating up my cheeks. "I was going to go anyway. By myself to Roaster's grand opening. It's not every day I have a babysitter."

"Haverford's new place."

"Haverford?"

"Charles Haverford. A local developer. He just bought the building that's in. He also owns half of downtown Barkley Falls."

I nodded. An awkward pause stretched between us where I felt like a complete nerd for admitting I'd been going on a date by myself.

Had been, past tense.

"Well as nice as this is, I'd better go and get Remy for you."

"You could still go," he said.

I laughed, then ended it abruptly when I saw he was serious. "My car isn't exactly functional."

"I'll take you."

I froze. "What?"

"I'll take you. It's their grand opening, right? Live music?"

"That the kind of thing you're into?" I asked.

"No," he said frankly. "But how often do you get out of the house to enjoy yourself?"

"Who says I'd enjoy myself with you?" I asked.

His lips twitched up. "I never said I'd go with you. I was just offering a ride."

I could practically hear the snow sizzling as it landed on my cheeks. I tightened my arms across my chest, staring Will in the eyes.

Just then the front door opened. "Dad?" Remy's voice was laced with confusion.

"Hey, sweetie."

"What are you still doing here?"

"Michelle had some car trouble."

There was a pause. "Oh," she said. "So... does this mean you don't need me anymore?" she asked me. I could hear the disappointment in her voice. I remembered babysitting when I was a kid—especially when they were good, easy kids. And while of course I thought my kids were the best, it was an objective fact that they'd be very easy charges for her. They'd been awed into beatific silence when they'd seen her and her cool leather jacket. Her buzzed undercut.

"Are the girls in bed?" I asked.

"We were just reading stories. I can keep them up for you if you want?"

The whole point of this stupid adventure was to show my readers I could have fun. Maybe I could show them the pictures of my car in the ditch and then me still going out after like the fun person I was. The fun, happy person.

I glanced at Will. He was looking directly at me.

"Don't you have your own plans on Friday night?" I asked, low enough that Remy couldn't hear.

"I don't know. Are you asking me out?"

I opened my mouth. The bugger!

His lips twitched once more, then, just as quietly, he said, "Listen, if I take Remy home right now, she's probably going to call Draco on the drive home. You could spare me that pain."

I tightened the smile away once more. Was I really going to do this? Go out with Will Archer? It's not like it was a romantic date. Just taking advantage of having a babysitter.

"I think we'll still go out, if that's okay?" I called to Remy. "I'll come back at eleven? Like I planned?"

Remy took a moment to answer and even though she was backlit, I could tell she was looking from her dad to me, running this through her head.

"Um... sure?" she said.

And just like that, I was going out with Will Archer.

6

WILL

I should have been desperate to get home—to change into pants not caked in drying mud at the knees. To maybe have a shower and get the damp snow out of my hair. But I felt good—as good as I'd felt in years. Better, maybe.

I'd be lying through my teeth if I said it had nothing to do with the woman standing next to the open door of my SUV.

Michelle's face was hidden by her soft curls as she bent down to brush her pant legs off—she was wearing jeans and sexy black ankle boots. But Michelle could be wearing gumboots and still be the sexiest woman I think I'd ever known.

It wasn't just her looks—though she was everything that made me attracted to a woman. Soft, with a good amount of curves. Those heavy-lidded eyes.

No, it was more than that. She exuded something that made me weak in the goddamned knees. Easiness. Her teasing maybe? And under that snappy exterior, something soft and vulnerable too. Something kind of... sad, maybe, but not the kind that needed pitying. It just seemed like she'd had a hard go, but she wasn't letting that keep her down.

It was dangerous. I should have stayed away. She even gave me an opportunity.

"You don't have to stay," she said as she climbed inside. "At the coffee shop, I mean. I can get a cab home."

There was a little voice telling me to run.

But I ignored it. "It's fine," I said, backing up. "It's good for me to know what's happening around Jewel Lakes. To get a feel for all the local establishments."

"Is that part of your job?"

"Yeah," I said. It was, sort of, but even I wasn't foolish enough to lie to myself. That wasn't why I wanted to go. Not at all. But it could be, I realized. There could be a perfectly neutral, non-Michelle-related reason I wanted to take her to this opening.

"I oversee all the departments who look after everything to do with Barkley Falls. From water supply to events in town spaces."

"But Roasters is in Millerville?"

"Barkley Falls and Millerville have a lot of crossover."

I wasn't sure who I was trying to convince.

As I drove, Michelle asked me more about my job, and I told her about how I had my finger on just about everything that happened in town. I told her about the time I spent outside my job involved in local community projects, charities, and events.

"So, you volunteer at things you do anyway for your job?"

"I spend a lot of time at work managing other people who get to do the fun stuff. It feels good to roll up my sleeves and actually get involved in stuff too. Plus, when I'm not getting paid, it feels more... pure somehow. Like I'm not just doing it for a paycheck."

Michelle smiled. "You're an asset to the town, Will."

"Hell, I wouldn't go that far. I just care about this town. About the people in it and visiting it. Even if they are pains in the ass half the time all wanting to get married on the same weekend in July every summer."

"You manage the weddings too?"

"Hell no, that's where I draw the line." As we passed the giant Welcome to Millerville sign, I explained how I had a whole events department that reported to me, and how it was one of the biggest departments in the city because of how popular weddings were at Barkley Falls Green.

"It's a beautiful spot," she said.

It was a beautiful spot. Barkley Falls Green might be my favorite spot in the whole county, and that said a lot, given how gorgeous the lakes and woods were. The Green was an immaculate lawn and garden on the edge of downtown with a hundred-year-old gazebo overlooking Opal Lake. I made sure the grounds were meticulously maintained and that the gazebo got a fresh coat of paint every year. As a consequence, everyone in the state seemed to want to get married there. While it wasn't my job to manage bookings, I usually stopped by to make sure no one was messing anything up.

"A couple years ago I went to twenty goddamned weddings," I said.

"You must really love weddings, huh?" she asked, as I pulled onto the street Roasters was on.

My stomach shifted. I'd walked right into that one. "No, actually," I said. "Can't stand them. I don't really believe in marriage."

"Don't believe in it? Like you think it's a myth?"

She was teasing me.

"They exist. Hell, I've been married myself. I just don't think—" how did I word this so I didn't sound like an absolute scrooge? "I just think they were transactional arrangements way back when, and, somehow, we got it in our heads that people had to be in love to get married."

We'd reached the coffee house. I pulled into the parking lot around back, killing the engine.

"That's generally what's considered a bare minimum for marriage, yes," Michelle said, her voice kind of strange.

"Look, I'm sorry if I sound like a cynic," I said, my hands still on the wheel. "I just didn't have a great example growing up. My mom was perfect, and my dad was... not."

Once, during an argument, my little sister Stella told me the reason I didn't get along with Dad was because we were so similar. I'd been pissed. But she didn't think it was a terrible insult. She was a lot closer to Dad than me and Hank, and later, she was the one who ended up taking over the garage. "Dad and I are nothing alike," I'd told her, my voice steely.

"He only got worse after Mom died," I said now. "Then my own marriage went mushroom-shaped well past the time I thought we were safe from that. So, not a lot of faith, you know?"

I could feel Michelle's eyes on me. I felt like a shit for bringing the mood down, but I didn't know how to fix it.

"I'm sorry about your mom," she said after a moment.

Something pricked in my chest. It had been years since someone had said that, and for a moment, the prick grew to an ache I hadn't felt in a long time. Mom had been my defender when Dad and I fought. She always supported me wanting to go to college and pursue a career in the public sector, no matter how hard Dad tried to push me to get my mechanic license and take over the family garage. She'd been there for me, and then she'd died.

"Thanks," I said, my voice stiff. "It was a long time ago."

"Doesn't mean it stops hurting. Or so I've heard."

I glanced over at her, suddenly feeling deeply insensitive. I'd lost a parent when I was already an adult. Mom may not have met my kids, but I'd had more than two decades with her. And my ex-wife had been around, even if our marriage had imploded. Michelle had lost her spouse. That was a whole other ball game. I wanted to tell her I was sorry about her husband—that I wished it had never happened to her, that it was goddamned tragic he'd died and she had to raise her two girls on her own. But she looked straight ahead as if knowing what I was thinking and clearly not wanting to go there.

"You know," she said brightly, "Other people might say you're a cynic about marriage because you just haven't found the right person yet."

I harrumphed. "My dad couldn't have met a better person than my mom and look where the hell that got him."

But I couldn't shake the voice in the back of my head that told me she was right. That I *was* just like him and I was doomed to end up just like him, alone and angry.

"You're incurable, aren't you?"

"Yes."

She frowned. Awkwardness clung to the air around us. It was my damn fault, of course.

"I'm sorry," I said, rubbing the bridge of my nose. "I didn't mean to start talking about this," I said. "You're going to think I'm a heartless ass."

"Oh, I already thought that," she said. Her lips twitched and something tight in my chest loosened.

"Well at least I know how to have a good time," I said.

"Unlike Ms. I want to smash my car in the ditch to avoid going on a date."

"I told you it wasn't a date!" Michelle gawped, but I could see the laughter in her cheeks, in the way she looked as if she was trying hard not to let it out.

"This isn't either," I said. It was supposed to be for me, that reminder. But I realized it had come out like some kind of insult.

The lightness faded in her eyes. "Obviously."

Fuck. I really was an ass.

∼

EVEN FROM OUTSIDE we could hear the music had already started. Good. I needed it to drown out my anger at myself for being such a dick.

What had possessed me to say that? *This isn't a date.*

You're pushing her away. Just like you pushed—

I interrupted the thought by quickly scrubbing my face with my hand. I wouldn't think about my ex-wife and how efficiently I'd destroyed that relationship.

Michelle strode ahead of me into the coffee shop, nearly slamming the door in my face.

So, things were going well so far.

The space was large, with high ceilings and exposed ductwork overhead, and the proprietors had clearly maximized the number of seats permitted by the fire department. At least fifteen round tables dotted the room, with several clusters of couches and easy chairs toward the back. Next to us, the coffee bar looked more like a bar-bar with the server handing patrons beer and wine. Every seat appeared to be taken. Great.

The band, a three-piece folksy ensemble with a bearded

hipster guy on the bass, a pretty young blonde woman, who couldn't be much older than Hannah, on the mic, and a stunning lanky brown-skinned woman with a completely bald head and about thirty earrings on the drums, made me feel old as dirt. All three of them were singing in harmony to an old Bob Dylan song.

At least there was something for me here.

I glanced at the back of Michelle's head as we stood near the doorway, not wanting to cross the room while the music was playing. Then I felt Michelle moving to the music beside me. Oh god. There better not be any dancing.

I picked out a few familiar faces in the glow of candles at various tables. While this wasn't Barkley Falls, where I knew everyone, I knew a lot of people in this town too. One woman, who I recognized as a staffer at Millerville City Hall —thank Christ not the one who'd been sidling up to me at the symposium last time—gave me a curious look and a wave.

Shit. Rumors hadn't been on my mind when I suggested joining Michelle on this outing. But now that I stood here next to her, I knew the Millerville city staffer could easily light one up in Barkley Falls if she wanted to. I shifted to hide my face— even though I knew I couldn't just hide all night. I'd have to ask Sheila on Monday if she'd heard anything. Actually, I wouldn't have to ask—I'd know by whatever look she gave me. Thankfully, as president of the Barkley Falls Rumor Mill, Sheila was also very good at correcting their course too, when I asked her. Of course, usually, I only asked her to help when the mayor had said something ridiculous that needed downplaying.

I'd have to keep things very clearly not-date-like tonight while we had an audience and make things doubly clear with Sheila when I was back in the office.

Not that it would be hard—Michelle was pissed off enough that anyone who thought we *were* on a date would likely assume we were in some kind of lovers spat.

Which we couldn't be because we weren't lovers.

Something hot spread in my lower half when I thought of the word *lovers* with Michelle next to me.

Really, Archer?

I tried to keep at least a few inches of space between us as we stood there waiting for the band to finish their song, but when a couple had come in behind us, we had to squish together to make room for them. I took off my coat and folded it over my arm like a shield between us.

"Kind of crowded in here," I said after the song had ended and the band announced they were taking a break. I'd had to bend down next to her for her to hear me over the sound of people talking and laughing, still buzzing from the music. The scent of her shampoo—or just her—had almost made me lose my words. It was a warm vanilla-honey kind of smell.

I closed my eyes, willing my olfactory senses to turn themselves off.

"There's a spot right there," she said stiffly, pointing to a small, plush, velvet loveseat in the corner. The two people who'd been occupying it were standing up and pulling on their coats.

My throat went dry at the thought of cozying up to Michelle. "It's kind of small, isn't it?"

But she was already heading over there. "We're going to lose it!" she said, giving the people next to us a look as if we were competing in some kind of amazing race.

We won, thanks to Michelle darting through the crowd like a slip of silk. I followed clumsily behind her, apologizing as I stepped on toes and nearly knocked a drink out of a woman's hand.

Michelle was already on the sofa when I got there. I wasn't quite sure how I was supposed to fit next to her, especially when I wasn't sure what would happen when we actually touched.

I hedged. "I'll go get us a couple drinks?"

"Or we could let the server do that," Michelle said, pointing her chin over my shoulder.

A woman in a black apron carrying a round tray was taking an order from a table on the other side of the room.

I frowned, wondering if it would be weird if I sat down on the arm of the couch. But Michelle had moved over, making room next to her. There was nothing to do but sit down.

Except when I did, the couch turned out to be much softer and significantly deeper than I'd anticipated. I sunk so low, Michelle rolled directly into me so her front was pressed up against my side.

"Oh!" she exclaimed.

For a split second, I was too stunned to move. Too intoxicated by the feel of her against me. Heat swirled in my gut. She was as soft and pliant as I knew she would be. Her scent filled the air around me, her hair against my cheek and neck. Was this what I had wanted? This very arrangement of our limbs, this closeness?

"Hey," I said, trying to shift so she could get off me.

"You're making this impossible!" she said.

"Me!?" I shifted over to my side of the loveseat, but that only made her roll further. The next thing I knew, her soft, ample breasts were pressed up against my tensed arm.

Heat shot through me, making my crotch jump.

No. Not the time, not at *all* the time.

All Your Fault 79

If I were watching this from the outside, this would have been comical. But I wasn't, and it wasn't. I needed her off of me.

"You need to stay over here," Michelle said and pressed her hand against my chest. "While I—" her face was scrunched in anger at me for some reason, as if I meant to be this big and meant for this couch to be so goddamned plush. But when she looked up, pinning me with her narrowed eyes, something hot ran through me. It was sharper than the desire already thrumming through my veins.

It sliced at the very core of me.

I didn't know this was how I'd react to us touching, though maybe I should have known, given I went fucking wobbly just looking at her from a distance.

"You know, if you wanted to sit on me, you could have just asked," I said.

"I promise I'm not trying to sit on you," she said.

"And yet..." But instead of getting her mad enough to get the hell off me, her lips twisted, like she was trying not to laugh again. For a moment, that vision of her in the imaginary hotel room flashed in my mind, her lips parting as she looked at me. She'd been naked in that fantasy.

My pants tightened. God*dammit*.

"I'll help you?" I asked, looking away as if she could see right through me.

"No, I can do it," she said, pushing off my chest. She shifted, and then her knee connected with my crotch, sending a searing pain shooting through me. I yelped, then nearly smashed faces with her as I bent forward.

"Oh no," she said.

At least my hard-on was gone. The pain had seen to that. But enough was enough. "I'm going to move you," I said, still grimacing as the bad kind of lightning shot from my boys. "Okay?"

"Okay," she said.

I twisted toward her and for a moment her face was in my throat, her breath on my skin. If my dick wasn't mortally wounded, I'd be turned on.

But it was, and I couldn't think about that now. Instead, I slipped my arm under her knees and back and lifted her over to her cushion.

She gripped the armrest next to her, staying still for now. "I think I'm safe," she said, after a moment.

But was I?

"You two all right?" a woman's voice asked.

I looked up, still melting in the pain that radiated from my crotch.

"Fine," I squeezed out.

Michelle nodded. "Great! Thank you."

"Can I get you lovebirds anything to drink?"

"We're not—" I began, but Michelle cleared her throat, shooting me daggers

"A beer please."

"And for you?" the waitress asked me.

"Same," I said, even though suddenly I wanted to leap to my feet—if I could—and bolt.

When she left, Michelle turned to me. "What is your problem?"

"I wasn't made for this kind of couch. And you kneed me in the crotch."

"I..." she huffed, and for a moment a look passed over her face that I knew wasn't frustration. It was defeat. She turned her eyes to the ground. Shit.

There I was, being an ass once again.

"Michelle, I—"

"No," she said. "This was stupid. I should never have come."

"No," I said, my voice hard enough that she looked back up again. "I'm sorry. I'm... Sometimes I'm not great around people I... women..."

Fuck.

"I like you," I said simply.

Michelle blinked.

Well, that was awkward. What the hell did I say that for?

But her lips did that little twitching thing again, and relief flooded through me.

"Can we start again?" I asked.

"Please," she said.

And just like that, I could breathe again. "Maybe you could tell me what kind of food blog involves taking photos of cars in ditches?" I asked.

Michelle laughed, sending something warm and loose through me. For the rest of the break, Michelle told me all about her blog. How she'd started it years ago as more of a personal recording device, and how she'd carried it on over the years. She told me about how it had grown in popularity and that she was even making money from it.

"Nothing to write home about," she assured me. "In fact, I really need to double down and figure out how to get it earning big. Some bloggers are hitting six figures."

"Six figures! For writing on the internet?"

"Writing's the smallest part of it," she said.

She described all the moving parts of how a blog operated, even allowing me to pull out my phone and visit Bella Eats while we sat there. Over my shoulder, she pointed me to her most popular posts.

They were, like she'd hinted at, the ones where she'd experienced misfortune. Where she opened up about her life, and not in a warm and funny way but a raw and real way, laying herself bare for her audience. It was brave, but also... it felt like it would be deeply painful to be exposed to this degree.

When she went to the restroom before the band came back on, I read through the most popular post called I GUESS I'M A WIDOW NOW. She'd opened up about her husband's death in the most poignant way. To hell if I didn't feel my damn heart tighten up reading her words. She was a good writer. A great writer, and the way she talked about her grief so poignantly, without being cloying, was a skill I knew I'd never have, as slick as I could be with my own words when making deals and negotiating giant public projects.

But reading through the comments, several of which had specific questions pertaining to the details of the fire, and some asking deeply personal medical questions, stoked something close to anger in me, like a spark from a flame of protectiveness I didn't have any right to feel.

Then I noted the number of shares on the post. There were hundreds of them. Did she want all these people OMG'ing her? Reposting her content with teary-eyed emojis?

I flipped through to the next post under the "Most popular" column. It was called *CAN WE BE FRAYNE'S?*

Emma's going to be okay, it started.

As I read, my jaw clenched as hard as my chest.

In the post, Michelle said she'd had to face her worst fears when she learned Emma could have the same condition as her father. It was so rare the medical community didn't even know if it could be inherited.

Technically, as you all know, she wrote, *my husband died in a fire, rescuing people trapped in a burning building, in his job as a NYFD firefighter. But Joe's condition had already been pronounced terminal, and we'd been preparing for his death a few months before it happened.*

The post was meant to be positive—she kept reiterating that Emma was going to be okay.

If she'd had it, her prognosis would still be good, thank everything above. Joe hadn't caught his illness until he was an adult, and people with Frayne's who catch it young typically lead very normal lives.

But the same thing happened on this post as with the last. Emojis. Probing questions. Requests for more photos of Emma.

"So, any new favorite recipes?" Michelle asked. Her expression was upbeat, but I could sense a wariness underneath it too. How long had she been standing there?

I smiled. "So far all the recipe posts appear to have taken a second seat to these life stories."

Something flashed in Michelle's eyes, but she shrugged, a brief smile passing her lips and faltering again, as if she were trying and failing to make it stick.

"There aren't actually that many of them, but either my recipes suck, or people like a side of tragedy with their carbonara."

It was supposed to be a joke I knew, but I wasn't laughing. I wanted to throw her damn blog in the trash. If there was a way to do that with something on the internet.

I shifted carefully so she could sit down without us smashing together again. As much as I wanted that to happen. At that moment, I wanted nothing more than to wrap her in my arms and tell her... what, that I was sorry her life had been so hard? That I would have given anything to know her earlier, to be able to protect her from all the lookyloos on her blog?

"I didn't know how serious that appointment had been,"

I said instead. "That day I first met you. I should have asked."

Her eyes flashed with that darkness again, then she straightened her shoulders and looked away. "I wouldn't have told you. I didn't want to tell anyone. That's why I wrote the blog post. Easier to say it once, you know?"

"Michelle?" I asked as the band began shuffling back on stage. The lead singer hooked a guitar strap over her neck and a few people cheered.

She looked me in the eye, her sharp gaze a challenge.

I didn't back down from challenges.

"Does the blog make you happy?"

She stiffened. "Of course it does."

I didn't say anything. In business school I learned that one of the best techniques to get people to reconsider their position was to allow silence. I wasn't negotiating with Michelle, but I didn't believe her.

I knew she didn't either.

"It was therapeutic for me to write everything down," she said, "and it was good for me to have a record of the life Joe and I had together, for the girls. Now—well, I love food, and showing people how to make delicious food."

That didn't mean she liked the direction her blog had shifted. I couldn't help but think of a ship drifting off course.

"Did you always want to write a food blog?"

Michelle huffed. "No. I used to want to run a restaurant." She softened for a minute. "A romantic Italian place. I'd keep the menu small. Serve the dishes my grandmother taught me, with farm-fresh local ingredients." Then she glanced over at me, her face flushing.

"It's not too late," I said. "If it's what you want."

"No. That was a pipe dream. A restaurant is a ton of work, and I have the girls to look after."

It might be. But there were ways around it, I knew. I helped businesses set up in the town all the time. And with all the new tourist programming we were planning a cozy Italian restaurant would kill here. I opened my mouth to tell her that when she folded her arms and fixed her gaze on me.

"What do *you* want anyway?" Michelle asked. She was being defensive.

"What do you mean?" I asked.

"You've been the town manager forever, right? You said yourself you have ideas for the place. Why aren't you making them happen?"

A flicker of anger ran through me. She was lashing out, that was all. But there was something in there that stung. "I *am* making them happen. I can get a lot of shit done with my job. I do, every day."

She raised an eyebrow.

But the lights dimmed before I could say anything else.

She'd won that one. Despite the finger she'd pressed in my wound, I couldn't help but admire her. Hell, more than admire her. I wanted to keep going. To keep doing this. To spar with her, to go out on dates like this with her.

To wrap my arm around her and know this was where I wanted to be.

The last dregs of my irritation drained away, and as the band launched into a song, I sat back, settling into the seat, thinking about the woman sitting next to me with something aching in my chest, wishing things could have been different for both of us.

7

MICHELLE

"Okay, this one's definitely going to make it," I said to Emma, Macy, and Reese, who sat at the kitchen table on the edge of their seats.

I shook the frying pan hard and the pancake inside flew up, did an arc, and... landed half in the pan and half on the floor in a surprisingly loud *splat*.

"Fail!" Reese called out like a referee while the girls shrieked with laughter.

"Thanks for the support!" I said, laughing.

"Mom," Emma said, "you should really stop trying to do that. You're not getting much better at it."

I gasped. "Excuse me! That one was halfway there!"

Reese stood and handed me the rag while I squeezed Emma's face with the other hand and pecked her on the cheek, then Macy too, who was still howling at the big mess I'd made.

"Here, let me take over," Reese said, taking the pan from me while I cleaned the batter off the floor.

Reese had shown up this morning with berries and a

carton of whipped cream, begging forgiveness for bailing on me last night.

"I'm here to spend all day with my favorite girls," she said. "If you'll accept my apology for last night. I hope you had enough time to cancel your babysitter?"

"No," I said as I let her in. "But I made the most of it. I went out anyway."

Her eyebrows had shot straight up, but Emma and Macy had come bounding down the stairs at just that moment and we got into pancake making instead.

Thank god Reese had shown up. Not just for the fun company but because maybe then I might be able to go at least five minutes without thinking about Will and last night.

I'd tossed and turned in my bed all night, replaying the evening in my mind. The way he'd rescued me from the ditch. How I'd accidentally, literally, thrown myself on him and how he'd felt against me.

It was like meeting him again at that park had lit up a dormant coal inside of me, and last night had brought it to a flame.

It was dangerous, and I didn't particularly like it.

But it wasn't just everything that had happened between us keeping me awake. It was what he'd said.

Does the blog make you happy?

Of course it did. I'd said that last night. So why was I still chewing on that when I woke up? I was sick of it. So when Reese showed up, I'd been deeply relieved. And I'd decided to make a big, messy morning of it, even if I'd have to clean it all up after. Anything. Anything to distract from last night and Will Archer.

Reese wasn't a bad cook herself. While she chatted away

with the girls, she turned the rest of the batter into gorgeous, perfectly browned, pancakes. I turned some frozen berries into a quick compote and whipped the cream. Then, of course, I took some photos—this would make good blog material.

After we ate, I made the girls take their dishes to the sink and told them if they got dressed and brushed their teeth on their own they could watch some cartoons, then I promised we could make a snowman later. I knew Reese wouldn't let me get away without talking about what had happened last night, and I didn't want the girls around to hear about it.

"I'll wash," Reese said.

I didn't bother arguing, just picked up a towel and started drying.

"So," my sister said, once her hands were immersed in water. "I thought for sure you were going to be upset about last night."

"I can't get mad at you for getting called into work."

"So, you went to the coffee house on your own?"

I didn't say anything, just picked up a plate and rubbed it dry with the towel.

"Michelle Franco!" Reese exclaimed, propping her dripping hands on her hips.

"I ended up going out with Will, okay?"

My big sister gasped.

I'd told her about running into Will again in the car on the way home from Emma's appointment but hadn't mentioned him offering his daughter's number for babysitting. Or that *that* was who I'd called last night. While she freaked out on me, I explained everything, emphasizing several times how it wasn't a date.

But she was rolling her eyes by the time I finished. "Michelle. It sounds like a date."

"It wasn't, Reese. Neither of us are looking for that."

She gave me a small smile and my stomach twisted. I suddenly wished I hadn't said anything to her. Because she was right—it sounded like a date.

"Honest," I said, drying the dish in my hand so hard I thought I might be wearing the enamel off.

She hesitated for a moment, running her soapy sponge over a cup. "Mich, why are you so adamant about not dating again?"

"Because I don't want to date Will." The answer came quick. Too quick.

"Why not?"

I frowned. Was it because he'd made his own stance on relationships clear? Partly. But that wasn't all of it.

Because you're scared.

No.

It was because I couldn't feel hopeful about anyone. I'd tried with Steve, and it hadn't worked. And for some reason, I didn't want to try that with Will. I knew he wasn't Steve. I never felt myself constantly thinking about Steve the way I did with Will. Steve didn't challenge me the way Will did.

But Joe had.

And I couldn't replace Joe.

"Reese, I just don't, okay? I'm happy where I am with the girls—except for trying to sort the blog out—and I don't want to mess that up. Plus, it's just too complicated."

That part was true too.

"The girls were so confused when I told them Steve and I were getting married... and then that we weren't. It's just easier this way. Maybe someday, when I'm an old lady in a retirement home and the girls are grown—maybe then I'll consider dating again."

Reese laughed, shaking her head.

"Besides," I said, "Right now I need to focus on the blog.

I want to do more than just struggle to get by. I want to feel comfortable financially."

"I do get that. Seriously, it's the only reason I'm sticking it out at Gastronomique—it's by far the best paying serving gig this side of NYC."

I was relieved the discussion about Will was over. Relieved I didn't have to justify my convictions or my feelings.

"These new owners are not what I signed up for," Reese said, handing me the last dish and draining the sink. "They never want me to miss a shift, then when I *do* have a night off, they expect me to drop everything to come in within minutes of calling."

"Reese," I said, pouring us the last of the coffee. I sat down at my kitchen table while Reese leaned up against the counter, cupping her mug.

"I know you keep saying you want to do something new, but you shouldn't hold yourself hostage by a dream that might…"

She stiffened.

I wasn't going to say might never happen. I wasn't. But I was thinking it. Reese dreamed of singing. But she wouldn't sing even for me.

"…that might take a while?" I finished lamely.

"I'd be letting myself down," she said, her voice sounding kind of pinched. She took a sip of coffee, not looking at me.

"I just want you to be happy," I said softly. "I don't think you'd be betraying yourself by looking somewhere else."

"You sound like Mom."

I sighed, lowering my mug onto the table. "I'm sorry."

"Anyway. It doesn't matter. The job isn't that bad. Besides, guess who I saw last night?"

"Who?"

"Eli."

I had to think a minute.

Will's friend.

"The guy from the park," I said.

Reese grinned, apparently forgiving me for alluding to the singing thing. She told me about how Eli had been having dinner with an older guy in an expensive-looking suit. Eli had looked stressed; he kept gesturing emphatically.

"I only heard part of it—something about a deal or a sale. Anyway the older guy left eventually and he asked me when my shift was over."

"And?"

"And we went out."

She was being obtuse on purpose. "Reese, did you—"

"What, take him home?"

Now she wasn't.

"Maybe."

I gaped. "Damn, Reese. I'm impressed."

Not to mention a little jealous.

It had been a while since I'd hooked up with anyone like that. I couldn't even remember when. Could I do that now?

Never mind that the logistics with the girls made it kind of impossible—what would it be like?

Would that put to rest the heat I felt when I thought of a certain single dad?

I tried to picture some random stranger, some faceless man I'd never see except in the shadows. But that face kept changing, coming into the light. Growing silver temples and a bunched brow. A hard jaw and a smart mouth.

Will.

I remembered the hard press of Will's chest under my

hand at the coffee shop last night; the feeling of his breath in my ear as the lights dimmed.

I want you, Michelle.

A tingle, over my skin. The press of his lips against the side of my stomach, the inside of my hip.

"Michelle?"

Reese's voice cut through my runaway thoughts. Oh god.

"Sorry—did you ask me something?"

"Yeah, if you could ask your friend about Eli? Like, if he's a... decent guy?"

"So, you're going to see him again?"

"I hope so. I mean, we had chemistry anyway. Lots of it."

"Um..."

"Unless you don't have Will's number?"

"I have his daughter's number," I said, pulling out my phone. I was momentarily distracted by a new text notification from an unknown number.

My heart jumped in my chest as I opened it. I didn't know it would be him.

But it was.

UNKNOWN: Hey, this is Will. I was serious about the tires—my sister's got someone else running her garage while she's away so I'll have to arrange it for you to make sure you get family pricing. Let me know when. And don't try to drive!

A FLICKER of annoyance went through me. He was all business. And who was he to tell me not to drive?

The guy who pulled you out of a ditch last night.

Okay, fine.

But there was a follow-up text, too.

. . .

Unknown: P.S. I had a good time last night. I'm sorry I was a dick.

Just like that, the annoyance drained away. Not completely, but his self-awareness made it hard to stay too mad. He wasn't a dick. Well, maybe a little. But if he was, I was too. He'd asked me about my blog, and I'd chewed his head off.

But I also didn't need to be hand-held with the car.

"What are you frowning at?"

I jerked my head up. My sister was too far away to see the screen.

"Nothing," I said.

"Really."

"My car," I said, standing up. I peered out the back door window at my car, currently under a thin dusting of snow. I looked at Reese, sheepishly explaining what had happened with the car.

She was aghast. "Talk about burying the lede! Why didn't you say something?" Suddenly she was in big sister mode. "How did that happen? Are you okay?"

"Fine," I said. "It was just embarrassing." I explained about the tires.

While Reese admonished me, I looked out on the snowy drive leading up to my house. I knew she—and Will—were right, I shouldn't have driven last night, and I shouldn't today. Even if I could make it to Barkley Falls. Maybe Millerville, which was more of a straight shot and had more garages—ones that weren't affiliated with the Archer family.

No. Not only was it just as ludicrous to think of driving

to Millerville on bald tires as Barkley Falls, last night Will had told me he could get my car fixed at cost. That could mean saving hundreds of dollars. Probably even a thousand, considering everything it needed. Was I really going to put my pride ahead of that much money?

The thought of calling Will and asking for help made my stomach somehow flip and sink at the same time.

Yes, I was. For as long as I could anyway.

"I'll drive you anywhere you need to go," Reese was saying.

But I shook my head. I didn't need to focus on my car or on Will Archer right now. "I don't need to go anywhere this weekend," I said brightly. "Not now that you're here. Let's get the girls and build a snowman."

8

MICHELLE

I survived three days without the car before my obstinance finally had to take a backseat to necessity. Technically, I could have gone a bit longer. The girls got picked up for school by the school bus, I worked from home, and Nonna had taught me years ago how to stretch very few ingredients into something delicious.

But by the time Tuesday rolled around, I'd used the last of the milk on the girls' cereal and there was no bread left for me to make a slice of toast. Macy got upset because we'd run out of glue for her take-home art project, and I'd had to get creative with making a flour and water paste to make repairs to her haunted house before rushing them out to meet the school bus.

I would have held out longer—glue was hardly a reason to go to town. But right after I waved them off, Hank had called asking if the girls wanted to go trick-or-treating with his stepson Sam on Wednesday. I felt like I hadn't seen nearly enough of Joe's best friend since moving here. I told myself I wasn't avoiding him—I loved Hank, and his fiancé Casey too. But it was always just the slightest bit triggering to see him; specifically, the scar on his arm, knowing it was from the same fire that took my husband. Still, each time I saw him, it hurt less. We were friends in our own right too. And the girls would never forgive me if they learned they'd been invited to trick-or-treat with Sam, the cool 'older' eleven-year-old boy. So, I told him of course we'd go.

But unless I wanted to ask Hank to pick us up, I needed my car back in commission.

Which meant it was time to reach out to Will.

Stop being a chicken, Mich.

Why had I heard that in Joe's voice? For a moment, I froze, picturing Joe sitting there at the kitchen table.

He'd never lived in this place; he'd never sat at that table. But there he was, sipping his coffee and shaking his head at me.

For a moment, my heart nearly stopped. This used to happen all the time. Right after he died, I'd see Joe everywhere. In the beginning, it was terrifying—and not only because I'd see him at the moment of his death. But just seeing him at all, in the throes of my grief—the breath would blow out of me as if by some cosmic vortex. I'd fall to my knees sometimes. Collapse right there on the floor.

As the years went on it got easier. My therapist gave me strategies for what to do.

Now, I hardly saw him at all.

But here he was, sitting with one ankle on his knee.

You're doing it again, Mich.

I barked out a laugh. Just like him.

You're dead, Joe! You can't tell me that anymore.

Ghost-Joe laughed. My throat tightened, that old familiar ache daring to press through. I grabbed a glass of water, tossing it down. I didn't want to see him right now. I didn't want him to tell me I was being a chickenshit about Will.

I didn't want him to see me thinking about Will at all.

Did you forget this was what I wanted?

He knew what I was thinking. I gripped the glass tighter.

You could try being friends with him? At least? C'mon babe...

"Babe?" I exclaimed. "How can you call me babe after what you did? You fucking left me!" I whirled back from the sink, clapping my hand over my mouth.

But Joe wasn't there. Of course he wasn't there. There was nothing there except the empty chair.

My heart pounded. Where had that come from, that anger? I wasn't angry at Joe—how could I be? He was gone. He'd died, tragically. He was a hero.

And he'd told you to find someone else.

But I couldn't do that. I couldn't. Steve had proven that. But maybe Joe—the one I'd concocted in my head just now —maybe he had a point. Maybe Will and I could be friends.

The thought felt crazy, but hopeful, too. It was something, without overcommitting.

I stared at the chair where Macy had sat pasting ghost and witch confetti to a cardboard haunted house only half an hour ago. Joe had never met Macy. But somehow, my picturing him there was like they'd sat there together. Like he'd held her on his lap. And as strange as it was, the thought brought me comfort.

Plus, Joe was right, of course. I was being stubborn. Stubborn because I was scared. Scared of the feelings I had around Will. But I didn't have to have those feelings, did I? Not if we were just friends. I lifted my chin, setting my shoulders back.

I grabbed my phone before I could lose my nerve and tapped on his name.

Michelle: Is the garage offer still available?

Send text.

If Will could be all business, so could I.

It was a workday, so I wasn't expecting him to text me back right away. But a moment later, my phone buzzed.

Will: I was beginning to think you liked overpaying for tires.

I relaxed, slightly, at his easiness. I wasn't sure what I'd been worried about. That he'd be cool maybe? Distant? I glanced at the chair in front of me.

Michelle: You know you sound like a tire ad.

Will: Technically I *am* a tire broker. For you.

I smiled. I wasn't sure if it was at the dumb joke or the words *for you*. Then I scrunched it off my face. Friends. That's what I was going for here. The word felt hollow, but I clung to it hard.

Michelle: The roads look good—I could bring the car down myself today if that works?

Will: >:(

Now I laughed out loud. *That* felt good.

Will: The truck will be there in an hour and a half. You can ride with the driver and take yourself home on new tires. Don't move.

He was awfully confident. How did he know he could get the truck here so soon? Or an appointment at the garage? Clearly, he was pulling strings for me. Not wanting to risk that he was overselling—I'd never not had to wait at an automotive shop—I texted Reese to arrange for her to be here when the girls got home from school.

Then, with one last glance at that empty kitchen chair, I went upstairs to change.

I wasn't sure why. My yoga pants and t-shirt were perfectly adequate for waiting around an automotive shop.

But I found myself pulling on my favorite form-fitting jeans, a snug navy tank top, and an oversized chunky cardigan on top of that. I dug around in the closet for those ankle boots I'd worn the other night. If I was making an effort with my clothes I might as well go all the way. I tried to tame my curls, finally deciding to pin them back. I tried tucking the few tendrils that fell out back in place but eventually gave up, heading back downstairs to wait for the truck.

With over an hour left to wait, I sat down at my desk and tinkered with the blog post I'd been working on this morning for Bella Eats. It was about pantry shopping for when you can't get to the grocery store. For the post, I'd framed the story around us being snowed in by last week's freak early snowstorm. I didn't say anything about how I drove my car into the ditch or how I got rescued by an irritating know-it-all.

How I'd put off fixing said car because of said know it all.

I said nothing about the man who made me feel all kinds of strange and confusing things I'd rather not face. The food ideas were good—a list of staples to keep in your pantry; the kind of sandwich spreads that mix together well; a no-knead bread anyone could make by mixing three ingredients and leaving it overnight.

But the rest—the personal note, the anecdotes about my grandmother—fell flat. It was like by trying not to say half the things my brain was thinking, the words on the screen were empty. Uninspired.

Will's words from the coffee shop kept coming back to me. Asking me if the blog was really what I wanted to do.

Joe would have asked me the same thing, I knew.

Well, not right now it wasn't, that was for damn sure. I slammed the laptop closed and stood up.

Really, Michelle?

Fucking Joe.

I sat down and opened the laptop again. Then I clicked over to a new page. They wanted personal? Fine. I'd get personal. Very personal. I started a new post, one about everything that had been on my mind. The car in the ditch. Will, coming to my rescue. The night at the coffee shop.

I added the photos I'd taken of Will—he'd given me permission, after all, and titled the post WHEN LIFE THROWS YOU SNOWBALLS, DRINK BEER.

I went back and re-read the post. It was good. Really good. Full of feeling. Authentic as Nonna's meatballs. I did have to tone down the stuff about Will a bit, making him a bit more anonymous and calling him a friend.

Maybe if I said it enough times, I'd believe it.

Before I could change my mind, I drew the mouse down to the publish button, hovered for a moment, and clicked it.

Then, for the second time that morning, I slammed the laptop shut.

Almost as soon as I did, I heard the rumble of the tow truck and put the post out of my mind. It was like now that I'd written that all down, I was no longer nervous about having to talk to Will. To call him to say thank you after I got this tire thing sorted.

I got up, reaching for my nice coat at the door, then hesitated.

Suddenly, I was embarrassed about how I'd dressed myself up. I was about to hop in the cab of a tow truck, probably with a big dude named Mitch with a mustache. I wiped off the smear of lip gloss I'd applied with a tissue and pulled on my bulky parka with the tricky zipper rather than the more form-fitting wool coat I'd worn that night at the coffee shop. Feeling slightly more nondescript, I stepped outside where the truck was backing up to my car. But when the door swung open, I froze. It wasn't a Mitch or a Bob. And there was certainly no mustache.

There was a gorgeous man in a cable knit sweater rolled up to reveal muscle-corded forearms. Expensive-looking slacks. Even more expensive-looking shoes.

It was Will.

I pulled the coat around me like a shield, picking my way through the soggy snow toward him.

He didn't hear me coming until I was a few feet away, and when he turned, it was fast, like he'd been caught off-guard.

"Michelle."

I couldn't help it—I laughed. "What, are you surprised to see me?"

Was it my imagination, or had he given me a once-over? Really? In this parka? I pulled it tight.

His eyes went to my lips, and I was hard-pressed not to raise a hand to them, to see if that was really what he was looking at.

"Those aren't exactly snow boots," he said, eyeing my stylish ankle boots.

Irritation flickered inside of me. "Neither are those," I said, eyeing his Italian loafers. I brought my hands to my hips.

Cold air brushed against my décolletage. I'd let my coat fall open.

His eyes were definitely on me. He flicked them away, abruptly turning and going back to hooking up the car.

"I came from work," he said, not taking the bait.

I softened. "I could have waited until the garage could do it."

"How long have you gone without a car?"

I hesitated. "Three days."

"Four, isn't it?"

But of course he knew how long it had been—he'd been with me the last time I drove it. Into the ditch.

"Why did you ask if you already knew the answer?" I asked.

He ignored me. "You're stubborn," he said. "Anyone ever tell you that?"

Yes.

"I didn't need the car until now," I said, defensively. He worked for a moment more, then turned around, rubbing his hands with a rag he'd pulled out of nowhere. His hands were gorgeous, I noted. He had long fingers. Skilled fingers. I wondered what else they could do.

"But... thank you," I said quickly, trying to get my mind away from those dangerous thoughts.

"You didn't have to come yourself."

His eyes met mine. "I wanted to," he said.

There'd been no hesitation there.

Something inside me went slippery. This man could say the most innocuous things and it just... did something to me. It was unnerving.

"Doesn't that take special training or something?" I asked, walking around as if I was inspecting his work.

"I worked at the garage all through high school. They haven't upgraded the truck or I'd be lost. Truck's as old as dirt, just like me." He hooked up the lights.

"You're not old," I said. "What are you, forty-eight? Fifty?"

Will glared at me. "Forty. Just forty."

Laughter bubbled up inside of me. This was better. Safer than whatever it was that had just passed between us.

"How old are you anyway?" he asked, turning back to the hitch. He was hooking up the lights now.

"Isn't that something you're not supposed to ask?"

"Hardly seems fair," he said. "Unless you're old-fashioned or something."

"Not in the least."

"Well?"

"Thirty-two."

Will grimaced.

"What, you think I'm young? I guess so—I was probably still in middle school when you had Hannah." I grinned, despite myself.

"That's... no. You really know how to make things weird, Franco."

No weirder than they already were.

"Let's go," Will grumbled, tromping around to his side of the truck.

~

The woman at the garage was very tall—maybe even taller than Will, who was definitely north of six feet. Her arms were made of pure muscle.

She introduced herself as Luciana.

"Just because you're William's friend, I'm going to bump my lunch for this job. But you better get back here by one because I get hangry. Just ask Jimmy."

Luciana threw a thumb at the kid working on a pick-up in the other bay. "She's not lying," he said.

"We will," I said. "I really appreciate it."

"I take it that's not your sister?" I asked Will, deeply confused as we walked out of the garage.

"Luciana's taking over the business while Stella's in

Michigan," Will said. He shoved his hands in his coat pocket as we stood on the sidewalk. "She said it was for the year, but I'd be shocked if she came back."

"Why would anyone leave Jewel Lakes?" I asked. I was joking, but he responded anyway.

"She's in love," Will said.

What was that in his voice? I looked at his face, trying to read something into him saying that word, but he wasn't looking at me. In fact, he looked as if he was decidedly not looking at me.

A man's voice cut through the suddenly tense silence.

"Archer!"

A man's voice hollered from somewhere above. I couldn't tell where.

"Shit," Will muttered under his breath. "Hey Fred," he called up.

I spotted him then, a red-faced man in a suit and tie, leaning out a window from the building across the street.

"Is that..."

"Mayor Billingsly, in the flesh," Will said.

"Lunch plans?" the mayor called.

Will hesitated. Then, out of the side of his mouth, he said, "Will you have lunch with me? Please?"

I could have refused, left him to his own devices, but instead, I shouted up, "Sorry Mr. Mayor! I've got dibs today!" Then I stuck my arm through Will's. Friend. I was being a good friend.

Somewhere, Joe laughed.

"Ho ho!" The mayor cried, clearly delighted. He held his hands up. Another man's face appeared in the window—a more discrete-looking businessman, handsome with silver hair, maybe in his sixties.

He gave Will a little salute but didn't holler like the mayor.

"Sorry, Fred," Will called. "Another time?"

"Thanks for that," Will said as we strode away. "You don't actually have to have lunch with me," he said quickly.

"It's going to be kind of awkward for you if those guys see me eating on my own," I said.

Will grimaced. "I'm sorry, I kind of painted myself into a corner."

"I helped," I smiled.

9

WILL

"I can't believe you yelled at the mayor," I said as we walked down Main Street.

She laughed. "You sounded like you needed the assist."

I did. The last thing I wanted was to be roped into lunch with the mayor and Charles Haverford. Charles would surely keep the talk appropriately on issues that didn't present a conflict of interest for the mayor. But Fred would stick his foot in it, and probably tell Charles I was gearing up my election campaign in the meantime.

"I did. I'm just impressed. Most people get nervous around him."

"Really? Him?"

"Damn, don't let him hear you say that. He's got an ego bigger than Opal Lake."

"Except Opal Lake is beautiful."

"You don't think Fred Billingsly is beautiful?"

Michelle pinched her lips. She was trying not to laugh again.

I loved this. Too much.

All Your Fault 107

The moment I thought it my stomach did a dip. Not the good kind, either. What was I thinking, finagling things so we could have lunch together? I should be back at the office, safe, and buried under piles of requests for new traffic lights and noise complaints about alpaca screams. Because that was really a thing here.

Instead, I was walking down Main Street with Michelle Franco, fighting a war against myself. One side wanted to do everything in its power to keep her close to me. That was the side that had me skipping out on my morning meetings to drive a goddamned tow truck to her house. Begging Luciana to bump her schedule to fit Michelle in despite knowing she wouldn't let me get away with claiming I was just doing a favor for a friend.

The other side was screaming at me to run. Far, fast, and permanently.

I was already in too deep. I knew that the moment I turned around and saw her in her driveway this morning looking so breathtakingly beautiful I'd had to grab a chain on the truck and hold on for goddamned dear life lest I open my mouth and tell her. Or, god forbid, try to kiss her.

I thought I could pretend it wasn't there, this deep, unyielding need I had for her—a need that was so strong it was like air to aching lungs. But I couldn't, and that scared the shit out of me. That was what was telling me to be hard and distant and to shut her out before she saw the truth.

"So... Aubrey's?" Michelle asked as we reached the end of the block. "Or Chinese?"

But I was helpless, in her presence. At her mercy. On my knees. And before I could stop myself I said, "How about my place?"

It wasn't the most outlandish suggestion. There weren't that many lunch options in Barkley Falls. Michelle had named the two big ones, and there was a fifty percent chance Fred and Charles would be at either one of them. There was a deli at the grocery store people from Town Hall tended to grab sandwiches at or the little coffee shop by the medical clinic, but really, that was it.

"I kind of need to hide," I explained.

"Are you ashamed of me?"

She was teasing me, but the thought I had was the opposite. *Never. I want to crow your name from the rooftops. I want to tell the whole world you're with me.*

"No," I said. "But this is a small town. If I have lunch with..." I hesitated. What I couldn't say was *a gorgeous woman I can't keep my damn eyes off of—*

What I said instead was—"With a new woman in town, I'll be answering questions for weeks."

"I'm not that new. We moved here over a year ago!"

"They don't start calling you established until you've been here a decade."

Michelle had hesitated a moment longer, glancing at the garage, then nodded. "Fine. Okay. But I'm scared of Luciana, so..."

"I'm only five minutes from here," I assured her. "I'm a little scared of Luciana too."

She laughed. I almost forgot how the sound made me feel.

As we walked down Main Street, we passed several people who wanted to chat. A couple of business owners; a colleague from work; one of the organizers of the Christmas fair happening in just over a month. Shit. I should have taken her straight down a side street.

But someone would have noticed that too.

Each of the people who said hi looked curiously at Michelle. And each of them I gave a polite hello but kept walking briskly as if I had a very important meeting to attend to. Which I did.

The only exception was when we physically ran into Barbara Chambers coming out of Sadie's Vintage. She put her hand up like a traffic cop. "Oh no, William. You are not walking by without introducing me to this lovely young woman."

When we finally extricated ourselves, I took Michelle by the arm, leading her around the corner onto the back street. Enough was enough.

"Barbara's like an Italian grandmother," Michelle laughed.

"I'm glad you find this amusing," I said.

"You know this whole town, don't you?"

I let out a breath as we got some relative anonymity on the leafy side street. Though I wouldn't be surprised if people were hooking their fingers in their blinds as we walked by. We were only a block away from my place anyway. "Between growing up here and managing the whole town it's hard not to."

"Maybe you should run for mayor."

I stiffened. "Funny you should say that. Fred's trying to get me to run. After he's done."

"You'd be good at it."

I frowned.

"Seriously—everyone seems to love you. And you're so involved in the community. Have you ever thought about it?"

Usually when people asked me this, I wanted to put them off. I did put them off, telling them I was happy with my current job. Which I was. Ish. But being with Michelle, I felt like there was no point in lying. She made me question why I hid so much of myself from everyone else to begin with.

"It used to be my dream when I was a kid. I saw the people working in my community, making a difference. I wanted to do that. I joined all the clubs, did all the things I was supposed to. While working in New York, after my MBA, I used to get calls from firms representing political organizations. They wanted me to run for office."

"So, what happened?"

Suddenly I wished I hadn't spoken. That I'd kept things to myself.

"Life, I guess."

"Life?"

What was I supposed to tell her? That I'd gotten scared? That all the things my dad used to say to me about how I just wanted to be a hotshot for not working at the garage got in my head? "I guess I discovered I could do just as much good working in the background running the operations."

Michelle nodded. She didn't believe me.

A flicker of anger hit me. I didn't have to tell her my life story. How had she gotten me to talk about this anyway? No one had before. Not even Jill.

We'd reached the steps of my house. I jammed my key in the lock. "Why do you care anyway?"

"Excuse me?"

"I mean, I could be perfectly happy doing this job. Why does it matter if I'm not?"

Fire hit her eyes now. "So, you're not happy."

"I am—I..." Goddammit. How had she done that? How had this turned into talking about me and my long-dead dreams?

"I spent a lot of years focusing on my family," I said

finally. "Trying to save a failing marriage. It takes a lot out of someone."

Michelle held her hands up. "I'm not trying to give you a hard time, Will. But... you asked me about my blog, if it makes me happy. I've been thinking about that a lot, that's all."

I pinched the bridge of my nose. This was going to shit. "I'm sorry."

Michelle smiled a little sadly. "It's fine."

It wasn't, but I didn't know how to extricate myself from this mess. This was what I did apparently. I fucked up.

"Maybe you could show me around?" Michelle asked, putting on a smile.

I didn't fucking deserve her. She was perfect and kind and I was not.

"Sure," I said, my voice tight.

We spent the next few minutes touring the house. She seemed genuinely interested in all the details my girls rolled their eyes at when I talked to guests about them. The original wainscoting. The lead panes in the study on the main floor.

"It looks like a beautiful place to have raised a family," Michelle said as we headed back toward the stairs after a quick run-through of the second floor.

"It was." Or it would have been if I hadn't messed things up so badly. What I wouldn't give to get a second shot.

It was only after that thought that I realized Michelle hadn't followed me down the stairs. She'd stopped to examine a photo from the wall of them lining the stairway.

"Is this your family?" she asked.

I came back up, stopping just below her.

She was looking at a framed photo of us, one of those Sears portraits, taken when I was around thirteen.

"Yeah," I said. Stella had given me, Hank, and Dad the same photo for Christmas a couple of years ago. I'd tried to get rid of it, but Hannah had gotten mad at me when she'd found it in the trash and hung it up. I'd almost forgotten it was there.

The boys—Dad, Hank, and I—looked less than thrilled to be there. Dad especially. He was actually frowning—a storm cloud next to Mom's bright and sunny smile.

Looking at Mom made my chest hurt.

"Oh my god, look at little Hank!" Michelle said.

Hank must have been around eleven. He looked like he'd rather be outside; like he'd been wrangled into his suit—one of the lapels was sticking out and I could see the metal glinting from his clip-on kid tie.

Stella, meanwhile, was grinning her face off, even though Mom had made her take out her customary ponytail, which she still wore to this day.

"You don't look happy to have your picture taken," she said, squinting at me.

I looked as miserable as Dad.

"My dad and I fought in the car on the way over. We didn't exactly get along." Mom had broken it up, tsking at Dad for getting so angry.

Michelle looked over at me. I was one step down, so our eyes were level. "How about now?"

"Still don't," I said.

I looked back at the photo. The way Michelle was looking at me was too much. I couldn't trust myself to meet her eyes.

My mom's smile radiated from the photo. "I don't know how my mom put up with him. Why she didn't just leave."

Like Jill.

"She must have loved him," Michelle said.

Somehow, she had. And Jill hadn't.

"We better get some food," I said, my voice feeling distant. "Your car's going to be ready soon."

∼

It was only when we got to the kitchen that I realized I didn't really have any food to speak of. I didn't really think this through.

"Shit—there might be some soup in the pantry?"

Michelle studied me for a moment, then let out a breath, appearing ready to drop the discussion of my goddamn future. "We can do better than soup."

After ten minutes of her scrounging around in my pantry, fridge, and cupboards, I was taking a bite of the most mind-blowingly delicious sandwich I'd ever tasted.

"How the hell did you do that?" I asked around a mouthful.

"It's kind of what I do," Michelle said. She sat on the barstool next to me at the island. "In fact, I'm finishing up a blog post about how to make something out of nothing later today when I get home. So really, you were just a guinea pig."

I finished my bite looking at her. As she took a bite of her sandwich, I sat back and ran a hand through my hair, feeling like an ass.

"I'm sorry," I said.

She looked over at me but said nothing.

"Michelle, seriously. I'm sorry. I've never really told anyone about my earlier aspirations before and I guess I felt kind of... called out."

"Now you know what it's like," she said, taking a sip of water.

"I still think you should be running a restaurant," I said. "I've never tasted a sandwich this good."

"It would have been even better with a pinch of fresh cilantro."

"Ugh," I made a gross-out face.

"What's wrong with cilantro?"

"You mean soap leaves?"

She gasped. "Will Archer—cilantro is a delicious herb! It's used in the most gorgeous dishes the world over."

"You mean it ruins dishes literally everywhere."

"My god. That is uncalled for."

"You know what's uncalled for," I said, taking another bite of her outrageously delicious sandwich, "an herb that makes everything taste like I'm eating a tin can."

Michelle laughed as I finished my bite. "You're nuts."

"I'm not. I can't believe you like it. I might never be able to speak to you again."

She laughed harder, throwing her head back.

My chest twisted. She was beautiful.

When she lowered her face, she took in my expression and bunched her eyebrows together.

"What, do I have something in my teeth?"

She ran her tongue over her teeth and the sight of it made heat jump in my crotch. For a terrifying, delicious moment, I imagined that tongue flicking elsewhere.

Like over the tip of my hardening cock.

Inwardly, I groaned. Her laughter still echoed in the room around me.

"No," I said, my mouth suddenly dry. At that moment, all I wanted to do was kiss her. I felt my hands rising, going up as if to cup her jaw.

What the fuck Archer?

I froze, forcing myself to keep my hands gripped on the seat of the stool.

I couldn't do what I wanted. I couldn't because it would ruin this. This perfect whatever it was between us. Michelle wasn't someone I could just kiss and walk away from. As badly as I wanted her, and as good as that would be, I wanted more from her, and that scared the ever-loving shit out of me.

"Michelle—" I said.

She smiled, waiting for me to answer. The heat of it felt like pain.

I loved her smile.

I loved how she called me out on the mayor thing.

I love every goddamned thing about her.

I swallowed. Then I noticed something sparkle in her hair.

"There's something there," I said. I needed this distraction; I clung onto it, focusing on the thing in her hair like it was the most important thing in the world. Leaning over, I reached out, my hand brushing her cheek.

Michelle's eyes fluttered.

Kiss her.

The urge was so strong, the voice so loud in my ears, that my other hand slipped around her jaw, sliding up into her hair.

Her lips parted. "Will—"

I tipped her head sideways, leaned in, then hesitated.

Her eyes were closed.

I wasted my best years on you.

The words echoed through my brain like gunshots. It was what Jill screamed at me during our final blow-out fight. She'd been shaking she was so angry. Red-faced. Teary.

I'd ruined her life. Just like my dad had ruined my mother's.

That moment, that fight, was the moment I vowed never to do it again—never to fall in love with another woman.

Michelle's eyes opened.

I didn't meet them. Instead, stomach roiling so hard it hurt, I plucked the thing from her hair. It was a ghost. A tiny, white, sparkly foam ghost no bigger than my fingernail.

"It's a sign," I said, holding it out on my fingertip. There was something papery on the back, dusty, like powder.

"A sign of what?" she asked.

She hadn't moved.

My hand was still entangled in her hair.

I slipped it out, my stomach churning hard like someone was punching me there, over and over again.

"I can't offer you anything good, Michelle," I said. "I'll only bring you down. You deserve better. You've been through so much; I don't want to cause you any more pain."

Michelle's eyes flashed. Was she mad? "I'm not asking you for anything, Will." Her voice was hard. Yes. She was pissed. See? This was what I did. It was the one thing I did brilliantly.

"I'm sorry. I shouldn't have asked you here. I didn't mean anything by it, I just..."

I wanted to be with you. I didn't want you to leave.

The four days without her had felt like torture. But so did this. My mind reeled.

"What about friendship?" I said, my voice strange, not sounding like me. The word felt hollow because it was. I didn't just want friendship with her. It felt like a substitute. A disappointment.

Michelle's mouth opened, her expression almost...

rueful? "Can we have that?" I asked. Pleaded, more like. I needed her to say yes.

Then her eyes glossed with tears.

Fuck. Of course, I was making her cry. "I'm sorry," I said. I reached up and ran my thumb under her eye, catching the tear brimming there.

The heat rushed back.

Fuck it. I needed to kiss her. Every cell in my body demanded it. I leaned forward, everything else be damned.

But just a fraction before our lips met, Michelle's hand landed on my shoulder, pushing me away. "Friends," she reminded me.

I opened my mouth, then froze. There were noises outside. Giggling. Stomping on the back steps.

The back door slammed open. I jumped in front of Michelle, arms up.

Remy appeared in the doorway. She screamed. Then, when she saw it was me, said, "Dad?!"

My heart thumped. "Remy! What the hell are you doing here?"

"I—" her eyes darted sideways. "Mom said I was supposed to be with you the rest of the week! She said she talked to you."

Fuck. Jill had texted a couple of days ago. I'd completely forgotten—she and her boyfriend were doing some kind of getaway this weekend. How the fuck could I have forgotten my own daughter?

You've been obsessing over Michelle, that's why.

Remy glanced sideways again.

What the hell was she looking at? I strode forward, confusion and anger at myself jolting through me all at once. I yanked the door open and there was Draco disappearing around the corner of the house.

"The hell?"

"Dad we just came home for lunch, I didn't know you'd be home, that you'd have—"

She peered over my shoulder. I turned to see Michelle wave. "I'm just leaving," she said. "Nice to see you again, Remy."

Just like that, I lost Michelle once more, and it was all my fucking fault.

10

MICHELLE

"He says he just wants to be friends," Reese sobbed, blowing her nose on a tissue.

That sounded familiar.

I lowered the last of the Thanksgiving dinner dishes onto the towel Mom had laid out on the counter next to the already-full drying rack. The open plan of the main floor of my parents' house meant I could see Mom pushing off from her seat at the table next to Dad and heading for the refrigerator as I headed back to the couch in the living room to be with my sister.

Reese. This was about Reese.

"I have just the thing," Mom said, pulling a container from the fridge. "Meatballs."

"Mom!" I said. "She doesn't need another meatball."

"Anyone sad needs a meatball," Mom said, tutting. Nonna used to call Mom her honorary Italian daughter because of how mom had taken to learning her classic Italian dishes. She'd started acting like Nonna used to, too, always worried everyone was going to starve.

"Ain't that the truth," Dad said, standing up with his after-dinner tea.

I glared at him as he began backing out of the room. "What?" he mouthed over his shoulder down the hall, back to his late-night football replays. I knew the sounds of him snoring in his chair would come faintly down the hall in only a few minutes, his tea forgotten beside him.

I smiled, glad for Dad's distraction. It was good being around my parents. Every time I was home it reminded me of how much I missed seeing them all the time like we did when we lived closer. I worried about them though—Mom particularly. While Dad had fully embraced retirement, Mom, even through her concern for Reese, was still looking around the kitchen to see if there was anything left to do.

Not only did she miss mothering us, she missed working too, I knew.

"It's fine, I'll have one," Reese said, sniffing. She got up in a cascade of bunched-up tissues and shuffled over to the table.

Thanksgiving dinner was long over, with the girls tucked in the guest room here at Mom and Dad's house.

"You could have one too, Michelle," Mom said.

"Mom, I don't need any more comfort food." The words came out more defensively than I meant them to.

Mom gave me a look, but I wouldn't meet her eyes. She'd been with me all day and knew I was distracted. But I wasn't the one who'd been dumped—not really. And I wasn't hungry.

So why was I looking at the plate dripping with tomato sauce with a kind of yearning?

Maybe I should take a photo of them. I could see the post now: *Nonna's Meatballs Cure All.*

I frowned, angry at myself for even considering it. Not only had I tried to capture every moment of the food's preparation, but I'd also spent half the meal taking photos too, to the point where Macy asked why I had to do that at Grandma and Grandpa's house as well as at home. The worst part was, it wasn't even that that'd stopped me. It was Emma, watching me with a kind of disappointment that finally made me guiltily shove the phone in my pocket.

I knew I was acting like a gambler and had been all month. Each time promising myself that this one would be the perfect post; that this one would win the readers over.

But the truth was, none of my posts were doing all that well. As usual, they generated enough interest to pay the bills, but not enough to write home about.

Not even the Thanksgiving preparation post from yesterday was doing much. It was a good post, full of useful info. I'd even stooped to including a mildly emotional anecdote, along with a gorgeous photo of Mom and Macy.

Who didn't love a robust instructional Thanksgiving post with a personal touch?

My readers, apparently. The stark truth I'd discovered over the past three weeks was that now even hints of my personal life wouldn't cut it—they only thirsted for one thing.

Will.

They're not the only ones, are they?

I could practically hear the teasing tone of Joe's voice. I shoved the plate of meatballs away.

Friends, I reminded Joe. *That* was *your suggestion.*

And Will's. My chest felt like lead. It shouldn't have— Will and I didn't have anything together, but it did. I knew Will was only protecting himself—I knew he'd felt what I had in the kitchen. It was fine—being friends was all I should want, too.

I could have backed away. Unfortunately, complicating things deeply, the post with Will in it was taking off. WHEN LIFE THROWS YOU SNOWBALLS, DRINK BEER was now the most popular blog post I'd ever written. Not just recently. But ever. By a long shot.

1500 likes. 255 shares. And 341 comments, mostly speculating who the handsome man with the winch was. My readers were losing their minds over the mysterious W. They couldn't seem to get over how handsome and chivalrous he was.

I should have been excited, but it only stung, knowing how much of a distance we were keeping each other. There wasn't any knock-on effect either. My next post, without Will, had tanked.

"You could always get him to pose for some more pictures," Reese had suggested. "It doesn't have to be real."

"I need to do this myself," I'd told her. I didn't want to be beholden to Will. I wanted my blog to be successful, full stop. The success with the SNOWBALL post felt like a step in the wrong direction, like I was back at square one.

But more than that, it hurt too much. Especially since Will and I *had* actually started growing close—as friends, and by text only.

Reese took a giant bite of meatball. She'd dried her tears for the time being and was inspecting me as she chewed. She knew I was thinking about him.

"How are you able to eat anything?" I asked, needing her not to ask. The last thing I wanted was to talk about Will.

I meant the question though—watching her eat made my stomach hurt. Two hours after I'd taken my last bite of dinner, I was still feeling uncomfortably full, having overdone it on pretty much everything. Of course, along with taking photos of everything as we went, I'd also accepted spoonfuls of everything from Mom, something I only did when I was cooking with her, and only because she insisted I wasn't eating enough.

"Crying takes energy," Mom said as she cleared away the container of meatballs. She eyed me with one eyebrow raised like I should know what she was talking about.

I did, of course.

Mom had stuffed me with all of hers and Nonna's favorite recipes that year the girls and I had moved home, after Joe. I half suspected she'd quit her job as much so she could cook for us as watch the girls.

A surge of love for her washed through my frustration as she returned to the table and rubbed Reese's back.

It had been a good afternoon—a great one really, with Dad playing with the kids and me and mom cooking as usual. She'd lit up when Pietro had called from London, and even I'd had fun talking to my annoying big brother. Plus, the food was quite possibly the best spread we'd ever created together.

Even if I had been constantly looking at my phone. And even if it wasn't just blog notifications I was checking for.

Reese had shown up just before dinner, and though she'd tried to hold it in, the moment I saw her I knew. It was only when I asked for her help with something in another room that she told me the short, blistering affair she'd had with Eli, Will's friend, had petered out.

Or more like been squashed.

I had asked Will about Eli over text this afternoon once Reese had opened up about what had happened. That's what we did now—text, like friends.

He'd said he thought Eli was a decent guy. He didn't know him *all* that well though.

We're divorce buddies, he'd said.

I'd asked him what that meant and he just said, 'picture another me, only younger.'

I could exactly picture another version of Will, with his handsome face and semi perma-frown. But was Eli a good guy like Will?

Was Will a good guy? Had he really done anything different than Eli?

I stood up and began putting the dishes away.

"Careful, you're going to break my china!" Mom scolded.

I realized I'd been taking my frustration out on the plates.

"Sorry."

"Let me help," she said, bustling over.

"Mom, you should go to bed."

She grabbed a dish, as defiant as ever. "I'm fine."

But a moment later, I caught her stifling a yawn with the back of her hand.

I shook my head. "Mom, the girls have a full day planned for you tomorrow, remember? They're going to want you wide awake for that."

The kids were Mom's Achilles heel.

She nodded then went over and kissed Reese on the top of her head. "You take care of her," Mom said as she came back and gave me a squeeze. "Tell her it's just a stupid boy."

"Mom," I said, trying not to laugh. "He's a man."

"He's a little boy if he's hurting our Therese."

I laughed, softly. "I guess you're right," I agreed.

Once Mom had finally gone off to bed, I gave up on the dishes, instead pouring two fresh glasses of wine and sitting with Reese on the couch.

"So? You want to tell me the whole story now that Mom's gone?"

Reese looked at me, her lip wobbling. She always felt everything with her whole heart, my sister. I hated to imagine what things would be like with her if she were ever pregnant. That was the last time I remembered sobbing so uncontrollably. Though that was also right after Joe had died too.

I sighed, pushing those thoughts away.

Reese took a long sip of wine and then launched into telling me how she and Eli had gone out on a few dates. Everything seemed to be going great. She used the term date liberally, given they went back to one of their places each time and had, quote, *animalistic* sex.

"What exactly is that?" I asked. I was no prude, but the images I had in my head weren't necessarily sexy.

"The chemistry was perfect, okay?" she said. "But it wasn't just that. We had a deep connection too."

"The guy was just recently divorced though, wasn't he?"

"Wasn't Will?"

A flash of something hot ran over me. "Will's been divorced a year, and we're not having a torrid love affair."

"Right. You're just friends. Just like Eli wants to be." She buried her head in her arms again, the wine sloshing in her glass. I pulled it away from her before she upended it on the back of the couch.

The reminder of what Will and I were pricked at me. Maybe things would have been easier if Will and I had just had a fling, like Reese and Eli. Maybe we would have gotten whatever this was between us out of our systems, and I wouldn't be plagued by constant thoughts of him at all times. Maybe I wouldn't want to text him with every little detail of my life like I had started doing.

But if that had happened, we surely wouldn't have become friends, either. And that part had been the most surprising thing.

Over the past three weeks, we'd settled into a comfortable friendship; albeit one that was texting-only, where we never mentioned anything that had happened between us that had been non-friend-like. Especially that moment at his house.

God, that moment. He'd been so close I could smell the scent of his skin. I could feel the heat of him on me. There had been desire in his eyes, as liquid and searing as I felt. It was like he'd barely been able to restrain himself.

Yet he did. He'd pulled back, just before Remy burst in on us.

He'd apologized again the next day, sending me an article about how cilantro-hating was genetic. I'd laughed, despite my jumbled feelings about what had happened. The next day, I'd texted him a photo of my perfect lasagna, and he'd told me I should frame it. The actual lasagna, not the photo. What started as a few texts here and there had turned into whole conversations.

Somehow, by sticking to text only, it was like a barrier had dropped. Maybe I should have run away after what he'd told me. But it seemed like he'd needed a friend.

And I realized, I had too.

I'd begun to tell him things I don't think I'd ever admit to in person. Silly things, like how I used to have nightmares about Big Bird when I was a kid, which he'd thought was the funniest thing he'd ever heard. Real things too like how I was worried about my Mom and Dad aging on their own in this house on Long Island. Just the other night, I'd even let a big one slip—we'd been talking about Hank and how much better he was doing since reconnecting with Casey and going to therapy. But talking about Hank only reminded me of Joe, and I'd told him I was scared Emma would grow to hate her father for how he passed. She knew he'd been sick, and she knew he hadn't died of that sickness. She'd been putting two and two together.

I hadn't even told Reese that one.

But Will had shared just as much. I now knew all about how he used to have a crush on his sixth-grade English teacher, and how he still blushed when he saw her around town, even though she was pushing seventy. I also knew Jill had told him she'd wasted her best years on him. Though he hadn't said it, I knew he'd blamed himself—squarely—for not having been able to save his marriage.

The only thing I wasn't sure of, that we also didn't talk about, was that blog post. The one with him in it. I was fairly certain Will hadn't seen it. He had to be making a concerted effort *not* to visit my blog. If he had seen the post, he'd know the two photos of him had made him practically a celebrity, at least in my readers' eyes. The only post that had done close to as well as that one was I GUESS I'M A WIDOW NOW.

I should have been happy about that. I'd achieved my goal of no longer being a pity-party. But even now, my frustration came back. The food was still taking a backseat. Plus, no matter what I tried, I couldn't replicate even half the success of the SNOWBALLS post.

"I need more wine," Reese said, holding up her glass. Somehow, she'd gotten it back from me and gone through the whole glass while I'd been thinking about Will. "It's the only thing making me forget I've lost the man of my dreams."

Guilty, and mad at myself for being so distracted, I took

Reese's glass once more and directed my full attention back to her. I was pissed at Eli too, for messing with my sister.

I was even angry at her for letting him get to her. "Reese, you barely knew the guy."

"But that's the thing, Mich. You're right, I did barely know him. But I felt like I knew more of him in the few weeks we saw each other than I ever knew of Simon."

"So, what happened?"

"He said he's moving away. He didn't tell me until yesterday. He said he has to take care of his family's business. A hotel or something. But it doesn't mean we need to break up. Honestly, I'm pretty sure he's just scared."

"So, he's running away?" I asked. "Maybe it's for the best."

She shook her head hard. "No. I didn't make up what we shared, Michelle. I'm not imagining it. I know I've had a few flings since Simon, but they've been nothing. Throwaway. This was bigger than that. And now…"

She slumped back on the couch as I set her empty wine glass down on the table. She'd forgotten about it, I hoped. The last thing she needed was to wake up depressed and hungover too.

"You know what he said?" Reese asked, resting her elbow on the back of the couch and leaning her head in her hand. "He said I could come and stay at the hotel if I wanted. That he couldn't guarantee he'd even be able to see me, but he could get me a room. A fucking room."

I narrowed my eyes. "What, so he's paying you off?" It felt good to stoke my anger.

"I don't know. I think he felt bad or something."

"Well, you should take it. Use the room."

"I don't want to see him!"

Suddenly I was sick of it. Sick of Eli making Reese—

normally so sweet and cheery—hurt so badly, and for chickening out and running away.

Sick of Will for dominating my readers' attention.

And mine.

"You don't even have to see him—book the room on the busiest weekend of the year."

"Christmas?"

"Mom would die," I said. "Pietro's not coming home then, either."

Reese smiled, wiping at her face with the heels of her hands. "Maybe I will."

"To hell with these guys, right?" I said.

She laughed. It was the best sound I'd heard in a while.

But if I knew anything, I knew Reese needed to help herself too. She'd been destroyed after Simon left. I'd had to scrape her off the ground to get her back on her feet.

She's the sensitive one, Mom said. She was, she had the biggest feelings. But she didn't have to let men be at the center of them. It was distracting her from what she really wanted.

I should know—I was letting the same thing happen.

I cleared my throat and put on the big sister voice she used on me in situations like this. "Reese, Eli did you wrong. But maybe you should take a break from dating. Find out who you are and what you want. You said yourself you want to do other things. That Gastronomique is going to be your last restaurant job."

I didn't mention the singing. I didn't want to set her off. But by the way she was looking at me, I think she knew.

"It's time to stop letting men interfere with your dreams."

Fresh tears glistened in my big sister's eyes. "You're

right," she said. "But I'm supposed to be the older, wiser one."

"You are," I said. "Except this time."

But as we hugged, I knew I was only really the wiser one if I took my own advice. I needed to back away from Will Archer. Stick to Reese, to family. Focus on me and my dreams—whittled down as they were now.

It was better this way.

11

WILL

I stared down at my phone, willing myself not to open my internet browser.

I won't be a stalker. I won't.

My thumb hovered over the keypad. Then I clapped the phone facedown on my desk, leaning back in my chair with my fingers over my eyes.

It had been weeks since I'd last seen Michelle. An eternity since I told her, in desperation, that I just wanted to be friends. It was a lie—the biggest lie I'd ever told, but it was a necessary one. I was sure of that. For her, but also for me.

The truth was, I knew, in that moment in my kitchen, with my hand in Michelle's hair, that I was doing the thing I'd promised myself I'd never do again.

I was falling for her. And it scared the shit out of me.

It was Friday night, and Sheila and I were the only ones left in the office as far as I could tell. The only reason I was still here was to meet an artisan who needed to measure her booth space in the room where the Christmas Fair was happening. I'd agreed to meet the artist personally as they were a friend of Casey's. Also because nobody else wanted to stay late on a Friday. There was no reason for my assistant to have to stay too.

"Sheila!" I barked. I could hear her voice through my door—she must be talking to someone on the phone.

I sat up straight, opening my email.

My eyes immediately glazed over.

Despite my inability to concentrate at the moment, I was grateful for my job this week. With Remy at her mom's until today, I'd stayed late every night this week, keeping myself busy so I wouldn't think about Michelle. Nights were the worst. I could read or watch a show, but once I crawled into bed, I was fucked.

In the dark, all I could see was Michelle's face. All I could feel was her body under my hands. Or at least, how I imagined it feeling. And God knew I'd imagined it enough over the past few weeks.

Last night, I'd imagined fucking her in the tow truck. Pulling over to the side of the road and pulling her down onto the bench seat next to me. Freeing those gorgeous, full tits; bending down and taking them in my mouth.

Another night I pictured us in the presidential suite at the resort the mayor wanted me to visit, just like I'd done in Fred's office. Only this time my imagination had no barriers. Given free rein, I pictured lifting her up onto the edge of the jacuzzi tub, her skin slick with water and soap, my tongue exploring every part of her.

But sometimes it was more innocent—or at least subtle. The sound of her voice, low in my ear. The scent of her, like my face was buried in her neck or hair. Even though it had been weeks ago, my brain kept taking me exactly where I worked so hard not to go.

This was ridiculous. I should just look at the blog.

Checking Michelle's blog was one line I hadn't crossed. I

hadn't read it since that night at the coffee shop. After seeing how personal it was, like a microscope on her life, I'd vowed to myself I wouldn't. I told myself it was because it was none of my business. But the truth was, I knew the line between me keeping my distance and driving right up to her goddamn door was paper-thin. Reading her blog, the most personal, candid stories about her life, would light a flame to that divide.

I picked up my phone again.

"You called?"

"Shit!" I said, startled. I shoved my phone in my desk drawer and looked up to see Sheila standing in the doorway with her coat on.

"Yes," I said.

Thank god she'd come in when she did.

"You should get out of here."

"You sure?"

"Definitely. Enjoy your weekend."

"Okay..." she said, but she didn't move. She was stalling for some reason.

"Don't forget to sign those," she said, pointing to a stack of files she'd brought in this afternoon. "All the signature lines are marked."

The names on the files looked familiar, and I had a strong suspicion Sheila had pulled the same stack off my desk earlier and brought them back in for dramatic effect. Or to get it through my thick skull that I needed to actually pay attention to work.

"Sorry, Sheila," I said. "I know I've been a bit distracted lately."

"You okay, Will?"

"Of course." I didn't look up, just pulled the files toward me. Luckily, Sheila was used to me not always plastering a smile on my face. "I've got a lot going on right now."

"If you ever want to talk about it—"

"I don't," I said, harder than I should have.

There was a pause where she hovered a moment longer. I looked up, extremely close to telling her she needed to go, when she said, "By the way, Louis will not stop pestering me about you booking a stay at that resort in Vermont."

Louis was the Mayor's assistant.

"Still?" I asked. Fred had been doing the same thing to me.

I'd pretty much decided I shouldn't go—Fred's insistence made me positive there was something else going on, but so far, he'd staunchly denied it was anything except taking notes to expand tourism in Jewel Lakes.

"Why the hell is he so adamant I go?"

The question was rhetorical, but Sheila answered anyway. "I don't know," she said. "But the funny thing is, one of those files is a request for you to give pre-Council approval to a project here under the same development company doing the renovations on the Rolling Hills Resort in Vermont."

I opened the file, suspicious. What the hell wasn't Fred telling me?

"Anyhow, on paper, it doesn't look like a conflict of interest," she said. "So you know, if you're not with the girls this year," —she knew I wasn't, and wasn't happy about it— "Maybe you should think about taking him up on his offer? The place looks wonderful."

She pulled a brochure out from where it was sticking out of the stack. It did look stunning.

"If you went," she continued, "it would get his assistant

off my back. He's driving me nuts—I swear, I'm about ready to bone him."

I dropped the brochure. "You want to what?"

"Bone him! You know, over the head."

I placed my hand over my mouth, making like I was rubbing my chin considering this, but really trying not to laugh out loud. A few weeks ago, I would have texted this to Michelle. Immediately.

The laughter died in my throat. Not anymore. Whatever friendship we'd struck up over the past few weeks had petered out recently. She'd only answered my texts sporadically, and I'd kind of given up trying.

I missed it.

I missed her.

"I'll think about it," I said finally. "In the meantime, just tell Fred's assistant to lay off. I'll let Fred know myself what I decide."

Sheila nodded, heading for the door.

Was it my imagination, or was she still lingering?

"Any plans this weekend?"

I frowned. "Nope. Remy's back tonight so probably just a pizza at home. Why?"

She smiled. "Oh nothing. Just... my girlfriend, she's a real foodie. She follows a food blog called Bella Eats."

My stomach dropped. "And?"

"And it's you, isn't it? In the photos? Getting her car out of the ditch?"

I'd forgotten all about the photo Michelle took of me, the one she'd asked if she could post. It felt like ages ago.

"Oh," I said, stupidly. I didn't know what else to say.

"I think it's *wonderful* you're dating again, and that sweet Michelle, she's been through so much..."

"We're not dating," I said.

Sheila blinked.

"We're..." I was going to say friends, but I wasn't sure we were even that anymore. "Remy's her babysitter. That's all."

"But you were in Millerville together—"

"I was just helping Ms. Franco out. That's all it is. And I'd appreciate it if you kept that to yourself." Then, because I knew how I sounded—and that I could trust her, I said, "Please?"

Sheila nodded knowingly. "Right. Of course."

I almost said something like 'it's not what you think.' But what did it matter?

After Sheila bustled out of the office, I pulled the drawer open and grabbed my phone.

Resolution be damned, I had to see what the blog said.

It didn't take me long—the most recent post she'd written was called *MEATBALL MADNESS,* published on Sunday. I opened and quickly scanned it—nothing about me, and no pictures except a delicious-looking meatball drowning in homemade tomato sauce.

Then, at the bottom I saw the button entitled PREVIOUS POSTS.

I clicked it, and there it was, a couple posts back: *WHEN LIFE THROWS YOU SNOWBALLS, DRINK BEER.*

There were the photos she'd taken. The first, me looking like a dufus getting my pants muddy as I hitched her car to mine. The second was a selfie, her smile dazzling.

I was suddenly thrown back to that moment—I'd been preoccupied with the feeling of Michelle's arm through mine as we cut across the parking lot. And in fact, the moment was captured. There in the bottom corner of the photo was my arm.

It was enough that the commenters below the article had clearly lost their shit.

Michelle, OMG, so happy you're on a date! Exclaimed one.
Who is THAT?!? Said another.

They went on. And on. There were pages of them. People chatting back and forth.

My stomach rolled around inside of me. I suddenly understood exactly what she meant when she said her readers were invested in her personal life. They were as bad as teenage daughters. Worse maybe, presuming they were all adults.

Last time I'd read her blog, back at Roasters, it had been a brief scan. This time, without her here, I scrolled back through several of her earlier posts, needing to see what they said about the rest of her life. If they were that eager about other people who appeared in her photos.

But somehow, my fingers hit a button that took me all the way to the beginning of the blog.

"Shit," I said out loud.

I went to scroll ahead but paused. These early posts were years old. The way she'd structured them was different—it was more like a personal diary than a cooking blog, though food was still a big part of it. My breath caught in my throat as I took in the photos of a younger Michelle leaning on the arm of someone else. She was still young now, but here she couldn't have been more than twenty-two or three.

Jealousy spiked through me, followed quickly by burning shame. How could I be jealous of her husband? The man was dead, for god's sake. I flipped to some later photos and my jaw nearly dropped when I saw Hank with his arm looped around Joe's shoulders.

I knew Michelle's husband had been my brother's best friend in New York. That they had met in firefighter training and had ended up at the same station together. I knew that was how Hank knew Michelle. But it was somehow shocking to see the two of them together. I thought of where I was around that time—here, in Barkley Falls, in the happier early days of my marriage, maybe, when the girls were young.

Hank looked kind of hollow-eyed in the photo, and I realized it must have been around the time he and Casey had split originally. Hank had confessed to me this summer, over more than a few beers, that even though he'd been devastated over his relationship with Casey—his first relationship with her, years ago—it was his fault they'd separated. He realized he'd been trying to prove himself to Dad. It was the whole reason he'd wanted to be a firefighter so badly—to make Dad proud.

I lowered the phone, shame rippling through me. Dad was in a care home now, not because he was elderly and frail—he was only in his late sixties but because he had such bad respiratory problems he needed around-the-clock care.

An argument I'd had on the phone with Stella only a couple of months ago ran through my mind. *Think of what he's been through!* Stella had said. She'd called me when she'd heard I hadn't been keeping up with the weekly visits to see him in the care home since she moved.

I knew about Dad's tragic past; that when he was a child, his family had perished in a house fire, and he'd been the only survivor. I'd only found out about it when Mom told me as a teenager. Mom said she told me because she thought it would make me sympathetic to him. But I'd been devastated that he'd lied. That he hadn't trusted me—his eldest son—enough to tell the truth.

At the time, I thought it explained so much. His stiffness. How he kept himself distant from his feelings. How he never wanted to talk about his past. How he hacked up a lung anytime he got a cold.

There was a time my heart hurt for him, but his bullheaded insistence that I live my life the way he wanted me to—no matter what I wanted—and all the fights that had brought out between us, had hardened me. As time went on, I knew it wasn't Dad's past that made him the way he was. It was him.

When Hank had been reconciling with Casey, I knew he'd wanted to resolve his issues with Dad. At the time, I'd told him trying to make Dad proud of him was a waste of time. I'd given up on Dad years ago. But the two of them seemed to be on good terms now.

I stared at the photo of Hank and Joe. Hank had been messed up about Joe's death. How could he not be? But he'd battled his demons and won. He'd figured things out with Dad, and he and Casey were happy too. I thought of that family photo again, that one Michelle had stopped at. The one with Mom and her glowing face. My heart twisted painfully. My eyes went to Dad. Was he the asshole, or was I?

For some foolish reason, Michelle's face flashed before my eyes, her scent swirling in my nostrils as if she were right beside me. And for the briefest moment, I allowed myself to imagine what it would be like being with her. Having the kind of relationship I thought I'd had with Jill. The challenging but rewarding days of being a family together. Sitting on a bench together looking out into the sunset in our old age.

But that kind of life wasn't possible. Some lucky people got it, but they sure as hell weren't me. I'd tried—for twenty years I'd tried with Jill. But I hadn't been able to hide the truth. I was just like my father.

My desk phone buzzed.

Morgan was here.

I closed the blog.

Morgan was a sweet, pretty, woman with clay under her nails and a slightly stressed-out air about her at the moment. After we made introductions and I'd shown her to the space the fair would be happening, she became intently focused on her work, pulling out a serious-looking camera and snapping photos of the space.

I wondered if Morgan was married—if she was someone who'd managed to figure out how to make a relationship work, or if she was messed up like me?

God, maybe I needed to spend more time with people who were actually happy. Hank and Casey. Graydon and Lucy. The thought buoyed me, and I pulled out the phone to text one of them. Or maybe both.

But when I unlocked my screen, I did a double take. I had one missed call from Michelle Franco.

12

MICHELLE

It was my landlord who made me call Will, breaking not only our unspoken texting-only rule, but the silence that followed after Thanksgiving.

That and the pizza.

My landlord, an elderly man who lived in the farmhouse up the hill, had hobbled down to our cottage in person this week, hat in hand. "I'm sorry Michelle, but with the three of you here, the water's been going up, and the electricity too. I gave you a discount when you first got here but..." He petered out. I knew he didn't have much money.

It was going to be an extra hundred and fifty dollars a month. Not the worst, but when I was barely scraping by as it was, it would hurt.

I told him I understood, of course I did. Then when I closed the door behind him, I broke down in tears, angrily kicking the garbage can by the back door. Luckily the girls had been at school.

I'd allowed myself to wallow for only a few minutes before straightening up and assessing the situation. We weren't going to be tossed out—not yet. Of course, I wouldn't let that happen.

"We could always move back to Mom's," I said when I talked to Reese about it.

"NO!" she'd said, emphatic. "You can't leave me—I came here to be closer to you! And what about our plan to get Mom and Dad over here?"

When we left Mom and Dad's place after Thanksgiving, mom had been bereft. It was Reese who'd suggested maybe we should try getting them to move to Jewel Lakes. I'd never thought about asking, mostly because I didn't want Mom to think I needed more help.

So far, when Reese asked a couple of weeks ago, it had been a hard no. They were attached to the home we'd grown up in. They had friends there. But we'd decided to keep trying, together, even though I wasn't sure it would ever work.

"I know," I said. "I'm just saying, if things got really dire."

"If things get that dire, you guys could move in with me." Reese lived in a one-bedroom apartment in Millerville. Hardly appropriate for a family.

I smiled, though she couldn't see it. "You're young and single. You don't need us cramping your style."

"First of all, I'm two years older than you. Second, cramping what style? My lifestyle is 'work and come home'."

"And dating?"

"I'm not doing that right now, remember?" she said. "Per your advice."

"Seriously?"

"Yes, seriously." She sounded annoyed.

"Okay," I said. "Sorry." Maybe I shouldn't have been so surprised she was taking my advice. But I couldn't help the note of suspicion in my voice. She hadn't said a word about Eli since Thanksgiving. I wasn't naive enough to think that meant he was out of her mind completely—I'd only ever known Reese to put her whole heart into her relationships.

I would have run it by Will—as an outside party, and my friend—if he and I were talking. But we weren't, not since I'd stopped texting beyond perfunctory replies to his now-dwindling texts. But thinking about that only added to my depression.

"Anyway we're not talking about me," she said, pivoting the conversation back to my financial stress. "What about the firefighter money?"

I hedged. "Yeah... I guess." I had a few thousand left in savings from the firefighter fund. But I was saving that. I wasn't sure for what yet—maybe nothing, but it was psychological at that point. Like I was holding onto a dream. But I knew if I used it now, I'd dip into it again, and the saddest thing in the world would be for me to run through it with living expenses over a couple of years.

Joe would tell me I was being stubborn, but when I listened for him, he wasn't there.

"Okay fine," Reese said. "You know what the other option is."

"What?"

"You know what I'm talking about."

I scowled. "I'm not putting him back in the blog."

"But it would be so easy! A couple of photos every other post. Bam. Rent increase covered."

"It's not that simple," I said. Though she was right—my readers were still sending me messages asking what had happened to the mystery White Knight.

Reese didn't know the whole story with Will. She didn't

know how things were between us. How it hurt to be around him and how I'd had to step back from even texting with him after it got too hard.

"You care about him, don't you?" Reese asked.

"Yes," I said, without hesitation. But that was what was so hard.

"Then why can't you talk to him?"

I didn't know if she meant asking him for photos or talking to him about what had happened between. "Because," I said, the words suddenly choking me.

"Because he's not Joe."

Reese didn't say anything for a moment.

"Mich, no one is."

But she didn't understand what I meant. My throat was thick from the pain of the words pressing at the top of my mouth. It wasn't that he couldn't live up to Joe. It was something else, something even harder.

But I couldn't say all that. I couldn't even say it to myself.

"I'll figure it out," I said. "I gotta go."

"Mich—"

I hung up before she could say anything else.

I was just going to have to step up the posts even more. That was all there was to it. Things had been getting better; I was generating more income, if only a trickle. I could do this. Never mind that last week I'd told Reese it was like pulling teeth. That I'd been breaking my back posting more often, taking more photos, trying new recipes, and I'd only inched up in revenue. It wasn't enough.

But I couldn't call Will.

You're doing it again.

I sucked in air. I hadn't heard his voice in a few days. A week actually.

I know. I know I am.
You know I'm dead, right?
I could have laughed.
You don't say, Joe?
Calling him won't hurt me.
My chest seized.
It'll hurt me, Joe. Won't it?
But Joe wasn't there. Of course he wasn't.

Impulsively, I threw my phone down on the table suddenly furious. When it thunked against the wood I sucked in a breath. What was I doing? I couldn't afford a new phone if it broke, and I needed it for the blog.

As I tapped the screen, saying a silent prayer I hadn't cracked it, a photo memory came up. Reese, making pizza with the girls last summer.

Pizza. That was it. The girls and I would make pizza and the blog readers would love it. It would be a hit and everything would be solved.

It had to be.

∽

HOMEMADE PIZZA with the girls was always a hit, both at home and on the blog. Tonight, I'd spent all evening perfecting shots of the dough-making process, the slow-cooked tomato sauce, and the various toppings. I'd caramelized onions and roasted red peppers. Meanwhile, Macy kept trying to stick pepperoni on her nose and Emma ate more cheese than she was sprinkling on the pie. It was cute, but was it cute enough? There had to be more I could do to make the post pop. Once it was finally in the oven, I left the girls with some coloring at the kitchen table, delaying clean-up for now in favor of setting up the studio equipment I rarely used.

Joe would say I was getting frenzied; digging my hole deeper while clinging to my stubborn refusal to do the thing I really should do. But Joe didn't understand. He never did. My doggedness—my relentless refusal to give up was what had kept us going when he went to that dark place after his diagnosis. It's what got him back on his feet, wanting to help and do good before he left rather than wallowing in self-pity. Because that's what he was doing, when he died. Good.

My stubbornness would see us through now.

It had to.

"Mom!" Emma called from downstairs. "Is the pizza supposed to smoke?"

I burst into the kitchen to see gray clouds puffing out of the oven. The girls were at the table where I'd left them, only now, Macy was hiding behind Emma's chair.

"Damn it!" I exclaimed, running to open the oven door. I hadn't been able to find the tripod. I knew it was somewhere in the boxes of stuff I'd moved from Rochester, but I'd gotten so involved in looking I'd forgotten I hadn't set a timer for the pizza. I always went by sight and smell, but that didn't work when I didn't stay in the kitchen.

Now, as I yanked open the oven door, a giant plume of gray billowed out, making me cough. Flames—actual flames—were licking the top of the oven. Then the sharp knife of the smoke alarm went off.

"Mommy!" Macy cried.

"It's okay, baby!" I said, grabbing the oven mitts. "Girls, go to the other room."

Emma grabbed Macy's hand and pulled her into the hallway.

Half the pie was in flames on the oven element.

Alarm shrieking, I hauled the burning thing that used to be pizza out of the oven and stomped the flames out, getting blackened dough, tomato sauce, and burning cheese all over the bottom of my slippers. Then I stood up on a chair and pried open the smoke alarm.

For a moment I stood there panting as the room went quiet.

"Mom?" Macy's little voice came from beyond the doorway.

The girls.

I whirled around, heart in my throat. I knew Macy was okay, but the realization of what I'd just put Emma through rocketed through me. Emma may not have Frayne's, but she still had the headaches. She was sensitive to bright lights and loud noises.

I sprinted out into the hallway. Emma was crouched against the wall, her head in her hands, Macy leaning over her like a tiny doctor.

"Oh my god," I said, running over. "Emma! Emma, honey..."

"I'm okay," she said, muffled into her knees. She didn't want me to worry. But when she looked up, I saw her eyebrows were sharply slanted. She was in pain.

"I'll be right back." I ran to the medicine cabinet for her painkillers.

Five minutes later, with Emma having swallowed her pill and Macy now crying, I sat in the hallway with a daughter under each arm, stroking the tops of their heads.

"I'm sorry," I whispered, shame rolling over me like water.

I couldn't believe I'd been so focused on this stupid pizza—and on trying to sort the blog out myself—I'd lost sight of what was the most important thing.

"Mom, what are we going to do?" Macy asked. I knew she was asking about the pizza, but I pulled her head tight under my chin and answered the bigger question.

"I'm going to get us help."

13

MICHELLE

A half hour later, lights flashed across our living room window, sending my nerves scattershot.

"They're here!" Emma cried. She and Macy bounded from their perch—pressed up in front of the plate glass—and raced to the door.

Emma seemed to have perfectly recovered from her flash headache, though I hadn't recovered from my guilt over not seeing it coming. Or not mitigating it quickly enough. Or a thousand other ways I'd failed my kids while I'd been preoccupied. But I couldn't think about that now. I'd asked him over to ask if he'd pose for the blog.

As my what—boyfriend? For a moment I blanched. I knew Will wouldn't go for it–not at first, anyway. But I only needed a few shots—we could even save them up to cover a few months.

That was all there was to it.

I let out a breath when I found Remy coming up the steps first. Seeing Will's daughter first was a relief, though the last time I'd seen her we'd both been in slightly compromising positions.

Macy threw her arms around the girl, then said, "I have to show you what Piggy-pop is doing right now," in a very serious tone. "It's a little embarrassing."

Piggy-pop was Macy's seen-better-days stuffed pig, who Macy frequently put in compromising positions, claiming the toy had done it itself.

"Not again!" Remy exclaimed, palms on her cheeks. Macy dragged her inside, barely giving the teen enough time to kick off her boots and wave at Emma and me. "Hi, Ms. Franco."

"Michelle, please," I said. I thought I'd said that last time but maybe I'd been flustered by the whole man in shadows thing—Will, waiting in his car outside to see she got in safe.

The same man who was stepping through my doorway now with two boxes of still-steaming pizza.

My stomach, already wobbly, pulled itself into a knot.

How long had it been since I'd seen him in the flesh? Since that moment in his house, more than a month ago. I'd forgotten how his stubble was flecked with silver. How his crystalline eyes bored into me, making my blood rush at double speed.

This was why I hadn't asked for him to help sooner. I couldn't be around him without my body—my everything—betraying me.

"Michelle," Will said in greeting. His voice, strangely formal, made something go loose inside me.

"Will."

This was like that first moment we saw each other again at the park. Like we were strangers but not at all.

Nerves jangled in my stomach. Just get him on his own and ask. How hard can it be?

"Will!" Macy called from down the hall. "Come see Piggy-pop! And no swearing!"

"I better go," he said.

I'd waited this long. A few more minutes wouldn't hurt. Not unless I lost my nerve.

"I can take those." I said, reaching for the boxes. Our fingers brushed as he transferred them into my arms, sending something snapping down my arm.

Shit.

"Mom," Emma said, tugging at my sleeve once Will had gone. "I feel better. Could we watch a movie with Remy while we eat? Just the kids?"

"Emma—" I said, ready to say no. I didn't want to leave my little girl. Not after tonight. But she wasn't so little anymore. I stroked her hair, so much like mine. "How's your head?"

"It doesn't hurt anymore."

"It's fine with me," Remy said from the end of the hall. She'd been leaning against Macy's doorframe and had popped her head out. "We can let your mom and my dad have some undisturbed alone time, right, Emma?"

Emma scrunched up her nose, not quite getting what Remy meant.

"I don't—" I began. I did need alone time with Will, just not for whatever reasons she thought I did. "Thank you, Remy. Come and get us if you need anything."

"We'll be fine," Remy said, grinning. She took one of the boxes from me, while Emma grabbed other supplies from the kitchen. Then it was just me, in the dark hallway.

I made my way to the kitchen, my stomach sinking when I saw it. The girls and I hadn't ventured after calling Will. It still reeked of smoke, and because I'd barely gotten a chance to start cleaning up while we were prepping the food, it looked like an Italian grocery store had exploded in it. Scraps of pepper lay all over the counter and the floor; a charcuterie board's worth of prosciutto scraps were stuck to the counter, and there was flour *everywhere.*

I didn't even have the energy to think about where to begin.

Wine. That would help, in the short term anyway.

I strode to the cupboard I used as a pantry, which was tucked into an alcove across from the kitchen table. The cupboard was narrow, with shelves all the way up. There was a bottle of red I'd stashed in there for emergencies. It wasn't great wine, but it would do the trick.

Of course, I'd hidden it a little too well. There was no light and I had to get down on my hands and knees to feel around for it amidst the various bottles and boxes on the ground.

"Hey," said Will from behind me.

I jumped, startled, whacking my head hard against the shelf above.

"Ow!" I exclaimed, as jars rattled and food packets rained down around me. Pain radiated through my skull.

"Jesus, Michelle!" Will said, rushing over as I slumped down onto my knees.

He knelt beside me. "I shouldn't have startled you."

"Yeah," I said, my eyes squeezed shut as I gripped the back of my head in my hands. "This is all your fault, Will." I tried a smile to show him I was kidding, but it hurt too much.

"It is, actually," he said, his voice serious. "Let me see."

"No," I said, fast. I couldn't have him touch me. It would be too hard. Too confusing.

Will went stiff for a moment, then stood up.

"I'm sorry," I said. I moved to get up but pain shot through my head again making me suck in air.

"I should take you to the clinic. The one in Barkley Falls should still be open—"

"It's fine. Just a goose egg."

Will inspected me for a moment but seemed to accept that I wasn't going to bleed out on the kitchen floor.

"What were you looking for in there anyway?"

"Wine."

"In the broom closet?"

"It's not a broom closet!"

"Looks like a broom closet."

I glared.

Will went over to the table. Did I see him smile before he turned? Why did I hope he did?

I gave up on getting up, instead leaning my head back against the wall, resting my arms on my raised knees.

I could do this. Just how to start? *Will, even though we're friends, kind of, and you think I hate my blog*—no, he thought my blog was hurting me. He'd said as much in the past. Was he right? Was it therapeutic sharing everything on my blog or was it a crutch, keeping me from doing what I really wanted? He'd kept sending me updates on that storefront down on Main Street in Barkley Falls, the one that had been vacant for a month. I'd thought he was joking–and he had been, sometimes. *You can call it* Michelle's Meatballs. Or *Canoodling At the Table*. I'd snort-laughed at that one.

I opened my eyes to find Will looking at me.

"You okay?" he asked.

He was a good man. He'd been a good friend, and I'd cut him off. I wanted to tell him I was sorry, that I'd seen what had happened with Reese and Eli and conflated it somehow to what we had.

But Will wasn't stringing me along the way Eli had been. We'd just been friends.

Right?

I could almost hear Joe laughing at me.

I nodded, unable to find the words, or worried if I did, everything would spill out. I stared at Will's face, at the line of his jaw with its silver stubble. At the way he was looking at me now, unraveling something inside of me. I didn't just want to be friends with Will. And that scared the shit out of me.

He studied me a moment longer, then began moving about the room, pulling plates down for us. Will looked good in a kitchen. At ease. Joe had been hopeless with everything except the barbecue. I let myself watch the play of Will's muscles under his shirt as he reached up into a cupboard, pulling down wine glasses. Had Joe looked like that? I couldn't remember now.

Will paused. "Are you sure you're up for wine?"

"It's a necessity," I said, barely able to find my voice.

"Okay. I brought a bottle. I can guarantee you're going to like this one better than whatever broom brew you were going for."

"Broom brew!" I laughed, forgetting myself. A dull ache followed the movement. I swallowed.

Will held up the bottle so I could see it. I recognized it as an expensive California red another food blogger I followed raved about constantly.

"That's expensive, isn't it?" I asked. Then I was embarrassed I'd said it. I'd always been too cheap to buy it. Or rather, I just couldn't afford it on my shoestring budget. Once again, I thought of the failings of my blog. How I'd ignored my family for it, framing endless photos of food and writing long soliloquies about tomato sauce—and for what?

"It seemed like we needed the big guns tonight," Will said, unbothered by the base question.

Was he just talking about my disastrous night? Or was he talking about the elephant in the room? That we hadn't seen each other for over a month and that the last time we had we'd nearly kissed?

Maybe it was none of that. Chances are, he was being sweet and kind. Bending over backward for me like he'd done ever since I met him, even if he acted like he wasn't sometimes.

I was the worst. The worst for treating him badly. The worst for ignoring my children while I beat my head against a wall trying to make this stupid blog work.

The worst for forgetting Joe.

Tears pricked at my eyes, and I tried to squash them with the heels of my palms.

"I felt like a terrible mom tonight," I whispered, latching onto only one of the things.

Will stopped what he was doing. "Why?"

"Because I got so caught up in trying to make this post perfect—I've been trying to do that for so long—I forgot about them. I nearly burned the house down trying to find fucking camera equipment."

Will was silent for a moment.

"I know what you're going to say," I said. "You think I should quit the blog. Follow my dreams."

"No. I mean, that may be true but I wasn't going to say that. I was going to say you're an amazing Mom." He gathered up the plates and wine glasses and came over to me—not even suggesting we move to the table. When he sat down next to me I had to fight the urge to tip my head down on his shoulder. *Focus, Michelle.*

I needed to remember why I'd asked him here. It wasn't to take comfort from him.

You sure?

"I had an amazing mom myself," Will said, reaching for the pizza. "So I should know."

I thought of a little Will, the oldest of his three siblings, with the difficult father he'd described, and the close relationship he must have had with his mother.

"Tell me about her," I said.

Will looked surprised, but he tipped his head back against the wall and told me about how his mom was his biggest fan. How she went to all his soccer games and debate meets. How she told him he could be president one day.

"President!" I said. "Are you still going to try that?"

"Maybe next year," he said with a smile, but there was a note of something in his voice.

"Are you still considering the mayoral run?" I asked.

"I never was."

"Why not? You'd be good at it."

He eyed me but said nothing. Just popped open the little knife from the corkscrew and cut a quick circle around the foil wrap.

"You're compassionate," I continued. "You care about people. Clearly, you're a problem solver too."

"I do like problems that can be solved with wine."

"I'm serious, Will."

"I am too."

Normally I'd drop it. But all my barriers were down right now—I had no restraint. "If it's something you always wanted, you should do it. Especially if the only thing stopping you is feelings."

"You could take your own advice," he said.

I pursed my lips. But I knew telling Will all this—that he could still see an old dream through—was a joke. Like I could make him some kind of proxy for my burnt-out dreams. It was the blog that was real. It had seen me through the hardest times and it was the thing earning me at least some semblance of an income now.

But the temptation of thinking about my old dreams—at least for a moment, was too strong.

I swallowed. "I used to carry around this little notebook, drawing diagrams of the seating chart at my future restaurant. Planning menus. I even glued paint chips onto the pages. I actually thought I could do that once."

"You still can."

"I know you think so. But that was an old dream, for the old me. It died a long time ago."

"What happened, Michelle?"

I considered. "Joe. It wasn't his fault," I said quickly. "He supported me no matter what. But after I got pregnant, it got harder to think of what it would be like to launch a restaurant at the same time as a family. Plus, I was happy then. The happiest I'd ever been."

Will was looking at me with an unreadable expression. If I had to guess, I'd say... sorrow.

I looked away, making my voice bright. "So, I started the blog instead. I still thought I might do it, somewhere in the back of my mind. Until... everything."

"Michelle," he said. "It's okay to still have that dream. We could... you could figure it out if you wanted to."

I'd heard the slip. For a moment, our eyes locked. Why wouldn't he let it go? Why wouldn't he let me settle for what I had? Suddenly I felt defensive. "What about you, Will? Why aren't you doing what you always wanted to do."

Will barked out a laugh, sufficiently surprised to shift the focus from me and my failed dreams.

"You should run for mayor. Your kids are almost grown. You'd have the support of the whole town."

Will shook his head. "My dad always said I was too damn ambitious for my own good. That I thought I was too good for honest work or something." I could sense the hurt in his voice.

"You work harder than anyone I know," I said.

"Even you?"

Suddenly, I was brought back to the reason I'd asked him here. I opened my mouth to say something, but Will had procured a bottle opener from seemingly nowhere, screwed the corkscrew into the cork and pulled it out in one swift, easy motion. His competence was... distracting.

Sexy.

I swallowed. I was losing my mind.

Will must have felt me staring at his hands, because he said, "Graydon and I used to have competitions to see who could open a bottle faster."

Will had told me awhile back that he'd worked at Gastronomique right after high school with his friend.

"Could you still beat him?"

"Absolutely."

He poured the wine. "You'd like Graydon," he said. "He's a family man. Two little kids. His wife Lucy is almost as feisty as you."

Will slid a glass over to me on the floor between two fingers. Somehow that was sexy too. I looked away. Focus.

"Would I like Graydon better than your friend Eli?"

I felt him pause beside me. I felt like a jerk for throwing that out there, but if I didn't, this night would turn into something else entirely.

"Eli's going through a rough patch."

"So is Reese, thanks to him."

"So are you."

Heat rose in my cheeks.

"To good wine," Will said, "or something else?"

I thought about it for a moment. To lost dreams? To burnt pizza?

To asking Will for more help.

Finally, I said, "To turning things around."

Will gave me this strange little nod. He lifted his glass and we clinked, the sound loud in the silence. From beyond the kitchen walls, I could hear the movie in the other room. I met Will's eye, and for a moment, we held each other's gaze. Then I got self-conscious. I hadn't even thought to take a look in the mirror. My hair was probably a nightmare. I knew I had flour and burnt pizza bits all over me.

I took a sip of wine.

"Oh god," I said, leaning back and closing my eyes. I took another, this one long and luxurious.

"That good?" he asked. His voice had shifted to something like gruffness.

"Sensational. Deep and rich and oaky. It's melting on my tongue."

I opened my eyes. Will was looking right at me. A flame licked across my skin.

"It's the best thing I've ever tasted," I said, my voice hardly more than a whisper.

But I felt like everything was getting away from me. My eyes were locked on his.

Tell him.

"Michelle—"

"Will—"

We'd spoken at the same time. "You first," he said.

I needed to say it now. Before I chickened out again. "I don't know if you saw my recent post—the one with you in it?"

"I saw it," Will said, surprising me.

"Right." I tore my eyes away. I couldn't look at him while I said this. "Well. You might have noticed that my readers got a little... excited to see a strange man in the photos."

"Yeah... it made me think you've got a food blog with readers who might not care all that much about food."

I stiffened. "They do. I'm going to help them see that they do."

"How?" He took a sip of wine. He was upset.

Too late to do anything about that now. "I was hoping you'd go on another date with me," I said. "I mean a date."

Will said nothing.

"Not a real one," I said quickly. "In fact, we don't have to go anywhere. Just take some pictures. I just... they really responded positively to you."

"Do you really think that's the answer to your problems?"

A spike of irritation joined the nerves thrumming inside me. "I do, actually. When the readers are excited, when they want to come back, it all translates into more people staying on the site, and clicking the links, and seeing the ads."

When I put it that way, I knew it sounded cheap. That sharing my thoughts on food and having people try my recipes wasn't the same as clicking on advertisements.

I didn't care. I was in too deep now. "It would sure as hell help pay the bills, anyway."

Will downed the last of his glass of wine, then abruptly stood up. "Well, I'm flattered, I guess."

He didn't sound flattered. "Will, it's not about you. It could be any guy, but you're here, you were in the photos, and they liked to see me happy."

"Now I'm really fucking flattered," he said, his voice hard.

This had gone south fast. How had things started on such a high note and plummeted so quickly?

You.

I shoved that aside, clinging to my anger like a weapon.

I gritted my teeth, standing up too. My head spun but I ignored it. I couldn't look right at him so I focused on what was in front of me. His chest. The little curl of hair rising from his collar.

"I didn't meant to insult you. It wouldn't be for very long. Just a couple of dates. I know there's not much in it for you, but... I could pay you? Once I start getting more revenue."

God, that sounded pathetic. But when I forced myself to look up at his face, I saw he wasn't just insulted. He was furious.

"Do you really think that has anything to do with it? I want to help you Michelle, I really do. It's just... fucked up. You don't even like the blog."

Heat raged inside of me. "That's not true!" I turned away from him, swiping for my wine glass. I couldn't look at him. He didn't understand. I needed the blog. I'd already broken my promise to Joe. I couldn't throw this away, too.

"Fine," he said. "You love your blog. So why don't you ask someone else to do it?"

I tossed my wine back and lowered the glass back down, avoiding his face once more. "Because you were already in it."

"You just said I could be any guy, Michelle. How the fuck do you think that makes me feel?"

Finally, i had to look at him. When my eyes met his, my breath felt as if it had been knocked out of me. He was staring at me, his eyes pinning me in place. My pulse surged.

I want him to touch me.

I was so confused, so sure I'd been right about everything. But as Will took a step toward me, I suddenly knew. Asking him over here to help with the blog wasn't all of it. Not by a long shot. It was him I'd wanted.

"Michelle," he said, fury still sending steel through his voice. "Don't you see? I don't want to be any guy."

My stomach lurched. I was standing at the edge of a sharp, precipitous cliff. Balancing on its knife-edge. Joe was on one side, Will on the other. And right now, I was leaning hard toward Will. Confusion roiled inside of me, but burning hotter was need. Need for this man, right here in front of me. This living, breathing, man radiating heat and fury.

Everything was falling apart, and I knew the smallest thing would tip me over.

"Michelle—" Will said, his voice tight. "I want you." His hands went to my jaw just like before, and there it was. Something cracked, sending lightning exploding through me in a sharp, jagged line.

I reached up, wrapping my arms around his neck. Then I kissed him.

A charge shot through me the moment our lips touched, snapping between us and making everything inside me go liquid.

Will was stiff, frozen where he stood.

Until he wasn't. Suddenly he was on me, fast and hard. He gripped the back of my head and placed his other hand at the small of my back, pulling me to him. Blood rushed in my ears, my pulse skipping at double-speed as Will's tongue, urgent now, parted my lips, finding mine. I stumbled and he caught me, walking me backward, pressing me up against the wall. My mind was suddenly and wholly filled with only one thought.

Will.

The length of his body was hard against mine. Crushing.

I wanted him. God, I wanted him. My nipples strained against my shirt, dampness growing fast between my legs.

"Will," I said when he pulled his lips a half-inch from mine. "I..." I wanted him, but I couldn't say it. It was like if I admitted it, I'd have to admit it to myself too. Instead, I brought my teeth down on his bottom lip.

He groaned, his one hand dipping behind my neck, the other popping the top button of my shirt open. Suddenly, I had no words. None at all.

We couldn't stay like this. We were hidden from the door of the kitchen in this alcove, but it wasn't really private. The sounds of the movie filtered in faintly, as if a reminder.

But I didn't want to stop. I couldn't.

"Michelle," Will whispered in my ear. "I can't stop thinking about you. Day and fucking night. You're like the air I breathe. I wake up with your scent on my fucking sheets as if you've been there."

One more of my buttons popped open under his fingers, and then his hand, skin rough and hard and hot, slid into my shirt, and under my bra, too. His palm cupped my bare breast, his thumb brushing against the point of my nipple.

This time I couldn't contain the gasp as his leg slid between mine. Heat and pleasure shot through me as he shifted his hands to my hips, rocking me on his thigh. He knew what he was doing.

Then something thumped out in the living room and he froze.

"Fuck," he said, backing away. There was a noticeable bulge in his pants. We both stood silent, waiting, a few feet apart. Our eyes were locked together.

One of the girls laughed and an explosion sounded on the screen, followed by happy shrieks.

Will was tense, his hands at his sides, like he was fighting himself. Then he closed the distance once more and kissed me hard, sliding his hands under my thighs and then lifting me so my legs were wrapped around him. He took a step and when my back hit the wall, he thrust his hips toward me as if he were actually fucking me.

I gasped, the sensation of his hardness between my legs too much.

Then he growled, lowering me to the ground and backing away once more.

"We can't do this," he said, his voice so tight it sounded like it might snap.

I stood there, panting.

He was still angry.

"Just say it," I said.

He worked his jaw, his hand going through his hair. "I can't believe you asked me to do that," he said, finally.

The heat of what we'd just done sharpened, funneling back into my own anger. "Is it really so bad? I'm just asking you for help," I said, biting the words out. I did up the buttons on my shirt in angry twists. Didn't he know how hard it was for me to ask? "I need this blog," I said. I couldn't explain how much.

"I'd do anything for you," Will said. "But I won't be your sham fucking boyfriend. Especially not—"

He shook his head, bending down and swiping up the wine glasses, which we'd miraculously managed not to break. "I should never have let that happen. I'm sorry."

The thing was, I wasn't. If he'd kept going, and it weren't for the kids out there, I would have kept going too. I wasn't sure I'd ever wanted anything more at that moment. But I couldn't tell him that. I'd already thrown myself out there, made a fool of myself by asking him about the blog. I wouldn't do it again.

And he was leaving.

Will moved to the sink, and for the second time that night, I watched his muscles work under his shirt. Only now they were tense. Hard with upset.

I wouldn't let him. I'd go first. Awkward, because it was my kitchen. "I'm going to go check on the kids," I said, my voice hard. "It's past the girls' bedtime."

"We should be going anyway," he said, turning. For a moment, our eyes stayed locked together. It was so different than that moment earlier when our eyes had met with anger, and again just now with need.

He'd wanted me. I knew he did. But he was a picture of self-flagellation. He didn't want this.

"Okay, well, thank you for coming. Thanks for the wine and... I guess I'll see you," I said, brushing by him.

I knew I sounded petty. But I didn't care. I stormed out the kitchen door for the living room leaving Will Archer behind me.

14

WILL

They say Christmas in New York City really is magical, but I was having a hard goddamned time seeing it as I tromped toward the subway with Remy hissing epithets into her phone at Draco.

It was only a week before Christmas, and as usual, I'd cut gift shopping close. Only this time, it wasn't because I was too busy with work. It was because I was dreading the day. Not only were the girls going to be with their mother this year, but on top of everything, I was still confused as hell about whether I'd done the right thing with Michelle two weeks ago.

It was dusk by the time we reached the subway entrance, and a light snow was falling. Strings of lights glowed in all the windows, and on every other corner, Santa Clauses clanged their bells. We even passed a group of carolers at the top of the stairs.

But I could barely register any of it. All I could think about was Michelle. How she'd felt under my hands. How she'd looked. How her voice and breath and body still clung to me. For a moment, the feelings came rushing back to me like a hot, burning blade. Every time I'd thought about that moment over the past two weeks I'd been brought to my knees, the air leaving my lungs.

Then I thought of the other part. How she'd asked me to be her fake fucking boyfriend for her stupid fucking blog.

How she talked about her dead husband the way... *fuck*. The way I wanted her to talk about me. I felt like a dick. And the whole thing felt like a joke. A cruel, shitty-ass joke that only underscored the whole reason I was never supposed to get involved with someone again.

I thought of my dad, the way he barely cracked a smile his whole damn life. How Mom kept up the sunshine for all of us. If, in some alternate universe, Michelle and I ever ended up together, that's what it would be like only worse because she'd still be in love with a fucking ghost. What kind of life would that be?

As the doors closed behind us and sweat beaded on my temple from the uncomfortably thick crowd in the subway car, I tried to focus my thoughts on the rest of my life. We were about to meet Hannah, who I hadn't seen since Thanksgiving, and that truly made me happy. I'd tried to keep that at the forefront of my mind as I trudged through all the shopping Remy and I had done today while Hannah finished up her last day working before the holiday.

But the city wasn't helping. The long lines. The cranky people buying overpriced gifts. I couldn't believe I used to live here—and that I'd liked it. Granted, it was only for a few years when I was doing my MBA and shortly after, but I'd loved the run-down apartment Jill and I had lived in with its clanging radiator and shouting neighbors.

Now, I longed for the winding roads leading back to Jewel Lakes; the peace and quiet after the first snowfall, and the spread of stars that reached all the way down to the horizon on a frosty winter evening.

"This is our stop," I said to Remy, who looked up from her phone and nodded.

I wouldn't think about Michelle.

Then I saw her.

We were almost to the stairs when she appeared—just her back. Thick brown curls springing from a white wool hat. A navy coat, snug against a body as voluptuous as a 50s pin-up.

Then she turned. And of course it wasn't her. This woman had a longer nose. A slightly dour expression. But it was enough to throw me back down into the dark place I'd been since leaving Michelle's place.

For fuck's sake.

"Dad!" Remy called. She'd slipped ahead of me, and I had to sidestep a slow-moving couple to reach her. I was supposed to be watching out for her. Not the other way around.

Not that Remy needed watching out for.

Finally, we got out onto the street level. It was quieter here, more residential, though there were still shops up ahead on the corner. "There it is," I said to Remy, pointing out the hole-in-the-wall restaurant down the street. Antonio's—my favorite restaurant in all of New York City.

For a moment, the darkness cleared.

"We're going to meet my sister now," Remy said tersely into the phone. I hadn't even noticed her answering it. Or had she called him? I was sick to death of Draco drama.

"Remy, for god's sake," I said, my mood faltering. Seeing that Michelle doppelgänger—and now thinking of her and a gorgeous restaurant that would never be in Barkley Falls—had me scowling.

That night at Michelle's place was only two weeks ago, but each day had been a battle. A hundred times I'd wanted to call her and tell her I'd do whatever she wanted. That I'd make a damn fool of myself if it meant I could be around her.

Instead, I'd texted her a couple of times and gotten nothing.

It didn't matter. I couldn't do what she wanted me to. There was no way. The idea of posing as Michelle's love interest for her blog—parading around as if we were together—was so deeply painful, it made me hurt. Physically.

Plus, I'd meant what I'd said to her. I didn't think it would actually help her.

Sure, I'd seen the blog posts—the one with me in it, which I'd scrutinized a thousand times over the past few days, along with the other one she'd posted this week about Christmas cookies. I saw the comments—one after another asking Michelle where her 'friend' was. If she had any plans with him over the holidays. Sure, the readers would probably go nuts to see Michelle pretending to be happy with a guy. But that was just it—she'd be pretending. Living a lie.

Just like you are?

"Hannah!" Remy exclaimed from beside me, startling me out of my distracted fog.

Remy ran up to her big sister, who'd emerged from the front door of the restaurant, and threw her arms around her. My heart swelled.

"Hey kiddo," Hannah said.

Remy snorted as she pulled away. "Kiddo yourself!"

I shook the lingering thoughts of Michelle from my brain, reaching down to pull my girl into a hug.

"Hey Ms. Banana," I said. "Let's have some spaghetti."

Antonio's Famous Spaghetti House hadn't changed one bit since Jill and I used to come here a lifetime ago. As we stepped through the bell-clanging door into the familiar space, I was hit with nostalgia. It wasn't like the first time I'd come back when I'd been bitter and angry at Jill. Now, it was just something old and familiar. The red-checkered tablecloths, dim lighting, and framed prints of bucolic Italian scenes hadn't changed since the first time I'd walked in. I knew digging into one of Antonio's famously oversized oval-shaped plates piled high with noodles and meatballs the size of my fists would cure whatever ailed me.

After we'd placed our orders and were sipping our drinks—sodas all around, given I had to drive from the train station back to Jewel Lakes on potentially slippery roads later tonight—I leaned back in my seat.

"I'm going to miss you guys over Christmas," I said, looking at each of my daughters. Soon, both of them would be having their own Christmases, with their own families. And where would I be?

"You already miss me," Hannah said. She smiled, tucking her long brown hair behind her ear.

If she weren't my beloved firstborn she might be tough to look at. She was the spitting image of Jill at her age, except with my mom's eyes and cheekbones. The combination of looking at Jill and my Mom, two women I'd loved who were no longer in my life, might have stung. But Hannah was her own person. A good, sweet girl who seemed to always know what to say or do—particularly when it came to her little sister.

"Don't worry," Remy said, "We'll see you next year!"

I clapped my hands over my chest. "Next *year!*"

Jill had requested she keep the girls all the way through New Year's this time, in exchange for me getting March Break. At eighteen, Hannah was old enough that she didn't have to partake in any of the custody arrangements, but she went along with them anyway, for Remy's sake. "It's easier this way," she'd said to me when she turned eighteen.

That was Hannah, agreeable as ever and always thinking about her sister.

"So where precisely is this place your mother's taking you again?" I asked.

"Dad," Hannah said. I couldn't tell if her voice was warning or pleading. I knew perfectly well where they were going—Jill's new boyfriend's parents' place. Or their summer home, down in Florida.

"It's not even going to be that hot," Remy said.

"Or that close to the beach," added Hannah.

I smiled. "I appreciate you guys keeping me from being too jealous," I said.

"We'll be back before you know it," Hannah said.

After Hannah had caught us up with everything about her first few months at school, Remy announced she had to go to the bathroom. She said it abruptly, sliding out of her seat without looking at us. But instead of heading to the back of the restaurant where the restrooms were located, she made a beeline for the entrance.

"Draco?" Hannah asked, sipping her Coke.

"They've been bickering the whole way here," I said, pulling apart a piece of garlic bread. "I think she knows I'm sick of it. I'm glad to hear school's going well, but hell, I wish you were around Hannah, just to show her what a normal relationship looks like. How's Geoff, by the way?"

Hannah took another sip of soda, not saying anything.

My stomach sank. "Oh no..."

"It's okay—it was too tough doing the long-distance thing, you know?" Her voice had a falsely chipper note. "Anyway Mom says I'm too young to get involved with anyone so seriously. That I should have fun—be wild and free, she says." Hannah rolled her eyes slightly at that last bit.

But I felt as if I'd been punched in the gut. One of the biggest, ugliest albatrosses in Jill's and my marriage was my suspicion that Jill wished she hadn't gotten together with me so young. Or maybe that she wished we hadn't gotten together at all.

I wasted my best years on you! She'd screamed during our worst fight. The words still burned into me. I didn't feel that way. And I told her so. That was the beginning of the end for us.

"Well, maybe she's right," I said. Given Hannah had already split up with her boyfriend I figured it was best to err on whichever side she needed to hear. And hell, maybe it was for the best. Maybe that was why Jill and I had ended so disastrously.

"Anyway," Hannah said, "Remy says you might be dating someone?"

I nearly spat my drink out. Just then, the server came by with our giant plates of food. I ignored mine. "What are you talking about?"

Hannah frowned, picking up her fork. "Remy said something about a woman she was babysitting for." She twirled her fork in her Alfredo. "Said you've been seeing her. That you guys text all the time and you went over to her house…"

"Wow, she didn't leave anything out, did she?" I said, anger building inside of me. I glanced toward the entrance of the restaurant. The windows had a curtain along the bottom and all I could see was the streetlights overhead and the odd lights from a passing car. Where the hell was she?

"I'm going to go check on her," I said, tossing my napkin on the table.

"Dad, don't get upset with her—"

"I'm not," I said, softening. I rubbed the bridge of my nose with my thumb and forefinger. "I—there is a woman I know and we did—I did take her out but..." God, why was I explaining myself to my daughter?

I stood up. I really was worried about Remy. "I'll be right back," I said.

When I stepped out into the cold night air, I spotted Remy right away. She wasn't on her phone—she was talking to a couple of people on the corner. She may be sixteen years old but since when was it okay to talk to strangers on the street? Especially in New York City?

Alarm shot through me. I couldn't see them from here, but it looked to be a man and a woman. "Remy!" I called out. All three of them turned to me, and that's when I saw at least one of them wasn't a stranger.

It was my ex-wife. And her boyfriend.

My stomach rolled making me slightly nauseous. Shit. Fuck. Shitfuck.

I wanted to grab Remy by the elbow and tug her back inside the restaurant.

"What are you doing here?" I asked when I reached them.

Not exactly Mr. Cordial.

Jill gave me a look that was painfully familiar. One that was clear she didn't need my shit. "Will, I'd like you to meet Gareth."

I glanced over at the man with them for the first time. He was good looking, in a seasoned, gray-goateed Ivy

League professor kind of way. Jill was currently doing some kind of advanced degree—really making up for lost time I guessed. "Really going all in on academia, huh?" I said to Jill.

"Will, for god's sake."

It wasn't like I was threatened in any way. I knew—at that moment and what I'd known all along—I didn't want to get back together with Jill. Yes, the divorce had been fucking awful. Yes, I'd tried to make a broken thing work for years past its sell-by date. But knowing the man was going to be spending Christmas with my girls? What used to be my family? I couldn't exactly clap the dude on the back.

But you could be a little less of an asshole.

Remy elbowed me. Shit.

"Yeah, hi," I said. "Will." I stuck out my hand, giving him a knuckle breaker just because I could.

"Gareth Jones," he said, his voice stiff. He handed the iron-tight grip right back to me, and I couldn't help being at least a tiny bit impressed. At least the guy wasn't a total coward.

"But seriously, what are you doing here?" I asked Jill. "We're supposed to meet at Union Square. They're still mine for the next" —I looked at my watch— "two hours."

"I wanted to bring Gareth to Antonio's."

"Really? Antonio's?"

"You seem to like coming back here," she snapped.

"With the girls," I lobbed back. For a moment we stared at each other, eyes hard. I was pissed, sure, but under that was a kind of sadness. I wasn't hurt at losing what we had so much as I was in pain because this is where we ended up. We were friends for so long—in fact such good ones that at times I felt like we were more best friends than husband and wife. Now, we were this. Angry. On edge.

All Your Fault

Or maybe that was just me.

You're your father's son, Mom used to say.

"Dad," Remy said. "Mom texted, okay? She asked if we were going to be north of downtown and said it might be easier for you if she picked us up here… I told her we were here and—"

My chest twisted. My sixteen-year-old was being more mature than I was. Jill was right—I didn't have any claim over Antonio's. Never mind that it was where we used to go —she likely had just as many fond memories of the place for its atmosphere and food as I did.

I held my hands up. "Fine," I said. "It's fine. I'm sorry, okay? I'm just… I want to spend every last hour with the girls before I have to pass them over."

"You'll get them next year," Jill said. "Besides," she said, sticking a stiff smile on her face, "I heard you're seeing someone? You'll have all kinds of free time for that."

I pinned my eyes on Remy, anger flaring. "Who haven't you told about Michelle?" I asked.

Remy's eyes went wide, a smile twitching on her lips before I realized what I'd just said. I'd named Michelle in the context of seeing someone.

We weren't seeing each other and to say that now felt like a cruel joke after everything that had happened. But Remy looked so bright-eyed, so pleased, I shut it again, the anger falling back just slightly. Seeing her happy like that… It wasn't like she was a miserable kid, but her main emotion seemed to be drama with all the shit she was going through with Draco.

Her phone buzzed in her hand. Speak of the goddamned devil. I wished I could grab the phone from her and yell at him to never call again. But Remy would never forgive me. And the thing was, he wasn't even a terrible kid. They were both just addicted to the drama.

I promised myself I would never tell my kids I knew better than them about their own lives. I knew what it was like to be on the receiving end of that all too well. So as long as Remy wasn't in any kind of real danger, I had to let her make her own choices.

But that didn't mean I couldn't guide her to the right ones.

"Yes," I blurted. "I am seeing someone. And she's great. She doesn't call me during family dinners and break up with me every other weekend."

Remy shot me a look. "I break up with *him* every other weekend."

"Remy, you're only with him because you don't know any different." I snapped.

Remy pulled her face back, blinking.

"Shit," I said, pinching my nose.

I could feel Jill's eyes on me. Was this what I needed to hear years ago? When I knew things weren't working with Jill?

Gareth chuckled. "Ah, young love."

The three of us all glared at him in unison. The smile fell off his face.

"Maybe, in this case, your dad might be right," Jill said, her voice on the edge of trembling.

"Jill—" I said.

But she shook her head, straightened up, and linked her arm through Gareth's elbow. "Come on. Let's go back downtown. There's a lovely bistro downtown I've been dying to try." To me, she said, "We'll meet you where we originally planned."

"Fine by me," I said. "Come on, Remy," I said. "Our food's probably cold by now."

As we walked back inside the restaurant, I swallowed down the sharp prickle of nerves in my throat. Why had I done that?

Michelle's voice rang in my head. *Just a couple of dates.*

"So, you *are* seeing Michelle?" Remy asked, her voice stiff as I pulled open the door to the restaurant.

We definitely weren't. But we could be. Not for real, but enough to show Remy that things could be different. That seeing new people could make a miserable old jerk happy.

Even if it was just pretend.

"It's complicated," I said. I didn't even know if Michelle would take my calls let alone see me. But the thought of seeing her once more, of being in her presence and feeling even a fraction of that feeling I got around her—it felt like something. A stick of something I could hold onto, even for a moment, while I floated in a vast and icy ocean.

"What took you so long?" Hannah exclaimed when we got back to our seats.

"Sorry," I began.

But Remy, sullen, snapped, "Apparently, Dad's got a girlfriend."

Hannah lit up. "Really, Dad? You're actually seeing her?"

I smiled, a hard line that didn't match my eyes. "Let's just eat, okay?" I said.

I stabbed my food with my fork. At least I couldn't mess up eating meatballs.

15

MICHELLE

I jumped at the sound of the kitchen window rattling violently in its frame.

Calm down, Michelle.

It was just a storm. Thank god school was out for winter break and that I'd gotten my shopping done early with Reese yesterday. It was only a few days before Christmas, and if we got snowed in tomorrow, the only question was whether Mom and Dad could make it here for Christmas. They were supposed to arrive tomorrow, but Christmas wasn't for a few more days. Surely the roads would be clear by then?

I walked around my house flicking all the lights off. Outside, wind howled through the trees in the yard. When I peeked out the back door I could see their naked limbs—barely, it was so dark—waving in the gale. Tiny flakes whirled around like stars, landing silently on the glass of the back door and melting.

Shivering, I shut the curtain, checking and rechecking the deadbolt. I don't know why I did that. Maybe it was instinctive because I was on my own with the girls. More likely it was just habit. I'd spent my whole life in and around New York City until Joe passed. Jewel Lakes was probably the safest place I'd ever lived, and yet here I was, jumping at every little creak and whine of the wind.

I had only a couple of gifts left to wrap, but I didn't have the stomach for doing that now. Guiltily, I'd blown what little I had left of the month's budget on them knowing my parents would insist on paying for all the Christmas groceries, and that I'd fight, but eventually give in. Their budget with their pensions was tight, but not as tight as mine.

I also spent the money knowing I was giving up on the blog. I'd given it my all—I knew I had when I'd stooped to asking Will to help. I was going to move back to the city so I could leave the girls with my parents while I got a restaurant job, if anyone would still have me—it had been a decade since I'd worked in a kitchen.

The idea of leaving Jewel Lakes broke my heart. I loved it here. The girls had settled into school, and I even had my big sister. But it didn't make sense to stay. Not when my parents wanted to stay where they were. And not when everything here reminded me of Will.

I grabbed my phone and headed toward the bedroom, glancing at it in the dark. There was nothing there. Not from the blog, and certainly not from Will.

Not that I'd reached out to him. We hadn't spoken since that night. After I'd run out on him and put the girls to bed, I'd come out to find my kitchen completely cleaned—even after all of that, Will, and presumably Remy, had still done that last, over-the-top, thoughtful thing. I'd sent him and Remy a text together, thanking them for coming and for the kitchen. For everything.

Somehow, that was the worst part, knowing he'd done

that even after I'd insulted him with my stupid, nonsensical plan.

Humiliation ran through me, still hot two weeks later.

When I'd told Reese, she'd felt terrible. "This was my idea!"

"It's not your fault," I'd assured her. It wasn't—I knew he wouldn't go for it. I'd known the minute he walked in that door and looked at me that way. And I'd done it anyway.

I climbed into bed, my bedroom window rattling in the wind. We were gearing up for a blizzard. I thought that would be sufficient to occupy my mind, but the moment I lay back on the pillow, the whole night came rushing back to me, just like it had every night since. Will rushing to our rescue. The girls having the time of their lives hanging out with Remy.

Will and I entwined against the kitchen wall.

I had felt like I might combust with the heat coming off of us. Even now it swirled in my abdomen as I remembered his hand in my hair and on my breast.

If I forgot about all the rest, I could live in that kiss we'd shared forever. I could dream about how it might have gone if we were on our own. If there were no kids, no blog, no dead husband. If we were different people in a different lifetime.

Maybe we would have made love right there on the kitchen floor.

God knows I'd wanted to. At that moment, it was the thing I wanted most in the world. But that wasn't us. We had our messy, complicated lives.

It's almost like you were trying to sabotage the whole thing, Joe said in the dark.

That thought was too big to even comprehend. I flopped back on my pillow. A week ago I might have extrapolated on what had happened with Will in my mind, playing it out while I slipped my hand between my legs.

Now, I knew I'd only feel worse after. I squeezed my eyes shut, praying sleep would take me now. Knowing it would be hours before it did.

That's when I heard the buzz of my phone.

A text message.

I reached over and picked it up.

Somehow I knew it would be him. With shaking hands, I opened the text.

∼

WILL: I'll do it.

∼

MY HEART THUDDED. I sat up straight, staring at the words.

"Now?" I said out loud. "Fucking now, Will? When I've already said goodbye?"

But we all know you're no good at goodbyes.

Joe's voice. I almost laughed. He only showed up when I was thinking about Will now. It was the worst, most painful irony.

I'd ignore it. I clapped my phone down on the bedside table and pulled up the covers, tossing and turning for a full minute before giving up and grabbing the remote from the table next to my phone. As soon as I turned the TV on, I was slapped in the face with a painfully familiar black and white image. It's a Wonderful Life. Through my anger, I felt my heart crack.

Joe and I used to watch this movie together. He watched it to indulge me—he found Jimmy Stewart annoying—

which always incensed me. It was something we used to tease each other about, every Christmas.

I pushed away an angry tear and picked up my phone.

Will answered on the first ring.

"No," I said. Then to my horror, I started to cry.

"Michelle?" Concern made Will's voice tight. "What is it?"

"I said no. You can't tell me it's a shit idea, kiss me the way you did, leave me for two weeks and then text me with that—"

"Whoa— hey, you asked me!" His voice was cut through with anger. "I thought this was what you wanted!"

I hesitated. Was it? Did I still want to pretend to date Will Archer for my blog?

Or did I really want him?

I sat up, muting the TV, my mouth suddenly dry. "What happened to you thinking it was a terrible idea?"

"I'm still not convinced it's the right thing to do."

"That's not for you to decide."

"It is if you're asking me to get involved."

Anger burned in my chest, but it was weak like the coals were cold; already burnt. I pinched my lips, then closed my eyes too. This was stupid. Beyond stupid. "It's fine, Will. You're right—"

"See, I'm not so sure about that, either."

I opened my eyes, shifting the phone to my other ear. "What do you mean?"

"I mean if there's a chance this can help you, I want to do it."

The anger inside me flickered like he'd blown on it. "So, it took you a whole two weeks to figure that out?"

"Yes. And also... it might be good for me too."

"How's that?"

On the screen, Jimmy Stewart, at this point an embattled banker, was running around the bank as a mob of people crowded him, demanding their money back. I wanted that too. I wanted to back out of everything. To start over.

"It's kind of... complicated," Will said, suddenly sounding kind of awkward. "It would make Remy happy. Plus, it might be good for her to see that I know what I'm doing, you know?"

Suddenly my chest hurt. Remy. "Will—it's all fine and good having her see her dad go on dates. But what happens when it ends?" Even though we were talking about the end of a fake relationship—one that was still hypothetical, even—it felt crushing, somehow.

"Remy needs to see what it means to end a relationship with someone in a way that's healthy," Will continued. His voice was slightly strained. He wasn't just talking about Remy and her relationship with her boyfriend or the fact that they broke up and got back together a dozen times a week. It was his divorce. It had been hell on him. So bad he'd decided he'd never try again.

"Okay," I said, simply.

"Wait, how did this turn into me asking you?"

Laughter bubbled up inside of me, like a pressure release valve. "You're desperate, I guess," I said.

For a moment we both said nothing.

Now that Will had agreed, I thought I'd feel differently. Excited. Optimistic. Instead, I felt empty inside.

"So..." I said. "I guess this means we need to go on a date. Or more dates?"

"I guess."

Then, on the other end of the line, a tinny voice echoed. *"Last stop..."*

"Where are you?" I asked.

"Just getting off the train, about to drive home."

I straightened, genuine alarm going through me. "You're driving home in this?"

Outside, through the gap in my bedroom blinds, snow whirled. It had thickened.

"Hey, I grew up on these country roads, remember? Besides, I have snow tires. Chains in the trunk, too."

"You can't drive through a blizzard!"

"I can't stay at the train station, Michelle," he said, his voice soft.

A vice gripped my chest at the thought of Will getting hurt. Sliding off the road. It was just normal concern for another human being. That was all. But it didn't feel normal. It felt like a fist gripping my heart.

"Maybe you could stay in Millerville?" I suggested, hating the way my voice sounded.

"Maybe... but Barkley Falls is only another half hour from there."

I grimaced. The country highway was windy, especially past my place. It got kind of hilly between here and Barkley Falls, and I had to pay close attention even in good weather. I was about to beg him to think about it—there were a couple of chain hotels in Millerville, I knew—when he spoke.

"Michelle?" He sounded hesitant. I heard the sound of train brakes, the rustle of his coat. He was leaving the train, heading to his car.

"Yeah?"

"Maybe you could stay on the phone with me for a bit? I have this headset thing in the car. It would be... nice to have company on the drive."

Then I'd know if he was okay, too.

The knot in my chest loosening slightly. "Of course," I said,

I wished he was closer. I wished he was right here, just around the corner. Safe.

But this was the next best thing.

We agreed he'd call me back once he got himself sorted with his snow chains and earpiece. The minutes stretched out like an eternity. I distracted myself by making some hot chocolate and doing the math on how long it would take him to make the drive. It was two hours from the train station to Millerville. For me, it was another fifteen minutes to get down to Amethyst lake. For Will, it would be an additional fifteen on top of that to Barkley Falls, longer in this weather.

And in the dark.

Just as worry started to creep again, my phone buzzed.

"Took you long enough," I said.

"I had to scrape the snow off. Two days' worth." He sounded contained now, and I could hear the faint sound of some kind of jazz on his car radio.

"Where were you?" I asked.

While Will told me about dropping Remy off in the city and seeing his oldest daughter again, I heard the rumble of his SUV. I pictured him there, the expert push of his hand on the gearshift; the calm, open-handed turn of the steering wheel. The quiet competence that was Will Archer.

For the next while, we talked. He asked me about the past week, and I told him about how I'd put up a post about Christmas cookies and described how adorable it had been. How the cookies had been cute, and how the only personal things I included were Emma and Macy existing in a couple of the photos. It had tanked. Hardly anyone commented on the recipe. No one said they couldn't wait to try. And not only that, more than one person had asked what I was doing over the holidays and was I spending it with anyone special.

"Well, that's going to change now, right?" Will asked.

A warmth spread through me. "Yeah," I said. "Let's see what they say to us kissing under the mistletoe. Metaphorically," I said hastily. "I meant."

Will was quiet.

Quickly I switched gears to talk about how my parents were supposed to be driving down for the holidays tomorrow. He talked about how Remy and Hannah were with their mom, so he'd be having Christmas dinner with Hank and Casey. And it went like that for two hours, until he announced he was approaching Millerville.

I let out a sigh of relief.

"It's pretty hairy out here, Michelle. And most of the town is dark."

My stomach clenched. "You need to stay there," I said.

He hesitated. "Are you worried about me?"

I didn't. "Yes."

"I'm okay, Michelle. Nothing's going to happen to me."

My throat thickened, my stomach dropped. "You don't know that," I whispered.

I saw flames. Fire licking under a door. Joe screaming.

"Even when we knew he wasn't going to live anyway," I whispered, "I lived in fear, all the time, that I'd get a call telling me he didn't make it. Then one day, I did."

He knew I was talking about Joe.

"I'm sorry," Will said. "With all my heart, I'm so sorry, Michelle."

"I know," I whispered.

"I'm not going to die," he said.

I swallowed. He didn't know that. But I couldn't control him, I couldn't control when people lived or died. I couldn't control that, but I could control how I felt. What I did.

"Tell me about the movie," he said. "You said you were watching It's A Wonderful Life."

I heard the rumble of his engine. He was continuing on. I had to stay with him. I tore my eyes from the window where several inches of snow had gathered on the windowsill.

"It's almost over," I said. "Jimmy's holding his little girl in his arms."

"What's happening?"

"His little girl is saying the famous line. 'Look, Daddy. Teacher says, every time a bell rings, an angel gets his wings.'"

The credits began to roll. Tears, too, were rolling down my cheeks.

Will was quiet, as if he knew I needed this moment.

"I love this movie," I said after a few minutes. Year after year I watch it and love it more."

A beat passed. Then Will said, "I have to confess something."

"What's that?"

"I can't stand Jimmy Stewart's voice."

I couldn't help it, I laughed. And laughed some more. Soon I was laughing and crying, I couldn't tell which. Finally, when I could breathe, I said, "Joe hated it too."

"Good man," he said. "Well, I'm willing to give it another try."

"You better."

There was a long pause. Then he said, "Michelle?"

"Yeah."

"It's rough out here."

I looked to the window again. The gap was almost

hidden by the gathered snow. The panic came back, wrapping itself around the inside of my chest. A fist, hard and unyielding.

"I had to stop," he said.

I blinked. "Where? There's no motel between Millerville and Barkley Falls. Nowhere to stop except..."

My heart thundered in my chest. I stood up, padding out of my bedroom and down the hallway in the dark. I held my breath as I went to the front door and swung it open.

Will was standing on my doorstep.

16

WILL

Michelle's hair blew back in the freezing wind, snow landing in it like stars in the night sky.

She wore only an oversized t-shirt, and it whipped against her body, her legs bare beneath.

"I'm sorry," I said, my voice raised over the wind. "I had to see you. But I should go—it's freezing, you're going to—"

But she shook her head, reaching her hand up and grasping my coat. She pulled me inside, closing the door behind us against the gale.

I looked at her for only a moment, to make sure the look in her eyes was need, like mine. But I didn't need to guess because she looked up at me then and said, "Kiss me, Will. Kiss me like you did before."

The whole world faded as I took Michelle Franco's face in my hands and bent down to kiss her. Heat engulfed me as our lips met. I slipped my tongue against hers, parting her lips, needing to feel her, to know her. I reached down and lifted her up while the damp snow on my coat soaked through her t-shirt. I pressed her up against the wall while heat ran through me, electrifying everything from my hips down, making my cock strain against my zipper.

I buried my face in her hair, her neck. Inhaling her like air.

"I was scared," she whispered. "So scared you were going to drive off the road and end up in a ditch."

"I'm sorry," I said. "I needed to see you. I would have driven a thousand more miles in that if it meant getting you here in my arms."

I pulled back, needing to see the beautiful woman before me. In the back of my mind, I knew my eyes burned with exhaustion, the muscles in my neck and shoulders aching with the stress of driving through that storm. And underneath everything was worry. Worry she'd think she was making a mistake. Worry I'd hurt her.

Worry she was still in love with a dead man.

But my need to be here was stronger. My desire was stronger. I shoved everything else aside. All I saw was her. All I felt was her.

Michelle didn't say anything, just took me by the hand and led me down the hallway.

Her room was lit blue from the TV, silent behind her. She grabbed the remote, flicking it off. Then she stood before me, looking suddenly nervous.

I took her hands in mine. They were trembling.

"You're cold," I whispered. "I shouldn't have let the cold air in."

"I'm fine," she said. She climbed into her bed, then folded the duvet back for me.

Maybe she needed more time. The thought of that was torture, but of course I could do it. I stripped down to my shorts and t-shirt and climbed into her bed, hoping she wouldn't see the need I had for her. Wanting her to feel no pressure.

I climbed in next to Michelle, and when she curled against me, something inside me swelled like a balloon. Joy, maybe. Elation. Whatever it was, I wasn't willing to do anything that would make the feeling go away.

I let Michelle take the lead, and when she placed her head on my shoulder, pressing her soft body against the length of mine, I knew, if this was all she wanted, that this would be enough.

I wrapped an arm around her and inhaled the soft scent of her.

"Are you okay?" I asked.

She hesitated. "I was worried about you. I didn't like it. I thought I'd figured that stuff out, but clearly there's something still there."

I wasn't quite sure what to say. Finally, I said, "I'm here now. Whatever you want, I'm here." A few months ago—hell, a few weeks ago—I wouldn't have ever imagined I'd say something like that. Not to Michelle—not to anyone. But right now, I'd say anything to keep her right here. And I'd mean it, too.

A long moment stretched out between us. Then Michelle took a breath. "I don't really know what I want." Another pause. "I thought I was ready before for something but I wasn't."

"It's okay," I said.

"I'm sorry."

"No," I said, stroking her hair. "Don't say that. You have nothing to be sorry for."

We lay there in silence, her breath on my chest a rhythmic warmth.

I could wait for her. I could wait a whole lifetime if I had to. So long as I got to keep this moment.

I BLINKED, disorientated, and more concerning, deeply fucking aroused, in pitch darkness.

I'd been dreaming of Michelle Franco. Of her whispering my name, and her pulling back a duvet to welcome me into bed. It was like that vision I'd had of her at the resort—the completely made-up fantasy my brain had concocted the moment the mayor had said *presidential suite*—had come to life.

My cock jumped. I lowered my hand to it.

But there was already a hand there.

I blinked my eyes open. Holy shit.

It was real. I was here. That was Michelle's voice in my ear. Her warm body pressed up against my back. Her arm was around my hip and her fingers wrapped around the hardness in my shorts.

I nearly came right there.

She squeezed me through the thin fabric and I let out a low groan.

"Jesus, Michelle..."

I had to see her. I had to look into her eyes to see if this was what she really wanted. Turning, I slid my hand up to her face.

Her hand stayed on me the whole time, stroking now.

It was so dark I couldn't see more than the faint outline of her cheek, the soft rippling of her hair.

"Are you sure?" I asked. I was thinking of her words last night. No, this night. It was still dark—dawn had to be a ways off still.

"No," she said.

I froze. But her hand kept moving, confusing both my body and my head. It felt so good I couldn't think.

But before I could say anything her lips were at my ear, her hair tickling my shoulder. "But I don't want to stop, either."

I struggled for words. I was immersed in Michelle Franco. I was breathing her. Feeling her. Wanting her.

Michelle.

Michelle. She wasn't sure. I wasn't sure. This was going to fuck everything up.

She slipped her hand inside my shorts, stroking my bare cock now.

But I no longer cared. The last bits of restraint left me and a low growl I didn't even recognize came out of my throat. I lifted myself up, turning around so her hand fell off me.

Then I was over her with my elbows on either side.

My mouth was on hers, my lips against her lips, my tongue flicking against her teeth.

"Is this what you want, Michelle?" I wedged my knee between hers, nudging them open. The question was no longer about feelings. It was about need.

I lowered my hips so she could feel mine, pressing my cock against the fabric between us.

It felt like fucking heaven.

She gasped. "Yes. This is exactly what I want."

As I kissed her again, I wanted to say this was what I'd wanted too—and it was true. But that wasn't all of it. I trailed kisses down her neck and along her throat, feeling her nipples harden against my chest.

"I've wanted you since the first day we met," I said as I lifted her shirt up. She raised her upper half so I could pull it over her head. I took in the curve of her breasts in the dark.

But it wasn't enough to touch her. I wanted to see her, too. "Light," I said, in between kisses. "I need to see you."

I wanted to remember this—all of it, with every sense I had. I wanted a picture in my mind of this perfect, exquisite moment.

"There's a candle there," she said, pointing to a gleaming object on the bedside table. I reached up, fiddling with the lighter next to it, lighting the single flame.

Michelle's face lit up in the soft golden light. Her cheeks were flushed, her lips parted, those long lashes at half-mast.

She was stunning. And she was mine.

I backed up onto my knees, wanting to see all of her. She tried to pull her arms over herself, but I shook my head. "Don't. Please. You're fucking... everything."

Michelle lifted her arms up over her head. I bent down and took both her breasts in my hands, holding them before me like a feast. Then I brought my mouth to one nipple, teasing and tugging it into a hard bud.

Michelle whimpered, writhing under me. I took her other breast, doing the same, until both her nipples were hard, gleaming nubs. I drew kisses down her stomach, trailing my tongue down to the hem of her underwear. I looked up, checking with her, and she nodded. I hooked my fingers into her waistband and tugged them down, revealing the glistening core of her.

She was wet for me. So wet. I dipped my head down and drew my tongue along her slit, tasting her sweetness. A shudder of pleasure went through me and for a moment I had to pull back so I didn't come right there on the sheets. I propped my hands under her ass and dipped my head down.

When my tongue met her clit she gasped. I went in slow, languorous circles, dipping my tongue into the center of her before returning to her center.

"Oh god, Will," she said as I slowed my pace on her clit, teasing her. I wanted to control this. I wanted to have her begging for release.

But not like this. I sat up. She sucked in a breath at my absence. "This way," I said. I sat her up and lay down on my back.

I crooked a finger at her. "Here," I said.

She was stunning in the candlelight, with her dark curls and parted lips. But I wanted her on me.

She gripped the headboard, lifting her hips so she was over my face then she lowered her pussy onto me.

I grabbed her ass as she ground herself onto me, as I sucked on her clit, flicking it fast and hard with my tongue.

Michelle swirled her hips over me, rocking against me.

"I'm going to come," she said, panting.

I couldn't help it, I stroked my cock as she arched her back, coming on my face. I used my free hand to cover her mouth; to quiet her screams as she bucked over and over again.

It was the hottest fucking moment I'd ever experienced.

I had to stop stroking—my cock was already dripping, ready for her.

Finally, she swung off me, falling back onto the bed.

"That was... incredible," she said. Her eyes met mine. "But I want more."

"Tell me what you want," I said, my voice thick with need.

"I want you," she said. "I want your cock inside me, I want you to make me—"

But I'd sat up, dipping my tongue back down to her

swollen clit. I slipped two fingers inside her, stroking and pulling while I flicked my tongue fast and hard once more. The change of pace was so sudden she cried out, clapping a hand over her mouth. She shuddered under me, instantly moaning, shaking, and drenching me with her wetness as she came. When she slowed, she lay there with her eyes closed, catching her breath.

I got off the bed and pulled my shorts off, dropping them to the floor.

Then I returned to the bed. I lay down next to her, cupping her cheek in my hand, and kissed her, soft, sweet, hard, all the ways I could. My cock grazed her thigh in delicious, slippery torture.

"Fuck, I need you," I said against her mouth.

She stretched her arm out, reaching for the drawer beside her bed, not quite making it. I leaned over her, pulling it open and taking out a foil packet. I tried to open it but she put her hand on mine.

"Wait," she said. She gently pushed me onto my back. Then she lowered her face down, her hair cascading over me, and took my cock in her mouth.

Pleasure shot through me, making my skin feel like a charge had gone through it. Her hands were working some kind of magic on me, massaging and stroking and tugging.

"Stop," I said. I pulled away as need coursed through me. I ripped open the condom, slipping it onto my cock fast.

Maybe I should have waited a moment, took some time to just look at her. Her whole body glowed in the soft candlelight. She was exquisite. A painting. A sculpture.

But I couldn't wait. I took her by the hips and gently flipped her over onto her front. I wanted her up where she was before with her hands on the headboard.

"Are you okay?" I asked, my hands on her hips.

"I will be," she said, "when you're fucking me."

I gave a low laugh. God, this woman. I pulled her ass up until the curve of it was under my palms.

"You're perfect," I said. "You know that, right?"

I got a moan in response. She pushed herself back to me. I slipped my hand between her legs, finding her swollen clit. I circled it, making her breath hitch, then slowly increased the pressure.

"Yes," she breathed. I could tell she was about to go over, and right at that moment I thrust my cock into her, maintaining pressure on her clit as I filled her.

She came hard against my cock, squeezing and bucking, sliding up and down my shaft with such force I came after only a few short strokes, the world spinning, waves of pleasure blinding me to everything except Michelle, Michelle, Michelle.

17

MICHELLE

I woke up to the sound of Emma and Macy shrieking. Blinking, I looked over at my clock. It was eight-thirty.

I sat bolt upright, remembering everything. *Will.*

The space on the bed next to me was empty.

"Rahhhhhr!!!" A deep voice exclaimed out in the hallway.

More shrieking. "You can't get us here!" came Emma's voice, muffled.

Will was playing with the girls. A warmth, shockingly deep and full-bodied, spread through me. Then, just as quickly, a flash of memory. Joe, chasing Emma as a toddler all over our house in Long Island. Her adorable little squeals.

My chest seized.

Don't panic. This is okay.

I don't know what I was thinking would happen last night when the girls found out Will had spent the night. I'd meant to figure it out, to get up early and bang around in the kitchen so they came to see me there. Or at the least maybe have Will move to the couch. But Will had taken care of it for me.

He knew what needed to happen. And he'd taken care of it for me.

The warmth grew in my chest.

Steve had always wanted the girls to go and watch TV, to go do *kid stuff*. He'd bought them presents—big, noisy toys they got bored of quickly. But I knew they were all a means to keep them out of his hair.

But Will—from the moment we first met, my kids adored him. He'd known exactly how to get down to their level. He'd *cared* about them.

And he cared about me. Then we'd... god, we'd done it all.

This is good. I was happy, or at least I should be.

Will wasn't Steve.

He's not Joe, either.

I scrubbed my face with my hands. Everything was messed up. My feelings. My heart.

The promises I'd made to myself—and broken.

My phone buzzed on my nightstand. Thank god. I grabbed it, needing the distraction like air.

Reese: You guys okay over there? You have power?

Michelle: We have power.

I hesitated.

I also have... a houseguest.

It wasn't that I wanted to kiss and tell, whatever that meant. I didn't know what to do. How to proceed. I needed help, and now, I guess I was someone who asked for it.

Reese: Have you heard from Mom and Dad?

Oh my god, I'd completely forgotten about my parents. They were supposed to arrive today. I scrolled back through my phone, ignoring, for once, the messages from Bella Eats readers, who were still—*still*—curious about where that mysterious man was and why he hadn't been making cookies with us last week.

Mom had called at six this morning—I'd slept right through it.

I thought back to last night, to the hours of waking up, making love, falling asleep, and doing it again. But we were asleep by six. Thank god.

I called Mom back, but it rang until it went to voicemail. Nervously, I put the phone down, lifting up the blinds. Snow blanketed everything. There had to be at least two feet of it.

Will's car was buried. He'd be stuck here. Suddenly I felt like I couldn't breathe.

Just then there was a bang behind me, followed by a cry of "Mommy!"

"Macy!" I said, laughing. "You know you're supposed to knock on doors before you come in."

Macy ran up to me, throwing her arms around my leg. "Will came over last night!" Macy said as if bringing me the news. I bent down and squeezed her to me, nuzzling her cheek. Even at eight, she still felt like a baby to me. At least there was no confusion here.

"Is that right?" I asked.

I wondered how her child's brain was computing this. How Emma's was. Emma, I knew, would have questions. Though it wasn't likely she'd understand the full implications of a man spending the night.

As if summoned, Will filled the doorframe. I couldn't help it, my stomach jumped at the sight of him. He was fully dressed, and besides his mussed hair and growth of stubble on his chin, he looked extremely put-together.

I lowered Macy to the ground. "Macy can you... go find

your sister? Tell her if you guys play for a bit now, I'll take you outside to build a snowman after breakfast."

Macy squeezed past him and ran down the hall.

"Morning," he said.

"Hi," I replied. Without warning, more flashes of last night hit me rapid-fire: Will's lips on mine. His face on the pillow, between my legs. The way he'd brought me over the edge the moment he'd entered me. The care he took to make sure I was okay before.

The warmth wobbled. I wasn't supposed to feel this way.

Will walked toward me and handed me a mug of coffee I hadn't realized he was holding.

"Thought you might need this," he said. Having him up close made my skin feel like it was burning. As if there was a charge coming off him my body was meeting.

I took it, gratefully holding it in front of my face as if that could offer a barrier between us. "Thank you," I said, taking a tiny step away from him. I couldn't think straight this close to him.

I'm going to make you come again.

Oh god.

Will's eyes stayed on me, even as I looked away. I could feel them, burning holes through me. But I couldn't meet his gaze.

"So," I said. "It snowed last night."

"Are you okay?" he asked.

I nodded. "Fine." It was then I realized there was an awkwardness to him. A stiffness.

"You regret what happened," he said, his voice tight.

"No," I said too fast. "I'm just... I didn't expect it. I didn't plan it."

"I asked you if it was okay," he said, his jaw working. "Fuck," he said to himself, looking down. He raised a hand up against the window frame, gripping it as if needing the strength. "I knew this was a bad idea."

"You came over here!" I said. I could hear myself and I hated it. I was picking a fight, needing him to get mad.

You're sabotaging this.

It was Joe's voice, but it was mine, too.

I didn't mean for that to sound so harsh. "I'm sorry," I whispered. "I don't know what I'm doing."

"Michelle," he said, making a fist against the wood. "I'm the one who wanted you to stay on the phone with me last night. I'm the one who couldn't go anywhere but here. So really—this is my fault."

"It's not," I said. "Truly. I thought I could do this but..."

"But you're not over your dead husband."

The words were like a gunshot in the air.

"I'm sorry," he said.

"I am," I said. My voice sounded defensive. Petty. "I've done all the therapy. The groups. It's been six fucking years, I'm over it."

I knew, with those words, that it sounded like I was very much not over it.

Pinching my lips, I looked out at the snow. He wasn't allowed to tell me I wasn't over Joe. That was for me to decide. I gripped the coffee mug so hard I was surprised it didn't shatter.

"Listen," Will said. "It's for the best, okay? Me, thinking I could have something like this, it was foolish. I should have known that from the beginning."

"It's not your fault—"

Will ran a hand over his head. "It's fine. I actually have to get to work."

Time had slipped away from me. I didn't even know it was a weekday.

"How?" I gestured outside. I wanted to laugh, but I knew it would come out sounding completely unhinged.

"The roads are clear—I just need a shovel to get my car out. You need your walk shoveled anyway, right? How else are your parents going to get up here?"

The fact that he remembered didn't soften my anger. It only cut deeper, the edge of it sharp as a knife.

"There's a shovel on the back porch," I said.

"Okay. Good." But he didn't move. Instead, he ran his hand over the back of his neck. "Did you want to take some pictures first?"

For a moment I didn't understand what he meant. Then I remembered: the blog. He was keeping the deal, even now. Taking posed romantic photos was the last thing I felt like doing right now.

It felt desperate. Cheap.

But I'd be an idiot to pass up the opportunity, wouldn't I?

"Right," I said. I was discombobulated. What the hell was I going to take a picture of? Did I really want to immortalize this moment?

Then I remembered the coffee in my hand. I thrust it at him. "Hold this."

I picked up my phone. There was a new text on there. I swiped it open—it was my mom; they were on their way. I opened my mouth to tell Will, then shut it again. Why had I had the urge to tell him? There was nothing between us.

Then I framed Will's hands in the shot. I remember being surprised how rough his hands were for a man who put out only figurative fires. He'd said it was from the regular work he did on Hank and Casey's farm. *Keeps me feeling useful,* he said, as if he wasn't useful in his job, or as a father. Or as a constant savior for me.

What the hell had I done? What was I doing?

For a moment I could feel his palms on me, the way they'd felt cupping my cheek. Gripping my ass. Holding my breasts while his tongue flicked at my—

I snapped the photo. I didn't include his face, just the mug, his hands, and his chunky cable knit sweater in the background.

"Can you turn and look out the window?" I asked. "Out toward the snow?"

He followed my instructions, and I got a few good shots of him looking out at the winter wonderland outside. His jaw was tight, his gaze hard. The angle of my shot, along with the brightness of the day outside, made him mostly a silhouette. A handsome, sexy as hell, conflicted enigma, who I knew only wanted to get the hell out of Dodge.

I dropped my phone back down on the table.

Will handed me my coffee.

"Thanks," he said.

"No, thank you," I flung back.

18

WILL

They put me at the kid's table for Christmas dinner.

Okay, so it wasn't a separate table. And there was only one kid. But Casey had definitely set up the dinner table so the two happy, loving couples, her and Hank and Stella and her new boyfriend Dean, were on one side, while the rest of us—me, Casey's son Sam, and Dad, were on the other.

"To family," Casey said, holding the glass of wine up at the head of the table.

Dad coughed. It was a long, wet hacking sound, and I caught Hank and Stella exchanging a worried look.

When he finished, everyone raised their glasses again.

"To family," we all said. All of us except Dad and me.

Sam threw me a sideways look. He knew his grandfather wasn't likely to join in on a cheery toast; he also knew he could give me a hard time about not doing it too.

"Don't you love your family?" Sam asked. He was eleven and didn't miss a thing.

"Of course I love family," I grumbled over a mouthful of turkey.

On his other side, Dad hacked again.

"How long have you had that cough, Dad?" Stella asked.

"It's fine," he said, tripping even over that word and coughing again.

Maybe I should have been worried, but I couldn't think about him that way. I was still too fucking pissed.

Luckily, Sam seemed to sense that today, I wasn't up for a roast, even from my favorite—and only—little nephew. Sam and I were buddies now, given I came over every Sunday afternoon to help with chores. It was win-win in my books—I got a good old-fashioned farm workout and he got to hang out with who I hoped was his favorite uncle. Though today, I wished I could even be away from him. I didn't want to be around anyone I cared about. I was too worried I might hurt them. I would have skipped Christmas dinner if Stella hadn't driven over to my house herself saying she wouldn't go if I didn't. I'd ended up following her car in mine, grumbling the whole fucking way.

"What's up with you?" Sam asked as he poured an obscene amount of gravy over his mashed potatoes.

Dad's cough seemed to have calmed down and everyone had relaxed. Stella had settled into a story about a car engine that had Dean and Dad deeply interested—both men were mechanics. Or at least Dad was before he retired. Hank and Casey, meanwhile, were leaning in and whispering at each other as if they were teenagers in love. Even Dean had an arm looped around my sister's shoulders.

"I'm just upset your cousins aren't here," I said, taking a way-too-big bite of mashed potatoes so I wouldn't have to talk for a minute. I'd spoken to Hannah and Remy on the phone earlier today. They were living it up by the pool at Gareth's complex in Orlando. "It's actually hot!" Remy had chirped.

"Remy and Draco are actually getting along, too," Hannah had shared when it was her turn. "Only two phone fights."

Then I decided a little honesty couldn't hurt. Only a little. "But I'm also always a little sad at holidays because my mom isn't here," I said.

"That makes sense," Sam said.

I softened. God, Sam was such a good kid. "My mom and I were really close, just like you and your mom are."

"Was she a single mom like mine was? Before Hank?"

"She was married to Grandpa," I said, jerking a thumb at my dad. "But she might as well have been."

Then I felt a surge of guilt. That wasn't totally fair—and I shouldn't be badmouthing Sam's granddad, especially not while sitting right next to him. "I just mean she was the one who spent the most time with us. Packed our lunches for school, dropped us off for all our sports stuff. Stayed with us when we were sick."

"Mom stuff," Sam said.

"Yeah, exactly."

Sam gave a glance over to his mom who caught his eye. "You okay honey?"

Sam nodded.

My heart twisted. Casey was a great mom. So was my mom.

So was Michelle.

I wondered, for the thousandth time that day, what her family was doing right at that moment. And for the thousandth time that day, I thought about our last night together. How incredible it had been. How *whole* I'd felt.

Running around with Emma and Macy had been so pure, so perfect, and had thrown me right back to when my girls were young. It was the one thing I was really good at.

And of course, I'd fucked it up. I hadn't been able to keep that perfect family I had together. But I'd even managed to put that aside on that perfect morning.

Then I'd seen her face. Michelle, looking at me like she was... scared. Like I'd stepped into this image she had of her life and I was the wrong fucking man.

What was it she'd said when she'd first asked me to take those stupid pictures?

It could be any guy.

But it couldn't. She couldn't be with any guy, and she couldn't be with me. Not when she was still living with a ghost.

Casey went back to whispering something to Hank, who threw back his head and laughed.

Anger roiled in my stomach. How could everyone be so happy? How had they figured it out?

"It's girl trouble, isn't it," Sam asked.

Since when had this kid become so insightful?

With everyone else occupied, it was easy to keep our conversation just between the two of us. I decided to tell Sam the truth. "You know about girls?"

Sam nodded sagely. "A lot of my friends have problems like that."

I suppressed a smile, nodding seriously along with him. "I'm impressed," I said. "When I was ten my problems were all about trying to beat my personal best on a test and worrying about getting picked for the baseball team."

"Oh, we have those problems too," Sam assured me. "So, who's the girl... I mean, woman?"

My heart squeezed painfully. "She's a friend of Hank's, actually."

"It's Michelle, isn't it?"

My jaw fell open. "You know her? Also, how did you know?"

"Hank said you had a crush on her."

"He what?"

"Not to her face or anything. I heard him tell Mom."

I glared at my brother who seemed to sense my eyes on him.

"What?" he asked.

I opened my mouth, but suddenly all eyes were on me. Hell. The last thing I wanted to do was air out my shit in front of the whole family. I looked at Sam, who suddenly looked nervous.

Dad coughed again, taking up the whole room with it. It rankled at me. It shouldn't have, but it did. He never cared about anyone else except the space he was taking up.

That wasn't fair, but I didn't care.

"It's okay," I said to Sam. "It's not you."

I clapped a hand on the table, making everyone startle. "I wanted to... give a toast."

Stella smiled. "And here I thought you were going to look like a thundercloud this whole dinner!"

"Hey, he misses Hannah and Remy," Sam said.

Don't stick up for me, kid. Not now.

"You're right, Sam," Stella said. "Sorry, Will."

"Well..." I cleared my throat, taking a sip of water. "I guess I did want to say I'm grateful to my siblings for putting up with me over the last couple of years."

I didn't say Dad. I wouldn't.

"I know I wasn't always a ball of good cheer, you know with the... divorce and everything. But I guess everyone's used to that."

I threw a look at Dad.

"Will," Stella said.

I kept going. "I also wanted to say I'm delighted that both my siblings have somehow managed to find their perfect matches. I thought because I failed that it wasn't possible. I guess I was kind of a scrooge about love."

"Will—" Stella repeated, her face suddenly serious.

"No—it's okay. It doesn't happen for some people, and that's fine. I'm just happy it happened for you and Dean and for you, Hank." I looked at my brother. "For you and Casey. Finally."

Dean gave a polite laugh. No one else did. Everyone else was looking at me like I had some kind of goddamned disease.

"Will," my dad said. "You're making a damn fool of yourself."

"Dad!" Stella admonished.

"Well, he is. If his mother was here she'd say so too."

"But she isn't, is she?" I said, my voice hard. It was only because of Sam that I didn't hit my fist on the table. "She's dead. She was the best thing that ever happened to you; she's gone, and you get to keep on going, your life improved a thousand times over because of her."

Dad coughed. Of course.

I knew I was sounding like an ass. That I was like the drunk family member at Christmas dinner—and I hadn't even had a drop to drink. I couldn't stop myself. All the pain and anger I'd felt toward him was sharpened to a fine point. I waited until he finished.

I stood up, talking only to my father now. "Do you remember, Dad, that she used to give us each a special, personalized thing she'd made every Christmas? On top of the regular presents? I still have that sweater from high school with me throwing a basketball on it. That she learned how to knit because I was the captain of the team that year and we won the goddamn..." —I bit my lip, glancing at Sam. "We won the tournament. Do you even remember that? I'm not sure how you could when you never went to a single game."

"You don't know the first thing about what I did for you," Dad said, his voice raspy. Was he wheezing?

I laughed. There was no humor in it. "Sure. I know what you did. You couldn't stand the fact that I wanted to do my own thing, that I had interests that didn't involve the family business."

"Will!" Stella said standing up. She looked furious but also like she was on the verge of tears.

My stomach lurched. I was an asshole. I knew I was. I hadn't meant to hurt her. But I'd spent my whole adult life avoiding this conversation with my dad and it was like my brain couldn't put the brakes on. My chest burned.

"It's true, Stella," I said. "You were too young to remember. But the minute I told Dad I wasn't going to take over the garage was the minute he stopped caring."

"Will," Hank said, standing across the table. We were eye to eye. His voice was hard. "That's enough."

I stared at my brother, every muscle in my body tensed.

"I know you're pissed," he said, "but you're going to ruin Christmas."

His eyes went down to Sam who was staring up at me, his eyes like dinner plates.

And just like that, the fire went out of me. It was replaced with a deep, painful wash of shame. I'd already ruined Christmas. I'd let Sam down. I'd let my whole damn family down.

I looked at Sam. "I'm sorry," I said. "I'm sorry to all of you." My voice felt like it was stuck in my throat. "Even you," I said to Dad.

Dad's eyes on mine were filled with anger. But they were glossy, too. From the coughing, that's all it was.

I shoved my chair aside and grabbed my coat at the front door.

"Will!" Stella cried, running after me. I stepped out into the freezing night. Snow blanketed the whole farm, and stars twinkled overhead.

"Will, wait!" Stella said, running up to me.

"I can't be around anyone right now, Stella," I said, my voice hard as I stomped to my car.

"Wait, goddammit!" she shouted.

I turned, my chest tightening as I saw my baby sister standing there with tears streaming down her face. She looked just like she did when she was a little kid and Dad and I were fighting.

I looked away, feeling like I ought to maybe crawl into a hole so I wouldn't fuck up anyone else's life. If it weren't for Hannah and Remy, I might.

But Stella walked up to me and threw her arms around me.

I was shocked. I didn't deserve to be hugged right now. I didn't deserve anything but getting shunned. "I'm sorry," she said.

"What the hell do you have to be sorry about?" I asked.

"I'm sorry things are so hard," she said, pulling back and looking in my face with deep concern. "I'm sorry you have to see Hank and I so happy when you've gotten such a raw deal. I know you tried with Jill. I know you didn't want this to happen. And I know Dad is hard on you specifically. I don't know why, but I think... I think he sees you in him. And Mom, too. He loves you Will, I know he does."

"He has an absolute shit way of showing it."

"Yeah. He does. But some people feel so much it hurts to

show anyone any of it. You're like that, Will. You care so much. The way you care about everyone at that table. Dad too, even if you don't want to admit it.

"I don't."

"Yes, you do. You were the one who drove all the way into the city to get him the right carrier for his oxygen tank. The one who talked the care home into giving us a better deal and insisting he have a room with a window because you know how much he likes looking out at that pond—"

"You have a skewed view of me," I said. "Because I'm your big brother."

"It's not skewed. You're the most caring person I know. And I bet if you asked the people who run all the organizations you volunteer at, and everyone who works with you, they'd all say the same thing. That maybe you're crusty on the outside, but you show up. You act where other people just talk about it."

I said nothing. They were just words.

"So will you come back inside?"

I shook my head. "No. I don't trust myself not to fuck up again."

"Then will you call her at least? So you have one good thing to come out of this Christmas?"

"How—"

"Hank told me about Michelle."

I stiffened once more, the anger threatening to come back. "Hank doesn't know anything about how I feel about Michelle."

"You're right. No one does because you don't tell us anything."

My heart ached. It ached as badly as if there was an iron fist around it, crushing the life out of it.

"You care about her, Will, I know you do."

I shook my head. "I'm falling in love with her," I whispered, the truth shocking me, rattling me straight down to my core. "Hell, I think I'm already there." My throat burned with the pain of it.

"So, what's stopping you from telling her?"

I could have told her what I knew, that she wasn't ready for me. That she'd probably never be ready for me. But it wasn't all on Michelle. It was me. I proved it tonight, right there at the table, I was my father's son.

"The last time I thought I could be with someone," I said, "I fucked it up. I couldn't..." my voice cracked. "I couldn't keep my family together. I'm just not the kind of person who can make someone happy."

"Do you realize how crazy that sounds?" Stella asked softly.

"Maybe," I said. "But I don't know how to fix myself. I look at Dad and I see me in thirty years. Bitter. Angry. Alone. Michelle deserves better. She deserves the best, and I'm too broken to give her that."

Then, before Stella could say anything else, I strode to my car, slammed the door and drove away.

～

An hour later, after I'd driven aimlessly around half of Jewel Lakes County, I found myself in downtown Barkley Falls.

The whole town was shuttered but all the lampposts were festooned with twinkling lights and wreaths. There was a constant debate at town hall meetings about how much money and effort should go into decorating for each holiday. I knew some people might imagine me on the side of not wanting to waste precious town resources on fanciful things like lights and giant stocking decorations or hanging flower baskets in the spring, but I loved them. I wouldn't tell anyone of course, but they helped make Barkley Falls the homey, magical place it was. The only thing besides my girls I could love unconditionally, and who I couldn't hurt with my shit.

Hopefully.

I parked at the top end of Main Street by the lumberyard. The whole of downtown took about twenty minutes to walk from end to end. I could probably do it with my eyes closed—I knew it like the back of my hand. I strode past the long, snow-covered logs. That's where I'd helped Hank pick up a bunch of wood last summer for the renovations on their barn and house. Further down the street, I passed the medical clinic where Mom once took me for a broken arm I'd gotten saving a kid from getting run over by a horse at a pageant when I was twelve. "You're my little hero," she'd said. Really, I'd been scared shitless, but I'd lapped it up. Her attention was like lifeblood compared to Dad's silence.

My feet crunched in the snow as I passed Aubrey's. Aubrey, who was actually Aubrey Junior, had retired this fall, and with the mayor on a golf trip, I'd served as proxy in honoring the spot as a municipal landmark. Her son now ran the diner, and I made a note to have the next few town events catered by them so they could keep thriving over the slower winter season.

There was the vintage clothing store, run by Casey's friend, and Graydon's sister. Further along this block—all of which was owned by Charles Haverford, the mayor's business associate—the empty storefront on the corner. The one I kept teasing Michelle about when we used to text, because it would have made a brilliant Italian restaurant, run by the brilliant, gorgeous, perfect Michelle Franco.

There was a *LEASED* sign in the window. It felt symbolic. Like an opportunity I'd somehow squandered.

I walked faster.

There were places I wouldn't pass on this walk down Main Street. Good Fortune, the Chinese restaurant where Graydon and I used to gorge ourselves back in high school after football games. Archer Mechanical, our family garage that Stella announced earlier in the day she'd be turning over to Luciana permanently as she was staying in Michigan. The place I used to change spark plugs while arguing with Dad about everything and nothing.

I thought about Dad at dinner tonight, how red-rimmed his eyes had looked. How bad his cough had sounded. I shouldn't have been so hard on him. I should have just let it go. That's what Hannah would have told me if she'd been there. How had I raised such a perfect diplomat? Maybe she was the one who should become a politician.

I didn't know where I'd been going until I arrived: The town green. Whereas a couple of cars had passed by on my hike through town, there was no one here at all.

The silence was glorious.

So was the open space—snow blanketed not just the green but Opal Lake too—it was a sea of pristine silvery white in the starlight. I tromped up the steps of the gazebo and sat down on the bench, not caring that snow soaked through my pants. I needed to feel.

I pulled out my phone, looking at it for the first time since this afternoon. I'd missed an email from the mayor's assistant sending me instructions for the stay at the Rolling Hills Resort over New Year's. I'd completely forgotten about that. I'd agreed to go sometime between pizza at Michelle's and the other night. The thought of staying at a fancy resort in a few days seemed absurd to me now, especially when further down in the email it said I was also booked for a couple's massage, dinner at the restaurant, and various other activities designed for two. There'd been a postscript from the assistant that said, "You're more than welcome to participate in any of these activities on your own, Will," which was so sad I had to laugh.

There were no other messages. I considered texting my daughters, but we'd already spoken at length today, and they'd probably worry about me if I sent a cryptic Merry Christmas.

The only person left was Michelle.

Despite every terrible thing about me, what I'd done, how I'd let her down, I couldn't let this day go by without telling her I was at least thinking about her. Even if it was the last thing I said to her, and even if she ignored me.

I pulled up her name.

WILL: Michelle I just wanted to...

I ERASED THAT.

What was I supposed to say? I'm sorry I'm such an ass? I'm sorry I can't make you happy? I fucking love you?

There was nothing she could do with any of that.

I leaned back, looking up into the rafters of this 100-year-old structure, wondering how many people had professed their love in here over the years? Not just the umpteen weddings, but couples on late-night walks. Teenagers on hot summer days, dripping in lake water, stealing kisses in their bathing suits.

Me, right now, with no one to hear it.

I love you, Michelle Franco.

If she were here, I'd say it. I wouldn't be able to stop myself. But she wasn't. I was alone, and it was better this way.

Will: Merry Christmas, Michelle.

I POCKETED MY PHONE.

19

MICHELLE

The double glass doors to the Rolling Hills resort opened in a swish of warm air and soft jazz.

"Wow!" Reese said, actually gulping.

"It's going to be fine," I said, though I wasn't sure who I was reassuring.

She wasn't nervous about the gorgeous resort, I knew. It was being here, at Eli's hotel.

Only a week ago, we'd been a couple of glasses deep into our eggnog after Christmas dinner, both of us trying to keep from losing our shit over our respective failures with our respective divorced men.

I'd just finished telling her what had happened with Will—toning down the gory details but leaving in the part about what he'd said.

The part I was so furious about still.

Reese had waved a finger at me. "I'm going to do it," she'd said, her overfull eggnog sloshing from the glass in her other hand onto the table.

"Do what?" I'd asked.

"Go to the hotel. Eli said it was an open offer. He thought I wouldn't take him up on it, but you were right. Why not?"

"You should!" I said.

"And you're going to come with me!" she'd tacked on.

"What? No." I was way too busy. I had the girls.

But in the end, it was Mom who'd convinced me to join Reese in Vermont. She'd not-so-gently suggested I needed the break. "We'll stay a couple days longer and look after the girls," she said, clapping her hand like it was a done deal already. Which I guessed it was.

When I'd gone wobbly at her kindness, she'd sat down next to me, tucking a strand of hair behind my ear like she used to do when I was a girl.

"Do I look that tired?"

"Yes."

At least she was honest.

It had been a good week. With Dad, the girls had built a massive fort in the living room with all the linens and pillows we owned. With Mom, we'd made lasagna, baked muffins, and watched a half-dozen Disney movies, which I think Mom liked even more than Macy, who was obsessed. I took the girls out on my own to let Mom and Dad recover. Ice skating, pedicures, and burgers and shakes at Aubrey's in Barkley Falls. I'd even put an 'on vacation' post up on my blog and turned off my phone for three whole days in the middle.

During that time, I tried to keep my mind a Will Archer free zone.

I failed, miserably. During the busy moments where I was distracted, thoughts of him would dip in around the edges. Once, during muffin-baking, Emma told this hysterical muffin joke (There are two muffins in an oven. One muffin says to the other muffin, "Man, it's hot in here!" The other muffin says, "Holy crap, a talking muffin!"). I'd picked up my phone to text it to Will before remembering we didn't do that anymore.

Both of us were too messed up to make this work, even though I could admit, now, that I wished we weren't.

"It's stunning," I said now, as we passed through the doors.

It really was. We'd seen the photos in the online brochure, but as I suspected, they didn't really do the place justice.

The Rolling Hills Resort was nestled on a hill in a thickly forested valley in Northern Vermont. The whole valley was blanketed under a thick layer of snow, which meant the golf course was closed (not that it mattered to me) and besides cross-country skiing, the emphasis appeared to be on indoor luxuries like the spa, massages, and various indoor sports, including tennis, under one of those giant domes.

Inside, the space opened into an expansive lobby. A modern chandelier, all metal and glass, the size of a minivan, hung overhead. At the far side of the expansive space, there was a rock wall adjacent to a floor-to-ceiling window overlooking the valley. Water trickled down the rock wall, running in a path along the base of the window in a replica of the river below, before disappearing into more rocks on the other side of the room.

This place really had spared no expense. The only shortfall from our already five-star experience, that I could tell, was the hallway on the right side of the lobby was completely boarded off with plywood. Outside, there had been scaffolding all along that wing of the building—they were undergoing some kind of major renovation, though I saw no workers or heard no sounds of it.

While we waited to check-in, a couple walked by in expensive-looking matching ski gear, speaking a Scandinavian language. They were heading for a doorway that said 'SPAS'. As in multiple.

"Reese," I said, feeling a little ill as I turned back to my sister. "I don't know if I can afford to add on all these extra activities." Even though the room was free, I knew we'd easily rack up a bill on food and anything else we decided to do for the two days we were here. Tonight was New Year's Eve, and I fully expected Reese would want to celebrate. Albeit, looking at her, maybe in the room.

"We're not actually going to *do* anything, Mich," Reese said, shocked. She was still wearing her sunglasses, her coat collar pulled up over her chin. "We're going to hang out in our room the whole time."

I couldn't help but laugh, even as I knew we couldn't hide the whole time. "Reese, I thought the whole point of coming was sticking your chin out and showing Eli you didn't care about him? That you can have fun without him at his own hotel? Also, you look like a celebrity," I said.

"Perfect. That's exactly the vibe I want to maintain here." Then her jaw fell open. "Speaking of which! Holy shit!"

I followed her gaze to where a very tall, athletic-looking man in a tracksuit was walking briskly through the lobby. Or would have been, if he wasn't pulling a toddler along beside him.

"Is he famous?" I asked.

"Mich, seriously? That's Jude Kelly! He's a tennis pro! He won the US Open three years in a row."

"Oh," I said. I had no idea who he was, but I could admit he looked like he could easily sprint around the whole hotel in about five seconds flat.

Then he looked right at us and lifted his hand up as if in greeting.

"Oh my god is he—"

But when I looked back, the woman behind the counter was giving him a curt nod.

"Not us," I said.

The woman smiled at the people in front of us. "Jude runs our recreation programs," she said to them. "We're lucky to have him."

There was something about how the woman said that that made me think she wasn't nearly as impressed with him as Reese.

But I was distracted. There was something familiar about the tennis player. Actually not him, though maybe I'd seen him on TV before or something. It was the boy I thought I'd seen before, with that adorable pointed nose and shaggy hair.

As the tennis guy pulled the boy up to sit on his shoulders, I had the strangest feeling of deja vu. The boy looked so familiar—even the fact that he was with a man.

When I looked back to the desk, the woman was giving a little wave to the toddler, looking decidedly happier to see him than the boy's father.

Then it clicked. This was Eli's family's resort. That little boy was the one Will had been with at the park that day, Eli's nephew, Jack. The tennis player must be related to him and maybe the woman behind the counter too. I looked at Reese to see if she had made the connection, but she was still agog at the celebrity factor—I don't even think she'd noticed Jack.

I decided not to tell her. I didn't need to remind her about anything related to Eli.

Especially not while I was suddenly thrown back to the

park. How Will had been flying Jack around like an airplane, the most comfortable and happy I'd seen him before everything happened between us.

My insides felt like they'd been hollowed out. I swallowed. *Not now.*

I was determined not to think about Will.

"Welcome to the Rolling Hills Resort," the woman at the desk said as the couple ahead of us strode off. "I'm Cassandra."

She was attractive, maybe my age or a couple years older, with blonde hair slicked back and wearing an expensive-looking suit. Everyone else working the desk wore matching uniforms, while this woman looked like she belonged in a Manhattan boardroom. A glance at her name tag said she was the General Manager.

The woman—Cassandra—saw where my eyes had gone.

"We're a little short staffed right now," she explained. There was a flash of something in her face—frustration? Exhaustion? "But I'm thrilled to help you myself."

She must be related to Eli, too. Now I prayed Reese wouldn't notice.

Luckily it didn't seem like she would—she was craning her neck around, looking more obvious rather than less. I knew she was looking for Eli.

As Cassandra entered our information into the computer, I glanced around too, only I forced my mind not to veer back to Will. There was a restaurant here I couldn't wait to check out. A little research told me it had been reviewed in international guides and publications, that the chef had been imported from France, and they carried wines I didn't know still existed.

Will probably knew them all. He was a small-town boy

with big city sensibilities. This would be the perfect place for him.

Damn it.

What was that he said?

I startled. Joe. I hadn't heard him since that day. I almost expected to see him shimmering in the glimmering sunlight on the waterfall feature.

Was he wrong?

I swallowed.

"Mich!" Reese was saying my name. "Michelle!" She poked me hard in the arm.

"I'm sorry?"

Cassandra was looking at me curiously. "I'll need to know your license plate..."

As I gave her the information she needed, I kept looking back to the waterfall, but there was nothing there except trickling water.

∽

OUR ROOM WAS JUST as gorgeous as the lobby, if a tiny bit less grand. And, as I peered a little closer, except for the furniture, a little dated, too, though they'd done a good job of making everything look as polished as possible. I imagined this side of the building was still waiting for its renos.

"I still can't believe we got the full package," Reese said, still looking slightly shocked. As the woman at the desk had handed us our cards, she'd noted the room came with a full deluxe resort package—activities, meals, and access to the spas included. As in multiple spas. My jaw had dropped when she handed us the brochure. I hadn't looked at the spa pages on the website earlier, but I saw now the whole lower floor of the building was a series of interconnected saunas modeled after a hot spring found in caves in Scandinavia.

As if that wasn't enough, a bottle of champagne that sat in an ice bucket in the center of the room with a welcome card attached. I handed the card to my sister.

She read it, her lips pursing.

She'd done a good job of expunging Eli from her system over the past few weeks, but I could tell by the way her face tightened that whatever was in the card wasn't a good thing. That despite the star treatment, he wasn't begging for her to come back.

"You were right," she said, tossing the card in the trash. "He's trying to absolve himself for dumping me."

"Then I guess we better take full advantage," I said. "Or do you still want to hang out in here?"

Reese lifted her chin and smiled, though the echo of pain was still there. "Not a chance."

Seven hours later, I was more relaxed than I think I've ever been in my life. The spas had been incredible, and later, after we'd gone back up to the room, I'd even taken a nap, which I don't think I'd done since the girls were babies and Mom would force me to. Now, while Reese was in the bathroom, I stood before the closet, holding out a cocktail dress I'd thrown into my bag at the last minute. I thought it might stay there, but Reese, apparently fully rejuvenated, had come around full circle and decided we needed to go down to the restaurant for dinner. "It's New Years," she'd said. "And I'm done hiding."

I was proud of her. And grateful I brought the shimmery black dress or I'd be ringing in the new year in this fancy place in jeans. But now that the dress was before me, I hesitated. I'd pulled it out of a box in my closet at home. It was filled with all the things I couldn't bear to part with when I sold Joe's and my house in Queens when I moved to Rochester with Steve. I'd rented the house out during the year I lived with Mom and Dad, and had kept a bunch of stuff in the basement— all the things I was too emotional to manage in the raw weeks after Joe's death. I'd gotten rid of all of it, except the things in that box. I'd bought this dress on a whim, for New Year's, actually, before discovering I was pregnant for the first time. But I'd never worn it, except once, to try it on. When I'd shown Steve, his eyes had gone wide and he'd suggested I never wear it out of the house. Maybe that was the beginning of the end.

Maybe I wouldn't wear it for Steve, but I would now, dammit.

It was a simple thing made with a lot of Lycra; it had a scoop neck and hemline just above my knee. But there was some kind of metallic thread spun through it, and it glimmered under the light. I certainly wasn't quite as lithe as I was when I first tried it on in the store years ago, but the Lycra gave it a good amount of give, and I think it actually looked good with the couple of extra pounds I'd put on since then.

"Good lord," Reese said when she saw me. "You look spectacular!"

I turned to look at my sister. She was wearing a long, silky green dress with a deep vee. The fabric flowed all the way down to her ankles, clinging to her body the whole way.

"Same for you!" I said, and I meant it. She looked stunning. She'd done her hair so that it fell softly down her back, and the sparkling earrings she wore lit up her whole face.

"I'm so proud of you," I said, feeling a knot in my throat.

"What for?"

"For embracing this trip. For living the life you want. Everything. And I'm grateful to you too, for always being there for me. Even moving to Jewel Lakes for me."

"I didn't move there for you," she said, waving a hand.

She was lying.

"You know, I want you to know that you don't need to stay there for me. I'm a big girl, and I can survive without my big sister watching out for me."

She smiled. "I love where I live, and I love being close to you. Maybe one day I'll move, but I doubt it. Not now anyway."

A surge of sadness hit me then. "What if I have to leave, Reese? I'm shutting down the blog, and the firefighting money is only going to last so long."

"You said you're getting a job?"

"I will, but only one that fits with our life. I need to be around for the girls. I've been distracted for so long."

During the break, I'd put my phone away. It had been eye-opening. While my mind kept wanting to veer back to what had cracked open and fallen apart between me and Will, the time with the girls had been everything. I was going to try to find something part-time in Jewel Lakes, but I knew I'd have to consider other options, too.

"I still think you should have used the photos you took of Will," she said.

I laughed, though there was no humor in it. "Yeah, maybe that would have been the smart thing to do. But it didn't feel right."

What I didn't say was after Will left, I'd gone through the photos I'd taken of him that morning with my heart feeling like a lead weight. He looked so handsome and so devastatingly sad, it would have been like posting the pages of his personal diary for my readers to see.

I didn't want them to have that. I'd already given them too much of myself, they couldn't have him.

"Anyway. Our reservation is in a few minutes," I said, blinking to keep the tears from falling. I was wearing mascara for the first time in years, and the last thing I needed was to smear it all over my face.

Reese embraced me in a tight squeeze. "I love you, Mich. And I'm proud of you too."

When she pulled away, there were tears in both our eyes anyway. I laughed, thumbing them away.

"But first," she said, "we toast."

She pulled out the champagne, pouring us two very full glasses.

"To love," she said.

When I raised an eyebrow, she said, "Of all kinds. This one is for sisters."

We clinked glasses and I felt, for the first time in a long time, like I was going to be okay.

∽

I WAS right about the restaurant anyway. It was absolutely five-star. Along with the renovations to the lobby and the new spa area, the restaurant looked like it was brand new, even though we'd learned from the chatty staff person down at the spa registration that the hotel had been here for over fifty years.

"Same family running it too," the woman said, with a note of pride in her voice. "Pillars of the community. Or they were until Mrs. Kelly passed last year."

I felt like I knew more about Eli's family now than I ever

needed to—especially since I was still mad at the man for breaking my sister's heart and trying to buy his way out of his guilt.

Which, granted, he didn't have to do.

Still, what kind of guy has a torrid affair with someone without telling her he's moving back to his hometown? Telling her he wants to be friends when, clearly, she fell head over heels at first sight?

We were seated at a small round, white-clothed table in the darkened room, right next to the broad floor-to-ceiling window overlooking the same valley view as the lobby. Outside, there was a wide terrace that looked like it would beautifully host some spectacular parties in warmer weather. Now it was covered in a thick layer of snow.

The hostess who seated us didn't look remotely like she was related to Eli, thank everything above. Soft jazz music played over the speakers, though there was a stage set up opposite us.

While we settled in, the manager from the front desk walked briskly through the restaurant. I watched over Reese's shoulder as she spoke urgently to a man with his back to me who then strode out of the restaurant at a clip himself.

Now she definitely looked stressed. Everyone working here seemed kind of stressed, actually, except for the woman down at the spa earlier. But then again, she worked at a place that pumped Tibetan singing bowl music and lavender mist around her all day.

"What are you going to eat?" Reese asked, bringing me back to the present.

I looked back down at the menu. "I'm looking hard at the filet mignon," I said, though to be honest, I wasn't all that hungry. We'd ordered a late lunch to the room after the hours we'd spent down in the spas. But damned if I was going to waste the opportunity to eat a good meal.

"How about you?" Reese shrugged as she took a sip of her cocktail.

I'd asked her when she ordered if she wanted to wait until dinner—she'd only picked at her lunch and had downed two full glasses of champagne. I knew she was trying to quell her nerves, but I also worried she might overdo it.

Well, so what? If there was one night of the year to overdo it, it was New Year's eve I supposed. I sat back in my chair, trying not to think of what Will was doing right at that moment. He was probably at home, scowling over a glass of scotch in his beautiful brick home. Maybe trying not to text Remy to tell her to start the new year without Draco.

Be single, like me.

My stomach turned.

"Lobster," Reese said.

"What?" I said, startled back to the table.

"For dinner. He's covered it, right?"

"Right," I said. "Good choice."

"Cheers," Reese said.

After our server took our order, Reese and I clinked glasses, chatting for a bit about how amazing the spa had been.

Then the lights flickered and we were plunged into darkness. A few patrons gasped and a moment later a terrific crash exploded next to us, nearly making me shriek.

Then the lights came back on.

A man had walked right into a server carrying a tray filled with steaming food.

"Oh my god," Reese said, jumping up. The man looked

hurt—something hot had sloshed on his hand and he was holding it against his chest, grunting.

"I'm so sorry," the server was saying, trying to pick up broken dishes. She was young and looked terrified, her hands shaking.

"Napkin, please," Reese said to me. I tossed her a linen napkin from the table next to us.

"Don't touch the plates like that," Reese said to the server, "You might get hurt. Come over here and hold this on —what's your name sir?"

"Abe," the man said.

"You don't look mortally wounded, but I'm going to get—"

"Kristy," said the girl, looking like she was about to cry.

"It's okay, Kristy. Sir, Kristy's going to hold this napkin on your hand and I'm going to help her with these items here."

The girl's hands were still shaking wildly. I went and knelt beside the girl.

"It's okay," I said. "You got this." She shouldn't have been carrying such an overloaded tray. If this were my restaurant, I'd have made sure of it.

"I'm going to get fired," she said.

"It wasn't your fault," I said.

Just then, Cassandra rushed over, along with another server carrying a broom and dustpan. "Tonight, of all nights," she said.

"Where's the restaurant manager?" I asked, feeling protective of this young server. She looked a little like Remy, if Remy were a lot more timid and had a full head of fine blonde hair.

"We don't have one," she said. "It's a whole... thing. I'm very sorry."

Suddenly I felt for Cassandra. She was the one holding

All Your Fault 233

this place together, I realized. By a thread. And she probably had no experience running a resort. She probably *was* supposed to be on a board somewhere in a tower in New York.

Reese had already begun piling the shards of dinnerware on the tray, expertly, so the sharp edges were pointed in. She'd also laid a cloth on the tray first. Somehow in a matter of seconds, she'd gained complete control of the situation, keeping everyone calm and preventing further injury. She'd done exactly what I would have done back when I worked in restaurants. Clearly, the staff here hadn't been trained the same way. In fact, as I looked at them now, I realized they all seemed a little nervous. New.

"Don't worry," Reese said. "I've handled much worse."

For a moment Cassandra stood there slightly stunned, then directed the other server to run and get something. "Thank you so much," she said to Reese, kneeling down beside her. "But please, you don't need to do anything else."

"It's fine," Reese said. "Honestly, I've been here a hundred times before and I'd rather see things get done right than someone get hurt."

The man on the ground, embarrassed, looked down at his hand. "I'm fine," he said to Kristy and me. "It was my fault."

He apologized profusely as we helped him to his feet, offering to pay for all the meals.

"We're just glad you're not seriously injured," the manager said to him. "Take him to the front and send the spa nurse to see him please," she told Kristy. "Call her from her room if she's off. And offer him a voucher," she added.

The girl looked like she was about to cry but nodded.

"It's okay," the manager told her. "It wasn't your fault. It's the damn lights, the reno— never mind. Just don't worry, okay?"

The girl gave her boss a grateful smile before leading the man away.

It was only then that I saw all eyes in the room were on us, some people clutching their napkins to themselves in shock.

"We're all good," Reese said to the crowd. All of her worry over not standing out was gone, apparently, as was whatever tipsiness I thought I'd spotted before. Shoved aside to do the right thing. I was deeply impressed.

The crowd broke out in applause as Reese stood up, taking a little bow. I realized how we looked then, especially Reese, getting down and dirty in her formal wear.

"You're in good hands with Reese," I said, standing back up.

"She's resurrected what could have been an absolute... well, more of a clusterfuck than it already is," the manager said. To Reese she said, "I don't suppose you're looking for a job?"

Reese laughed. Then she saw the woman wasn't joking. "I'm..." She glanced at me. "No, I'm not. But that's very kind of you."

"Reese," I said, but she gave a quick smile and shake of her head.

She wouldn't leave because of me. But she couldn't keep working at Gastronomique, either, with how poor the management was now. The only thing absolving the quick rush of guilt I felt was knowing she couldn't exactly work at Eli's hotel either.

"Well, thank you so much, again," the manager said as Reese stood. The other staffer came back and hefted the tray

All Your Fault 235

as we returned to our seats and the other diners finally turned away with the excitement over.

"I don't think we've ever had a guest save our skin like that," the manager said. "And we were already in disaster mode with the restaurant manager gone."

The manager was definitely stressed. Beyond stressed. "This is not what I was supposed to be doing," she said, almost to herself. She looked up at us, her cheeks going pink. "I'm sorry, there've been a lot of changes here recently. We've got all new staff, including myself. And this reno has been an unmitigated disaster."

She waved at a passing server. "Please bring these two a bottle of the DuMaurnier Pinot Noir," she said.

"Well, thank you again," she said, clasping her hands. "The only thing that could have turned everything around is if one of you told me you were a singer," she joked.

Neither Reese nor I laughed. We just looked at each other.

"You're not, are you? Oh god, please tell me you are. Our entertainment quit on us tonight too, on top of everything."

That must have been what she was dashing across the restaurant to deal with earlier.

Before I thought too hard about it, I said, "Actually, Reese has a gorgeous voice."

Reese's eyeballs went wide.

"You do," I said.

"Well," the manager laughed. Then she went serious. "If that's true, please let me know. The dinner guests are expecting music at nine. It's a paying gig, of course."

After she told us she'd be at the front desk if we could possibly help, Reese looked at me, her eyes brimming with anger. "I can't believe you said that."

"Why? It's true, isn't it? I know you keep your voice in shape. I've heard you."

"Where?"

"In your room at Mom and Dad's. In the kitchen at my place with the girls when you thought I couldn't hear."

"You were eavesdropping?"

I ignored that. "Is it a lie?"

She pinched her lips. Then she grabbed her cocktail and tossed it down her throat. The server came just at that moment with our food, along with the bottle of wine. He offered to let us taste it but I shook my head and he nodded, deftly pouring two glasses and slipping away.

Reese ignored the food, grabbing her glass of wine and taking a giant gulp of that, too.

Somehow, this was what made me flip to anger. Not toward Reese, but to Eli.

To Will.

"Reese, remember how we said we weren't going to let our reaction to these men dictate how we live our lives? That we wouldn't let our past control our future? Whatever Simon did to you—whatever Eli did to you—you're still you. You're still my beautiful big sister with the gorgeous voice. There's still time for you to take back what you always wanted"

I took my own sip of wine. Then another.

She stared at me, her hands flat on the table. Her eyes flickered to the stage. Was she actually considering this?

I ran with it. Her challenging her own terror would be everything. For both of us.

"Listen," I said. "Do you want your nieces to hear about how you let a man squash your dreams? Or do you want to show them you persevered? You took your life by the horns even when you felt like you wanted to crawl in a hole and never come out again?"

I could feel the effects of the wine loosening me up, emboldening me. "Since when do you give the big sister pep talks?" She said, swigging her wine once more.

I ignored her. "Do you know what I found when I pulled this dress out of that old box?"

I didn't wait for her to answer.

"I found that restaurant notebook I used to carry around with me. I opened it up for the first time in years, and when I did, I felt..." My voice cracked. "Like a failure. I had a dream once and I never saw it through. When my life went absolutely sideways, after I lost the one man I'd ever..."

I swallowed. Was that true? Was Joe the one man I'd ever loved?

Had Will been right?

I looked out across the room, my eyes blurring with tears. Will was wrong about that. But he'd been right about me giving up on my real dreams. I'd been clinging to the blog because I thought it was how I'd stay connected to Joe. But he'd always be there, a beautiful part of who I was. That would never change.

But I had to.

"When I lost Joe, I gave up on my dreams. I shouldn't have."

I won't.

"What do you have to lose, Reese?"

Reese was staring at me, her eyes now wet with tears. "Okay, that was good," she said. "I guess you're doing the pep talks from now on."

She stood up, wiping the tears from her eyes with her fingertips.

I held my fingers over my mouth, my heart leaping in my chest. She was actually going to do it.

Reese wobbled a little as she took a step, but quickly recovered. Her glass was empty. She hadn't eaten enough. No matter how impressive my speech had been, the liquid courage was the only thing actually making her stand up and *do* this thing that terrified her.

I stood up too, giving my big sister a hug. "You're going to be amazing," I whispered.

Then I let her go, watching as she strode off in the direction of the lobby.

I only hoped I hadn't sent her to do something she might regret. I was all nerves.

Food.

Food was always the answer.

Our meals were sitting on the table untouched. I sat down and picked up my fork, glancing over in the direction Reese had gone one last time, wishing she'd eaten something before running off.

Then I froze with my first bite only halfway to my mouth.

There was a man at the entrance.

A gorgeous man with salt and pepper hair wearing a dark, well-tailored suit and tie.

My stomach dropped. It was Will.

20

MICHELLE

For a moment, I just sat there, blinking.

Will Archer was standing at the entrance of this restaurant. At this resort. Where I was.

My only saving grace was that he hadn't seen me.

The hostess, who even from here I could see was flirting with him, flipped her hair and laughed a little loudly before pointing somewhere over by the bar.

Will didn't laugh. He looked like he wished he was anywhere but here. I watched as he walked away from her, a dark cloud practically hanging over him.

Why did I have the urge to run up to him? To throw my arms around him and make a stupid joke to get that cloud to part?

And what the fuck was he doing here anyway? We were three hundred miles away from Jewel Lakes. I couldn't help but think of the line from Casablanca. *Of all the gin joints in all the towns...*

I watched as he sat down at the bar next to another man.

Eli.

Of course. They were friends. That had to be why he was here.

Oh god, Eli was here.

I'd been banking on him not being anywhere near this restaurant. Reese told me he was an electrician, which somehow I'd stuck in my brain as keeping him far from anything like this place.

Thank everything Reese wasn't here.

Then I realized what that meant: I glanced at my phone. In only five minutes, Reese *would* be here, getting up on stage, singing for the first time in years.

In front of the man who'd broken her heart.

He'd ruin this. It was Reese's chance at reclaiming her most precious dream. But if she saw him... I knew she'd barely gone to talk to the manager in the first place. This asshole would destroy this moment for her and be just as bad as Simon for stealing it away once again.

I looked away and turned back to my food. Suddenly my appetite was gone. I took a giant sip of wine instead, which instead of helping, burned as it went down, making my stomach turn.

That was it. I couldn't stand by and watch this happen.

Nerves spiking in my stomach, I stood up and walked over to the bar.

Eli saw me first. We'd never actually met before but I could tell he knew who I was, maybe from the park? Or the blog? If Reese had ever shown him.

If Will had ever shown him.

Will turned on his stool and nearly fell off.

"Michelle?"

Heat tore through me but I knew if I looked at Will, I wouldn't be able to do what I needed to do.

"You need to leave," I said to Eli.

"What?"

"Michelle," Will said, "what are you doing here? How—"

"Me," Eli said. "I invited Reese."

From the corner of my eye, I saw Will had his hand on his forehead, trying to make sense of what was happening. I hazarded a quick glance at him while he wasn't looking.

My chest seized. *Will.* Did I think I'd never see him again? Is that what I'd wanted?

But I had to stay focused. "Eli, I don't know what you were trying to do inviting her here, thank you—it's a lovely place, but--"

"I'm sorry," Eli said. "For hurting her. It was the only thing I knew how to do. I'm not in a position to be anything good for her."

"God *dammit,*" I said, incredulous. "Can you hear yourself?" Now I turned to Will. "Do you hear how that sounds?"

Will stared at me, his eyes so deep for a moment I couldn't speak.

No.

This wasn't about me and Will.

"Eli, you need to leave. If she sees you here, she's going to lose her confidence and I won't allow that."

"What's she—" he began, but the lights dimmed slightly, the music coming from the speakers going quiet.

Fuck.

I turned to see Reese walking across the stage. I could see the tension across her whole body, but just like we'd talked about, she stuck her chin out and walked right up to the mic.

She glanced over at our table, blinking as she saw it empty.

Fuck again.

"Hello," she said into the microphone. It gave a little feedback, but when she backed up, stopped. She laughed, nervously.

"Holy shit, is that—" Eli said.

"My sister," I flung at him in a whisper.

A spotlight flooded the stage and Reese squinted. But I let out a breath. She definitely wouldn't be able to see Eli now.

"Oh god, I hope that holds," Eli said.

I jerked my eyes toward him. "The electrical," he whispered. "It's a mess in here. The whole reno—"

"I don't care," I said. "You broke her heart."

Even in the dim light I could see him blanch.

"I'm going to sing a few songs for you," Reese said from the stage. She pulled the mic from the stand.

There was some scattered applause around the room. The clinking of dishes and conversations continued, though people had dropped their voices lower.

I could feel Will's eyes on me.

You broke her heart.

"Michelle," Will whispered.

I refused to look at him. I looked up at Reese instead, my whole body a live wire.

She opened her mouth and let out the first line of Adele's *Someone Like You*. It was just Reese, no background music or vocals, and it was breathtaking, the melancholy strains silencing the whole room.

Someone lowered the lighting further.

At that moment, in the room's stunned silence, with my sister's gorgeous voice singing about heartbreak, about love not lasting, and with tears streaming down my face, I dared to glance at Will.

He was looking at me. Only me. He stood up from the stool, stepping toward me. Eli craned his neck to see until Will was out of his way.

In the darkness, all I could hear was the song, the words —talking about how it wasn't over—as Will came to me.

When I took a breath it was him, that familiar scent. On my skin I felt heat radiating from him.

Will stood before me, the whole world in his eyes, and in the dark, he reached for my hands.

I was powerless to stop him. Heat and heartbreak, love and pain, all of it rose like a crescendo in my chest as he dipped his face down, his lips at my ear.

"I'm in love with you," he whispered.

The words echoed, falling through me like fluttering feathers. A sob stuck in my throat as he pulled back, his eyes on mine. He didn't care if I didn't say it back. He'd do whatever I wanted him to, I knew. He'd leave or he'd stay, he was a man in love. My heart ached, stung, and swelled as Reese hit the chorus.

And then the lights went out.

Reese's voice cut short.

"For fuck's sake!" Eli exclaimed.

A murmur shot through the crowd.

I pulled my hands away from Will's.

Then the lights came back on. Only it was the restaurant lights now, and Reese looked out onto the crowd, as stunned, scared, and silent as a rabbit.

"Reese," I said.

She couldn't have heard me, but she turned in our direction anyway; that's when she saw Eli, walking forward, looking straight at her.

She dropped the mic. Feedback screamed and Reese ran off the stage.

The lights flickered again. "What the hell is wrong with this place?" I exclaimed. I needed to go after her, but the lights were once again out.

"The contractor," Eli said. "It's been a disaster, we just fired them."

When the lights came on again, I looked at Will. He said nothing, and neither did I. Then I ran to find my sister.

∽

I RAN AWAY FROM WILL. Away from Eli.

When I hit the lobby, I stumbled. It was crowded with people, laughing, tittering over the excitement of the lights. Half of them held champagne flutes. New Year's seemed so meaningless right now. I pushed my way through them, praying Reese had run to our room. Then I froze.

Over by the window, by the waterfall, stood Joe. He was smiling at me, holding up a glass of champagne.

It's time, Michelle.

I blinked.

"I have to find Reese," I whispered. I ran, ignoring Joe. When I reached the corridor and looked back over my shoulder, he was gone.

It was only as I was smashing the button for the elevator, praying Reese had gone back to our room, that I saw I wasn't alone. Eli had followed me.

"Hey," he said.

"Go away."

"No."

Anger hit me then, anger I'd been storing up for a lifetime. "I said, go the fuck away! Get away from me; get away from my sister."

Eli held his hands up, but I saw anger of his own flaring in his face. "This is my hotel."

"Your family's." He did have a point. But I wasn't ready to hear it.

"Listen," he said. "Your sister—she's a good person."

"She's the best."

"I never meant to hurt her. We just—we just met at the wrong time. Everything is shit in my life right now. I'm in the middle of a divorce, my wife—my ex-wife fucking... cheated on me. I wanted to get her back I—"

"You're not helping your case," I said. The elevator dinged.

I stepped inside. Eli hesitated then stepped in after me. He stood next to me and we both folded our arms.

"I wasn't using her if that's what you think," he said. "I just can't be with anyone right now."

I turned to look at him as the elevator doors closed. He looked wrecked.

He cleared his throat. "I had to move here to look after everything—my mom passed and my dad is off his rocker and—we're all just trying to get this place back on its feet. My sister hates me, my brother's barely talking to me and... I just feel like shit."

Something inside of me softened, only slightly.

"You have to... Will told me you lost someone. So, you have to know what it's like to have your world fall apart?"

I was shocked. This man knew about me?

"Don't get mad at Will, he only told me because I made him. I was worried about him. He's even worse off than me. Anyway—"

The elevator dinged, the doors sliding open.

"I know it's not the same," he said, following me. "But

having my wife do that... I lost the person I loved most in the world. I still don't know how I feel. It's so complicated. You have to relate, right?"

I spun on my heel. We were alone in this hallway. I could knock this guy out if I wanted.

But he hung his head and suddenly and the anger went out of me. The man was in pain. Pain I recognized.

I knew exactly what complicated feelings were like. I knew what it was like to be furious with someone you used to love so much. Because that's what it was. It wasn't just that I was devastated we lost Joe. I was furious at him. He'd left. He'd run into that building, knowing the risks, not letting us say goodbye.

I thought of Will, down in the dark, whispering in my ear. His hand holding mine, the knowledge that, at that moment, he'd do anything for me.

"It'll get easier," I said.

Eli lifted his head. "What?"

"It will be easier with time. The feelings for your ex. But you have to say goodbye."

It was like a light had come on, a spotlight, pointing directly into my heart.

The elevator dinged behind us and I knew Reese was there.

I turned around. She shook her head when she saw Eli. "No."

"You should go," I said.

He stood there a moment, his face stricken with pain, then he nodded and walked toward Reese.

"341," he said to me, without stopping.

"What?"

"341. That's Will's room."

I didn't even have time to digest that. Eli stopped in front of Reese. "I'm sorry," he said. Then he kept going, catching the elevator doors.

I took Reese's hand and together we strode toward our room.

"You were incredible," I said.

"I ran."

I opened our door, holding it for her.

"Yeah, but first, you sang."

She stood in the doorway, blocking my way. "Hey," I said, confused.

"You're not coming in."

"What?"

"I saw him there."

Will.

"I'm not—"

"Yes, you are. I saw the way he was looking at you. I saw the way you looked at him. Michelle, you need to go to him. To tell him the truth."

"What's that?" I said, my heart thudding now.

"That you love him."

I stood there a moment, then I took a breath. "I can't leave you—"

"341," she said.

I took in a shaky breath, then it was my turn to run. I ran as fast as I could in the heels I'd put on. I wasn't used to them. I made it to the stairwell before taking them off. I flung them aside, running down the stairs in my bare feet.

I had to stop and look at one of the little directories—341 was in the third wing. I'd have to run through the lobby first.

Heart pounding, I raced as fast as I could. What if he was gone? What if he'd decided to drive off in the night? What if that was it?

The lobby had even more people milling about, if that

was possible. Everyone was laughing, the mood jovial. Once more, I had to slip through all the people, apologizing as I knocked into one and then another. Then, before I knew what was happening, I was standing in front of the waterfall.

So was Joe.

I told you, he said.

Told me what?

That it was time.

Time for what? I said, even though I knew. I knew exactly what he was talking about. He didn't answer, just smiled. His image flickered in front of me. Only this time, I didn't reach for him. I didn't pray he'd stay.

It was time to say goodbye.

I waved at him. "Goodbye, Joe," I said out loud.

What are you waiting for? He asked.

"For you to go first."

Stubborn. Then he smiled, lifting his hand up. *Goodbye Michelle.*

I laughed as my eyes blurred. Then he was gone and I knew exactly where I needed to be.

~

THE DOOR to room 341 said Presidential Suite in curly lettering. I pounded on it, but he wasn't there.

I'd missed him. He'd left—it was too late. I leaned my back against the door, sliding to the ground.

Then I heard the click. I looked up toward the sound. Will stood at the end of the hallway, staring at me. "Michelle," he said, voice choked.

I jumped up, and then I ran. I ran as fast as I could, laughing, sobbing, probably looking like a crazed woman.

Then I leaped into Will's arms.

"Michelle. God, Michelle," he said, his face buried in my neck. Then he pulled back and we kissed—the longest, deepest, most perfect kiss I'd ever known.

"I love you, Will. I love you with everything I have."

Somehow, we stumbled back to his room, crashing through the door of the presidential suite. For a moment I paused, holding Will away as I looked at the room, my mouth hanging open.

"Good lord," I said. The space was as big as my whole cottage. There was a whole living area with a fireplace, a giant freestanding tub behind a frosted glass partition, and on the other side, a massive bed loaded with plush pillows. And just like the lobby and restaurant below, one whole wall was windows looking out onto the valley.

Then Will was picking me up, walking me to the bed. He lowered me down onto it as if I weighed nothing.

"Seeing you tonight," Will said, "was nothing short of a miracle."

He kissed me, sending sparks flying through me, my skin tingling like I was lit up from the inside.

"I'm sorry I said that about your... about Joe," Will said.

"You were only half wrong," I said, rising up on one elbow. "I loved Joe. He was my husband, the father of my children, and he was taken from me too soon. But because I was through the worst of my grief, I thought I could move on. When it didn't work out with Steve, even though I wouldn't admit it to myself, I thought it was because no one could ever fill Joe's shoes. But it wasn't about that. The thing is, no one has to fill his shoes."

I looked down at Will's nice loafers hanging off the end of the bed.

"You have your own shoes to fill."

Will smiled, reaching a hand up and running his thumb over my temple.

"What if I hurt you, Michelle?"

"I'm not going to get confused, Will. I don't expect you to be perfect."

"What if I'm exactly like my father?"

"Maybe he's not as bad as you think he is."

Will's eyes flashed with something like pain. "I was cruel to him, the last time I saw him."

"Then you'd better sort things out before it's too late."

He nodded. "You're smart, Michelle. You don't give up until you figure things out."

"Some might call it stubborn."

"That too," he said, grinning. His eyes twinkled. "Thank you for not giving up on me."

I bent down and kissed him, and suddenly, everything else disappeared. All that mattered was us, here, together.

Will put his hands on my waist and turned onto his back, taking me with him so I landed on top of him, laughing.

"You're going to kill me, in this dress."

"How about out of it?"

His pupils dilated before me. "Even better." Then his eyes went to the massive jacuzzi tub in the corner of the room. "How about over there?

Ten minutes later we were sitting together, immersed up to our necks in bubbly water. I leaned back against Will's body, every part of him hard. Then I angled myself next to him–there was enough room in the giant tub–and reached down, idly stroking his chest, slipping my hands down beneath the foam.

"Remember that night in the coffee shop?" I said. "Where that couch threw me onto you"

"I couldn't stop fantasizing about it afterward," he said, reaching his hand up and drawing his dripping fingers along my temple, down my neck.

A shiver of pleasure ran through me.

"I kept imagining you getting up onto me in the dark, with everyone all around us."

"Like this?" I asked, swinging myself over him with a splash.

He tipped his head back, groaning as my hand reached down between us, gripping his cock. It was like a rock under my fingers.

"What about this giant window?" I asked.

"Unfortunately, it's got some kind of fancy thing in it so people can't see inside."

I laughed. "One-way glass?"

"Fancier."

"In that case..."

I lifted myself out of the water. Will groaned as he took in the soapy water sliding off my body.

I backed up to the other end of the tub, which had a wide enough rim that I could sit on its side comfortably. Then I opened my legs for him, sliding my hands over my soapy breasts and thighs.

"Fuck, Michelle," he said, pouncing like an animal. Water sloshed over the side of the tub. "You're breathtaking," he said. Then his tongue hit my clit.

I gasped, gripping the edge of the tub, crying out as he dipped his fingers inside of me. I had no words except his name as he worked his tongue on my clit in a rhythm with his fingers inside me. He played with me, bringing me close and then slowing down again. Soon I was nearly thrashing as Will finally brought me all the way, sending waves of pleasure coursing through me so fast I cried out, my voice echoing through the room, water cresting the edge of the tub.

When Will stood, his cock was at attention. I reached for it but he shook his head, instead stepping out of the tub and grabbing two fluffy towels from the rack. He reached for something else, too, from his satchel on the counter.

With both of us wrapped up, he led me into the living room where he flicked on the gas fireplace. Outside, snow glistened beneath the moonlight, but in here it was warm enough that I dropped my towel, once again presenting myself to him. I couldn't stop—the way his eyes went dark with desire when he looked at me sent my body to the brink, before he even touched me.

"You are the most beautiful woman I've ever known, Michelle Franco."

There was an oversized padded ottoman in the middle of the room, and I knelt on it, feeling it steady under me. My back was to him, so I was looking out the window, Will behind me. I got down on my hands, tilting my ass up, making my message clear.

"You want it like this?" he asked, his voice husky.

"Right now."

I heard the crinkle of a wrapper and then Will was behind me once more. We were reflected perfectly in the window, and faintly beyond I could see the whole world.

I was at just the right height for him to tease my opening with the tip of his cock. Then he gripped my hips and guided himself inside me, filling me with excruciating slowness.

"God, yes," I breathed, seeing stars.

He withdrew, at the same speed, all the way to the tip.

"Please, Will," I said. "Give me everything. All of it."

"I'm all yours," he whispered. Then he thrust himself into me, making me gasp as my ass met his body, his full length inside me.

Will lowered himself back onto his knees, taking me with him so I was upright, his cock still deep inside me. I watched in the reflection as one hand went up to my tits, pinching my nipple while the other hand slid down to my clit. Then he thrust with his hips, bouncing me on his cock.

"I love you, Michelle. I fucking love you."

"I love you, too," I whispered. "Will Archer."

I fell then, into Will's arms, as pleasure rocking me hard against him.

Later in bed, we lay curled next to each other in a nest of feather pillows. Will was behind me, his hand resting on my hip, stroking my thigh.

"I'm going to shut down the blog," I told him.

For a moment, Will didn't say anything, just paused in his hands' idle movement up my leg.

"Is that what you want? I didn't pressure you into it?"

"No," I said. "You knew what I couldn't admit to myself. That I was holding onto it for the wrong reasons. I know now that that's why I couldn't get it to work–at least not without pandering to the things I didn't want to do. The blog was a part of my past—not my future. I'll always love it and be grateful for how it shaped my life, but it's time for a new chapter."

I think Will knew I was talking about Joe, too. That I'd finally said goodbye.

He flattened his palm against my stomach, pulling me closer against him. "I'm here," he said. "For all of you."

We talked then about everything—everything we'd

wanted to say to each other but held back on, everything we hoped for the future. It was liberating, sharing these words with Will, and by the time the fireworks went off outside I knew, this was the man I would love for the rest of my life.

Right here, right now, forever.

21

WILL

I was awoken by the scent of vanilla and caramel. I inhaled deeper, nuzzling my face in Michelle's neck, my heart swelling.

It was so big, so full, that for the briefest moment, I edged into panic.

My instincts, which I was learning were not to be trusted when it came to this topic, were to stiffen up and hide. To retreat into myself.

But Michelle had made me step past those old barriers. Last night I'd opened my heart to her—my everything. I'd told her all about my fear, that I was destined to be just like my father, and she'd told me not just that I wouldn't, but when shit came up, that she'd be here to help me through it.

I thought I didn't deserve her, but the truth was, I would fight to make sure I did.

I rolled onto my back so as not to wake her, my hand going to my cock. Shit. I don't think I'd sustained a hard on for this long in a decade. Maybe more. Maybe never.

Then my phone buzzed. It was coming from the floor. I vaguely remembered knocking it off the bedside table in a particularly rambunctious spate of fucking. The memory made my cock twitch once more.

"Down boy," I whispered, as I peered over the bed to see who it was. Stella's name flashed on the screen. My sister never failed to call at completely inopportune moments. I tossed the phone back on the carpet. She could wait.

I rolled back next to Michelle. A glance at the clock told me it was seven in the morning. Outside the winter sun was only just rising, golden light coalescing on the other side of the valley,

Michelle stirred, stretching an arm over her head, revealing the delicious curve of the top of her breast.

She blinked.

"How are you awake already?" she murmured.

"It's late," I said.

Michelle turned to the window, scrunching her face at me. "The sun isn't even up."

"It's after seven! I'm usually out the door by this time."

She groaned and threw a pillow at my head. "Not me. I work from home."

I laughed, dodging it.

Then her smile faded. "What if I can't find another job?"

"You'll just have to make your own."

She laughed. "You make it sound so easy."

"It will be," I said. "And if it's hard, I'll be right by your side." It was a mirror of what she'd said about my feelings around my dad last night. She knew I meant it.

She kissed me, winding her arms around my neck. "Now, what are you going to do to me?" she asked, her smile taunting me.

My cock stirred against her in response. Her eyebrow went up. "That all you got?"

"I've got more." I bent my head down and nudged the sheet aside so she was exposed from the waist up.

Michelle gasped. When I took her nipple in my mouth she gasped more while arching her back. I swirled my tongue around, bringing her to a hard point.

"That's better," I said, doing the same to the other. Meanwhile my cock, slick at the tip, slid across her leg.

"How are you ready again?" she asked between breaths.

Last night we'd made love and slept and made love again in a cycle where I'm not sure which one happened more.

"It's a new day," I said. "Hell, it's a new year."

"Happy New Year," Michelle said.

"Happy New Year, my love," I said, coming back up to kiss her.

We spent the early hours of the morning like this, exploring each other's bodies, me ignoring my phone after the first time when I checked to make sure it wasn't important—it had just been Stella, who had a tendency to call me first thing in the morning. She could definitely wait.

Eventually, Michelle pushed away from me, her face holding all the regret I felt.

"I need to go check on Reese," Michelle said. I could hear the guilt in her voice. "And call home to check on the girls."

"Me too," I said, though my kids were probably basking poolside, not having any use for their dad until they flew into Newark in a few days. "Eli's promised to squeeze me in for a lunch meeting with him and his sister too, even though it's a holiday."

I still couldn't get over seeing Eli here, though of course that's why Michelle was here too. I'd been flabbergasted when I ran into Eli in the lobby yesterday afternoon.

"*This* is the hotel your parents own?"

The coincidence was too strange until I found out it wasn't one—Eli had done lots of work for Charles Haverford back in Barkley Falls, and it was he who'd first piqued Charles' interest in the property, who in turn had gotten Fred interested.

"He's actually here right now," Eli said of Charles. "Though my sister is pissed I suggested we might be up for selling the place."

"Shit, half of Jewel Lakes seems to be here," I'd said, only half-joking. Next I'd find out Stella was downstairs. Though of course, she lived in Michigan now. I always forgot.

I'd also forgotten, until just this moment, about the drunken pact I'd made with Eli. To never get involved in a relationship again. I would have laughed, instead, I just felt sorry for him. And for the guy I'd been back in that bar when we'd made it.

Now, when Michelle and I finally said goodbye, it was with as much angst as if we didn't live in the same small town.

"Will," she said, between kisses, "I need to stay with Reese tonight."

"I understand," I said. I did, even though the thought was awful, having her so close but so far away.

It wasn't until she'd left and I'd taken a shower that I finally checked my phone, aware I'd ignored my own sister. But my heart nearly stopped when I saw there wasn't just one missed call from Stella.

There were five.

Plus a series of texts.

STELLA: CALL ME.

STELLA: Will what the hell, please call.

STELLA: Dad's in the ICU.

All Your Fault

∽

"It's watch and wait at this point," Dr. Ruiz said, pushing her glasses back up her nose.

The doctor was an older woman who looked like she'd be mom's age if she were still alive. Close to retirement. She had her pen up against the lightbox, pointing at an x-ray of Dad's lungs. It was two days after we'd first learned Dad's home had found him close to unconsciousness, his lips blue from lack of oxygen.

"Pneumonia this developed can, unfortunately, be quite dangerous anytime in a man your father's age. But with his comorbidities..."

The respiratory problems from his childhood. The smoke inhalation from when he lost his family.

Hank, Stella, and I looked at each other from behind our masks. They'd made us suit up to come in here and advised us that the fewer people who came in here the better, so our respective partners were waiting downstairs in the cafeteria.

Dad lay on the bed, a tube under his nose, a respirator helping him breathe. While he'd barely been conscious when they brought him in, now he was fully out, deep in a medically induced coma.

"If his counts are looking good in a few days we'll try giving him a chance to breathe on his own, see how that goes," the doctor said.

"That's a good thing, right?" asked Hank.

"If he can do it, yes. If he can't, he'll go back on the respirator."

She looked between the three of us.

"Now this is something I always ask—is there anything, any favored object or item your father might like to see in the event he wakes up and none of you are here?"

"We'll be here around the clock," Stella said.

"I'm afraid you can't sleep in his room," the doctor said.

Stella looked ready to fight, but I laid a hand on her arm.

"That's probably a good idea, just in case," Hank said.

"What kind of thing would Dad want?" I asked. "A carburetor?"

Stella, still looking incensed that she couldn't sleep on the linoleum, let out a laugh. Even Hank smiled. I think; I couldn't see it behind the mask.

Stella was crying, and I could tell Hank was trying not to.

Me, I was the hardened asshole who wasn't. It wasn't like I was feeling anything good or bad. I was just... numb. And what I wanted was to be far away from here. I wanted to be with Michelle and our girls. Never mind that mine were still in Florida for two more days.

God, I'd have to tell the girls.

"I'll look around his place," I said.

My siblings looked at me, not arguing. I could tell they were grateful. They'd needed their big brother to take charge.

But I needed to as well. Taking care of shit was the only useful thing I could think of to do right now.

∽

"You okay?" Michelle asked as she handed me a cup of coffee from the hospital cafeteria. I took a sip, then nearly spat it straight back out again.

"I was, before this coffee."

Michelle turned to me as we walked to the car after saying somber goodbyes to everyone. "You want to talk about it?"

I grasped her hand with my free one. "Not yet. But I will."

She nodded. We'd given our significant others an update when we'd gone back to meet them in the cafeteria. But none of us had gotten into anything more than technical details. I think we were all still in shock, processing what was happening in our own ways. I'd caught Hank looking at me with something like sorrow. He'd made his amends with Dad last year, after him and Casey had gotten back together. "It's not too late to tell him how you feel," he'd said to me while the others talked about the roads.

He was right. Even if Dad couldn't hear me, I could tell him how I felt—that I might still be holding onto anger, but I wanted him to live. I wanted us to at least try to exist together without losing our shit on one another. I'd come back tonight, I vowed to myself, on the way to the city to pick up the girls, who were flying in late from Florida.

"We might as well go to the care home now, seeing as we're here," I said to Michelle now. This part I wanted to get over with. I knew Dad's room was going to be depressing as hell. I'd never actually been inside it, not since he moved in. The few times I'd visited him we'd been in the common area.

Despite the dreary, gray day and depressing as shit hospital parking lot, my chest swelled when I thought of how lucky I was to have Michelle with me right now.

"I'm just going to check in on Emma and Macy," she said when we got to the car.

She sent off a few texts, smiling and showing me the text her Mom sent—a photo of her and her dad with Emma and Macy building a fort in the backyard.

"You know, Hannah's the queen of fort-making."
"Really?"

"Yeah. I think it's why she's an engineering student now. Your girls are going to love building them with her." I considered. "I hope. Remy couldn't stand building forts with her. She used to say, 'who measures their snow blocks?'"

Michelle laughed, and a glow poked through the gray. I'd never tire of hearing that, even on the hardest days.

∼

JUST AS I SUSPECTED, while the care home itself had done its best to put on a cheery visage, with a big HAPPY NEW YEAR banner strung across the front desk and balloons pinned to the chairs in the dining area, the hallway leading to dad's room was a grim, too-bright-with-fluorescent lights space.

Then the orderly opened the door to Dad's room.

"Oh god," I said. It was the first time I felt anything besides blank nothing at the situation with Dad. Ironic, because the room was a whole lot of nothing. Nothing on the walls, not even any hospital-issue landscapes. Not even a damned calendar. The only things that indicated someone lived in the bachelor suite were Dad's coffee maker, the same yellowed plastic machine he used to keep at the garage, and a model car kit half opened on the table.

I turned away from that, not liking the strange feeling it stirred in my chest.

"Maybe there's some piece of clothing or thing in the closet?" Michelle said, her voice imbued with false cheeriness. I appreciated the effort.

I nodded, the numbness spreading now.

"How about I look?" she said.

I nodded again. "Thanks," I said, moving to the window.

It was a beautiful day, the snow crisp and white, the sky sparkling sapphire.

Too nice for what was happening here.

I peered down at the pond Hank said Dad liked to feed the ducks at. I'd fought for this room—they hadn't wanted to give it to him, saying because of his respiratory issues they wanted him in a completely depressing room next to the nurse's station that had a view out to the side of the parking garage next door.

Hell, maybe dad would have liked that. He'd get to look at cars, and maybe the nurses would have noticed his cough going on longer than it should have.

Maybe this was my fault.

I was about to leave the window to join Michelle at the closet, where she was on her tiptoes pulling things off the top shelf, when I caught a glimpse of green.

It was Millerville Central Park, I realized. I didn't know Dad could see it from his room. Maybe, in some split second, Michelle and I had been visible to him that day.

I squinted. No, it was the wrong end of the park. It was where Eli had sat on that bench, taking the call from his sister.

Life felt, at that moment, like a series of serendipitous moments. What if I hadn't gone with Hank to see his best friend's widow that day? What if I hadn't met with Eli at the park during my break? What if I hadn't agreed to go on that work trip to Rolling Hills?

I almost had to laugh at that one. In the lobby, waiting for Michelle on the way out of the resort, I'd run into Charles Haverford. He'd been so surprised to see me—and I didn't want to dump my personal business on him—I'd pasted on a smile. I told him I was there at Fred's behest.

"I'm sorry I have to head out," I told him, "Family business. Maybe we can have a chat about the..." I couldn't remember the name of the proposed resort that had been mentioned on the files Sheila had stacked on my desk. "The version of this you're hoping to develop in Jewel Lakes when we're both back in town?" I waved my hand at the lobby generally.

Charles had given me a strange look.

Something ticked in my brain. An awareness—that strange feeling I'd had when Fred had asked me to take a look at the resort. "You're not building a resort in Jewel Lakes, are you?" I said.

"No..." Charles had said. "I'm here to make an offer on this resort. Between you and me, the organizational structure here has gone completely mushroom-shaped. Did you notice there's no one actually doing the renos?"

"Yeah, they were fired," I said, my mind still reeling over the implications of what Charles said.

His eyebrows, dark black slashes compared to the full silver of his hair, went up. "Is that right?"

Shit, I probably wasn't supposed to say that. Eli hadn't exactly told us to keep it under wraps last night but... we were all a little preoccupied.

"Fred's not going to like that," he said.

"Why's that?"

"It's his company doing the renos!" Charles said, sounding surprised I didn't know.

Consolidated Holdings. The same company proposing the development in Jewel Lakes.

What was Fred doing? Getting town approvals on a project while an elected official—mayor of said town, was not just a conflict of interest, it was illegal. It violated several statutory acts in the town's charter, and even if it wasn't, it was unethical as hell.

Heat rose up my throat. He was getting me involved, unwittingly, not just because he hoped I might make the approvals if I were elected, but because he wanted to implicate me in his scheme.

That way I'd be forced to push the project through.

"So, you were never intending to purchase property to do a development like this?" I asked, wanting to make sure I was crystal clear. This was something I couldn't accuse Fred of lightly. This would impact his seat in office, and that would just be the beginning of it.

"Oh, I certainly thought about it. When Eli told me about his folks' place a couple of years ago, I thought it sounded great. Don't you?"

"In theory."

"Right. But I couldn't figure out a place to put it. With the golf course and all. Anyhow, I kind of put the idea on the back burner, and now, with this place being all gone to hell with Eli's mom—the matriarch—having just passed, well, maybe it's time to diversify, you know? Start expanding out of state."

As I peered out my dad's window now, I tried to muster that same anger I'd felt standing there talking to Charles for Fred. Back at the resort, the only thing that had stopped me from throwing Fred under the bus right there was wanting to make sure I had my facts straight. I knew I had to get back to the office to know for certain, but I was pretty confident that there'd be an election a lot sooner than Fred anticipated.

But now, even though it wasn't, it felt insignificant. I was on the brink of losing my dad, and all I had to show for our relationship was the burning coals of resentment. All the anger I'd felt at Fred funneled into the bigger, roaring fury that burned inside of me over my dad.

He was going to die, and I'd never get to say my piece with him.

I'd never get to forgive him, either. Or myself, for keeping it going so long.

The last words I'd said to him were cruel. Thoughtless.

I was his kid, alright. Maybe I was able to move past the fear of falling in love again, but I wasn't sure I'd ever be able to shake that feeling.

"Will?"

Michelle's voice, the sweetest sound in the world, cut through the thundercloud of my thoughts like a rainbow.

At some point she'd finished with the closet, and had tried the space under Dad's bed. She'd pulled out a shoebox and was kneeling before it.

"Let me guess," I said, "more model cars. No—car parts."

"Just come and see," she said softly. The box was the kind where the lid folded open, and it was up, so I couldn't see what was inside.

She stood up and placed it on his neatly made bed.

I went over to the box. Inside were stacks of paper—it looked like a mix of newsprint and printouts, with some objects I couldn't really see stuffed in around the edges.

I picked up the paper on top. My heart felt like it had stopped beating. For a moment, I heard nothing but the sound of my own breathing.

It was a newspaper clipping from the local paper we used to have that had switched to online only a few years back. The date was twenty-two years ago, while I was still in high school. *CAPTAIN WILLIAM ARCHER LEADS JEWEL LAKES TIGERS TO VICTORY.*

"I don't—" I said, laying it down and picking up the next. It was a photo of me in the kitchen at home, holding up a medal. "Debate club," I said. I reached into the box. The medal in the photo was tucked in there along with stacks of ribbons from what looked like all the races of any kind I'd ever won. There were letters in there from summer camp, notes from teachers on things I'd accomplished. A record of everything I ever went to.

"Did your mom save this stuff?" Michelle asked.

I shook my head. "No. She made these big scrapbooks for each of us. I have mine at home. This is..."

This was all Dad.

The knot in my throat swelled, growing so thick and prickled over I couldn't breathe.

I lowered myself onto the side of the bed, and for the first time since I heard my dad was in a coma—hell, for the first time I could remember in adulthood—I put my head in my hands and sobbed while Michelle sat beside me, her hand in mine.

~

Later, as we walked out of the care home, Michelle suggested we take a walk. Somehow, it was still early afternoon—plenty of time before I had to start the drive out to New Jersey to pick up the girls at the airport. I'd missed them so much I was actually looking forward to the long, boring stretch of highway that would take me there.

The end of it anyway.

Michelle sent another text off as we stepped out into the cold, then tucked her phone in her pocket.

"You're not working on the blog, are you?" I asked as I buttoned up my coat. I was teasing her by habit. But I was too vulnerable; too raw from what I'd just learned to put much fuel into it.

I was still reeling with the new truth that my father had

followed every one of my accomplishments. Hank's and Stella's too—there'd been a box for each of us. When we thought our medals and pins had been thrown away, he'd been tucking them away in those boxes. Clipping and printing out news stories when the news was long forgotten.

All the things I thought he'd despised about me, all the ambitions I'd buried long ago—he'd cared. He'd been proud.

"I still have to write my goodbye post. But no, I'm not." Her breath plumed around her in the cold.

"You don't have to quit the blog, you know."

"Yes, I do. That chapter's over."

I squeezed her against me, swallowing hard as we rounded the corner. We'd ended up in front of Millerville Central Park. I looked back in the direction we'd come—there was Dad's building. And there—I counted windows—I thought was his room. When I turned back, I sucked in a breath. Hannah and Remy were standing before me, holding hands with Emma and Macy.

My heart really did feel like bursting. I couldn't help it, those damn tears came back.

"Dad," the girls said, both of their eyes filled with concern. "We're sorry about Grandpa," Hannah said.

I hugged my girls against me, squeezing them so hard Remy made a sound. From the corner of my eye, I saw Emma and Macy run to their mother.

"Thank you for cutting your vacation short," I said.

"It got cloudy anyway," said Remy.

Hannah shot her a look. "Actually, we missed you."

"She also missed her boyfriend."

"Remy!" Hannah said through gritted teeth.

"And I broke up with Draco," Remy said.

"So, when are you getting back together?" I joked.

"I'm not, Dad," Remy said. "I thought about what you said, how I was only with him because I didn't know any different. You were right. So I ended it for good. I told him I was giving him back all his crap. So, I'm going to need a ride to his house to do that. It'll go better with you there."

I pulled her in tight. For a moment I was so shocked I didn't speak. It was music to my ears. I hadn't realized how worried I'd been about Remy. How sure she was going to repeat my mistakes. But we didn't always have to follow in our parents' footsteps, did we?

When I finally let them go, Remy said, "I can't wait to start playing the field. There's a whole world of people out there."

I grimaced. "What have I done?"

Both girls laughed.

"Was Mom upset you left early?" I asked.

"No," Hannah said. "She understood. She also said she was sorry about Grandpa."

She'd sent me a text, saying the same thing. "She's a good mom," I said, meaning it.

"Except she and Gareth were being gross," Remy said.

I laughed, but then quickly shook my head. "I'm glad your mom's happy. She deserves it."

Michelle's girls had been hanging out with her, waiting, and once Hannah and Remy stepped aside, Macy came flying at me. I bent down so she could give me a giant hug. Emma gave me a soft handshake. "I'm sorry about your Daddy," she said. "I hope he gets better and you get to spend a long time with him. But if he doesn't, you can be okay, too."

My heart twisted at her profound words. "Thank you, Emma. You're really smart."

"I know," she said.

I bit my cheek so I wouldn't laugh. Or to stop the damn tears, I couldn't tell which.

Macy ran to the older girls, taking their hands and tugging them along with her. She yelled over her shoulder at her sister. "Come on, Emma! Let's play!"

Emma turned on her heel, and the four of them ran off.

I scanned the park, searching for Michelle. I spotted her, walking a line through the snow to the giant maple in the center of the park.

The same tree she'd been standing under when I first saw her again. Now the tree was bare, its limbs waving against the crisp blue sky, leaves long dead. But Michelle was here. She was alive and vibrant, as beautiful as the day.

I followed her footsteps, tracing the path she'd made, until I ended up in front of her, looking down on her perfect face, my hand brushing her curls from her cheek.

"Thank you," I said.

"It was nice," she said. "Easy. The girls were ready to come back as soon as they heard."

"What about you?" I said. "Would you come back to me if I needed you? Even if I pushed you away?"

"I wouldn't have to," she said, "because I'd already be here at your side. I'm not leaving Will. I'm here to stay."

"I love you," I managed to croak.

Then I kissed her, long and deep, her face in my hands and our hearts entwined.

After, I pulled her close and we turned around to look for our girls, finding them on the swings together, flying high.

EPILOGUE
MICHELLE

The moment Will and I stepped through the heavy wood door of Gastronomique's main entrance, I was hit with the warm, rich scent of French cooking, along with soft classical music streaming from small black speakers tucked subtly in the corners of each room.

"This is *perfect*," I said, reaching up and kissing him on the cheek. We both had news to share with each other and had decided to make a date out of it, with Remy watching the girls at my place.

We'd talked so much I was pretty sure we each knew what our respective news was, but it was nice to have the atmosphere and ceremony to do it in anyway.

Will gave me his dazzling grin. A shockwave of desire ran through me. It was like a magic button. God, I couldn't even look at the man without wanting to jump him. Luckily, we got the chance most nights, so long as the little ones were in bed.

"I can't believe I've never brought you here before," Will said as we hung up our coats.

"I can't believe I've never *been* here before." Somehow,

even with Will's and my appreciation for good food, not to mention my own sister working here, I'd never stepped foot through the restaurant's doors.

Now, I was mad at myself for missing out. The place was gorgeous.

Gastronomique had been converted from a giant old country manor perched at the top of a hill, with views to Amethyst Lake. If my own cottage were closer to the water, I might even have been able to see it from my window. From the foyer waiting area, I could see the tables were split into three rooms—each with only peekaboo views into the others. With the soft music, low lights, the soft clink of cutlery and murmur of conversation divided into smaller rooms, it felt cozy, even though Reese told me it seated around a hundred and fifty people.

As we hung up our coats on the row of hooks in the entryway, my chest bloomed with happiness at being here. Not just because the food was definitely going to be incredible, or that I'd get to see Reese, but because Will and I'd both had a busy February. Mine was a purposefully relaxed kind of busy, with seeing a career coach and taking care of all the things I'd never found time to do while running Bella Eats, like volunteering on a bunch of activities with the girls at their school.

Will's was much more packed. He'd been helping his dad with his rehab since he'd been discharged from his extended stay at the hospital.

He'd spent the whole day at the hospital the day they took his father off the ventilator. "I needed to be there when he woke up," Will told me later that night. "To tell him I was sorry."

"Why were you sorry?" I'd asked him.

"For holding onto my anger for so long. For my last

words to him being so cruel. He fucked up, but he also wanted the best for me, just like Mom used to try to tell me. Me being angry was trying to keep myself safe. But it was only hurting me, and everyone around me."

My heart had squeezed for him, this man I loved, at finally seeing past his anger and hurt. Just like how I'd seen past my stubborn need to hang onto the blog, conflating it with loyalty to Joe. But while I thought losing the blog would hurt the way losing Joe had, it had been cathartic. Will had helped me see that.

Will and his dad hadn't officially talked things out as far as I knew. Maybe his father would never figure out how to apologize for how things had gone when Will was a boy, but Will showing up for every appointment—and being with his Dad without anger—that might be reconciliation enough for now.

Besides spending time with his dad and being a dad himself, Will was also running Town Hall without a mayor at the helm, now that Fred had stepped down. He'd come home late every night this week, exhausted but happy. I knew that even if this was how our life would be forever, we'd make it work.

Though I suspected it wouldn't be. One of the reasons we'd managed to get out on a date was because we'd both discovered we had news to share. I suspected his was likely to do with his job.

I knew Will was skipping a Council meeting to be here tonight, and I rose up on my tiptoes to kiss him. "Thank you," I said. I was talking about the restaurant date, but I meant everything else too.

"Thank *you*," Will said, pulling me into his arms.

Reese appeared just as the kiss was getting a little not-restaurant-appropriate. "Ew!" she said.

We jumped apart sheepishly. "Sorry," Will said.

"I'm not," I said.

Reese elbowed me. "Come on, I can't wait to show you your seat."

She was smiling, clearly happy to see us, but maybe as only sisters can, I could see the strain on her face.

"You okay?" I asked as she led us through the doorway to one of the smaller rooms.

She glanced around, then leaned in. "No, actually. I'm at the end of my fucking rope. We've had three of our best servers quit in the past week, and now, our owner is here tonight, micromanaging everything. I swear to god, I'm this close to taking off myself, backup plan be damned. In fact, if you guys hadn't made a reservation, I probably would have."

"I'm sorry!" I said. "Guess I shouldn't have waited so long to make one."

Reese gave a wry laugh. "It's my own fault for waiting until it got this bad. Anyway, how's this?"

The table she'd led us to was right next to a gorgeous lead-paned window. Outside, stars twinkled over an expansive view of the lake, reflecting like diamonds on the water below.

"It's the best seat in the house," Will said.

"Damn right it is," came a voice from behind me. I turned to see a handsome silver-haired man in his fifties, wearing a suit that rivaled only Will's. He was sitting with a petite woman of about his age, maybe a little younger but who looked like someone I'd see in a New York lifestyle magazine, with her razor-sharp gray bob, Wednesday Addams-style high collared dress and wine-colored lipstick.

"Charles," Will said, shaking his hand.

It was the man I'd seen up in the window that day with Will, a lifetime ago.

"This is Michelle Franco, the love of my life."

Reese snorted with laughter, quickly covering her mouth.

"You really did that," I said to Will, flushing.

Charles laughed heartily. "This is mine," he said, introducing the super-cool older woman as Sal.

"Hi," she said, winking at me. Somehow I felt starstruck.

"Those two are couple goals," Reese whispered as she lay our menus on the table.

"Seriously," I said as she slipped away.

"So," Charles said as we sat down. I angled myself sideways for a moment so as not to have my back to them. "Are the rumors true?"

His eyes were on Will.

"Which ones," Will asked, hedging.

Charles leaned in. "Fred's retirement. I heard it wasn't voluntary."

Will put his hands up. "No comment."

"Well, you know I've always said I'd never back any candidate in a mayoral race. I like to keep business and politics separate, though of course, Sal says that's impossible."

Behind him, Sal murmured "mm-hmm" and took a sip of wine.

"But say if a real community-oriented player decided to run whenever the election's called—well, I might just change my tune."

Charles was a big player across Jewel Lakes, I knew. Will had even told me he'd tried buying the Rolling Hills resort up in Vermont, though he hadn't been able to secure the sale. His endorsement would be huge.

Not that Will had made any decisions around that—he was still working as town manager, holding the whole city together while Council floundered on making decisions about legal action. He'd told me they were still reeling, two months later, from the news of Fred's underhanded dealings.

"Isn't Will supposed to remain a neutral party, as an employee of the town?" I said.

"Right you are," Charles said. "Let's just say I'm telling you, for future reference. In case you know anyone."

"Thanks," I said. "I'll keep that in mind."

"You need to let these two get to their romantic meal," Sal said.

Charles grinned. "Right, I'll leave you to it." He was about to turn when he perked up and said, "Oh, Will, you were right about this place."

"Oh yeah?" he said, with a quick glance at me.

Charles lowered his voice. "This place looks good on the outside, but it's falling apart. The books are a mess. I put in an inquiry with the owner's wife, and it looks like they'd be willing to sell—quick, too."

"Would you be looking at redevelopment?" Will asked.

"I quite like this place as a restaurant, don't you?"

"Yes," I said, though he wasn't talking to me. "It's the property's best use, and the community needs a higher-end place for those special occasions, and to snag the New York tourist crowd. If it were better managed."

"You know about restaurants, do you?"

A twinge of embarrassment hit me for speaking up, but I nodded. "I worked in them for years."

"She's also the person behind Bella Eats," Will piped up.

Sal, who'd been sipping at her wine, lowered it to the table. "I adore that blog! I've been following it for years. I was so sad to see you were ending it."

"Me too," I said. "Though it was time."

Sal's eyes went to Will and then back to me. "I understand," she said, her face capturing everything I'd been feeling. If she was a long-time reader, she knew my whole story. It was always strange when I met a reader in real life and they knew so much more about me, but this time, it didn't make me feel uncomfortable, it felt like maybe I'd done the right thing, both in sharing so much, and shutting it down the way I did, with a love story.

And Nonna's killer meatball recipe.

"Sal's been wanting to start a blog of her own," Charles said.

"I could definitely give you some pointers," I smiled at her.

"Well, let me know if you know any potential restaurateurs, too," Charles said, handing me a card.

When I turned back around a few minutes later, Will was grinning like a teenager. "Mich, can't you see it? Bella Eats—the restaurant."

My heart, soft from hearing about how my blog had touched someone, did a little skip-beat. For the first time, I could see it. Here, in this place, Nonna's recipes come to life for everyone to enjoy.

I thought of the last of the firefighter fund. Had I been saving it for this? It felt... right somehow. And I knew Joe would have approved.

Then the nerves hit. "I don't know, Will. The thing I keep getting hung up on is how to balance the huge, time-involved endeavor of starting up a restaurant with being around for my kids."

"Delegate," Will said. "It's my secret. People want to help you, Mich."

My heart warmed once more. He was right. If Will had taught me anything—on top of how to love again—it was that.

"What's this about a restaurant?" Reese said, setting a plate of still-steaming baguette and freshly churned butter on the table.

My mouth watered as I reached for a piece. "Will's trying to convince me to start a restaurant. Bella Eats, the live version."

"It's about time," she said, pouring us wine without asking. She knew it was my favorite, and she'd promised to have it ready when I'd made my reservation. "Hell, you can hire me."

"I thought you weren't going to work any more restaurant jobs?"

"For you, I'd make an exception. Just while you found your footing."

"You are the best in the biz," I said.

I knew she'd still been thinking about that offer at the Rolling Hills. She'd mentioned it, jokingly, a few times. I told her, in no uncertain terms, that she shouldn't stay here just for me. "That way we could visit the resort where Will and I confessed our feelings anytime we want," I'd said. The only reason she hadn't jumped on it was because of Eli, I knew. While it had been a fairytale ending for Will and me, Reese had left her encounter with Eli worse off than when it started. Even if I now knew Eli wasn't a horrific sociopath, I was still mad at him for what he'd done to her. Even if I did feel a little sorry for the guy and the mess his life was in.

After Reese left with our orders, Charles offered a cheers from the next table. "I'm getting more and more pumped about this place the more I think about it," he said to me in a conspiratorial whisper. "Sal says your specialty is Italian food—I can't think of a better cuisine to fit this space. And I'm a helluva landlord."

"Charles! Leave them alone!" Sal laughed.

After we'd turned back to our own tables, I leaned forward and reached for Will's thigh under the table.

"You know, seeing you and Charles together is like watching a battle of the silver foxes," I teased.

"Silver foxes?" Will said, overly loudly.

"Shh!" I said, stifling a laugh.

"Remy told me what those were. You think he's handsome, don't you."

"My god, Will, keep your voice down."

He frowned. Was he really agitated? Do I give it a rest? Or continue to play with him?

Since when have you not given everything your all?

"Charles *is* very attractive," I said, as if admitting the fact. Like I'd been admiring the wealthy businessman.

Will stabbed a scallop with slightly overdone violence. "I could take him," he said.

"What?"

He leaned forward and lowered his voice. "He's a small man."

"Maybe compared to you." Charles was very compact, it was true. "But he looks very fit."

Will scowled, looking down as if to inspect his own fitness. I was surprised he didn't flex right there at the table.

"I can't believe you're insulting his size," I whispered. "He's completely average height. Besides, I've known plenty of attractive men smaller than you."

Will gaped.

Yes, having fun with him was the right choice. I spread a pat of butter on another baguette slice. "Anyway I'd have thought you'd be more focused on his kajillion dollar suit."

Will harrumphed. "Yeah, size small."

I nearly choked on my bread.

Then, somewhere in the kitchen there was a loud crash,

followed by the sounds of someone yelling. It quickly quieted—I could just imagine what was going on in there. A moment later, a furious-looking man in a white chef's coat stormed through the dining area next to us into the foyer, followed by an even angrier looking man in a suit. The owner, I imagined. Reese ran out behind them, her face hard with anger.

The patrons murmured to each other and Charles waggled his brows at us. He was clearly here for this—the restaurant imploding would only help his potential offer.

All three of them came back through a few minutes later, none of them speaking but at least calmed down enough to continue working. Reese had probably been the only reason the chef stayed.

"What happened back there?" I asked Reese when she came by with our food shortly after. She looked flustered, her hair still windblown.

"The head chef walked out!" she said. "Our owner was breathing down his neck about how to cook the duck—completely outrageous given his twenty-year history as a blue-ribbon chef. I only managed to talk him into staying because half the tables haven't been served. He hates people going hungry. I'm just so—"

As if on cue, the owner appeared in the doorway.

Reese saw me looking and turned.

The man, red-faced, jerked his head toward the kitchen.

Reese took a calming breath. Then said, "I'm sorry if we're ruining your night."

"Not at all," Charles said, eavesdropping.

I could see Will restraining himself from rolling his eyes. He'd picked that up from Remy, or maybe Emma, I was sure. I would have laughed except for Reese's stress.

Reese stalked out.

With the drama apparently over, we dug into our food, talking about how everything could look if I ran my own place. "You could run a restaurant any way you want," Will said. "Be an arms-length advisor. Hell, get another person wanting part-time work to project manage the opening with you. A retiree, maybe?"

I thought of Mom with her charts and lists. How much she missed work.

"Actually, that brings me to my news," I said. "I finally convinced my parents to move!"

Will smiled, taking my hand. He knew how important it was for me to have them close. Then his eyes sparkled. "Does that mean you'll need to find a place for them to live? Like, say, a cottage on Amethyst Lake?"

Will had been trying to talk me into moving in with him since the moment we got back to Jewel Lakes after New Year's. It made sense, given we spent almost every night together anyway.

"Maybe," I said. It would actually be perfect—Dad had even talked about getting a dog, now that they were moving to the country. I could just see him walking a rambunctious puppy around the lake.

Reese had just brought us our tiramisu when I realized Will hadn't shared his news.

"Well," he said, as Reese was walking away, "I had a meeting this week with Barbara Chambers."

"The former mayor?" I said. I knew where this was going, but I played along.

"The very one. She and Pearl Bradley wanted to tell me that the Ladies Auxiliary—a surprisingly powerful lobby here in Jewel Lakes as you know—like Charles, are considering offering their endorsement to a candidate when the election is called. I said I'd need to talk it over with you, but I was thinking about—"

Will was interrupted by a crash. I looked toward where the sound had come from but couldn't see anything. I was reminded of the collision at the restaurant at Rolling Hills on New Years.

"I'm sure Reese will take care of it," I said, keen for Will to continue.

"Actually, I think Reese caused it," he said. From his position, he could see further into the room where the commotion was.

Reese came storming out to the foyer, followed by the angry man who'd been chasing the chef earlier. That had to be the owner.

"Don't even think about walking out!" the man said. He'd probably meant to keep his voice low, but it reverberated through the hushed restaurant.

"Listen to me," Reese said, spinning and shoving a finger in the man's chest. "I've had it up to here with you. Everyone has. Just because you're the only fine dining restaurant around for miles, doesn't mean you can treat us like garbage." Then she undid her apron and held it in front of the man's face.

"You can take this job"—she stepped forward, giving a quick scan of the restaurant, to make sure there were no kids around, I suddenly knew— "and shove it up your ass!" The man gasped, along with half the restaurant.

But she wasn't done. She tossed the apron in his face and added, "IF YOU CAN FIND ROOM NEXT TO THAT GIANT STICK!"

Then, while everyone's mouths still hung open, Reese strode over to our table, picked up my wine, and took a giant swig, letting out a satisfied "ah" when she was done.

Not knowing what else to do, I held my palm up. "High five?"

My sister grinned, slapping her hand against mine. "Love you," she said, before spinning on her heel and brushing past her stunned ex-boss.

"Good luck finding a job in this town again!" he spat after her.

"I'll hire her," Charles said smoothly. "In a heartbeat." He cupped his hand around his mouth. "SEND ME YOUR RESUME!"

The whole crowd gasped some more.

"I'll hire her too," I said, emboldened by my sister's act of bravery.

"Hell, me as well," Will chimed in. "I'll need people willing to stand up to bullies on my campaign."

"So it's true!" Charles said.

I grinned at Will, and now it was his turn to wink at me.

Outside, Reese's tires squealed as she drove off. The owner had disappeared somewhere and the restaurant came back to life with tittering voices.

"Brilliant!" Charles said, slapping a palm on his table. As Will took out his wallet Charles shook his head. "Oh no. Dinner's on me."

"I'm running a clean campaign," Will said.

But the older man shook his head a second time. "Don't worry son, I'm bribing your woman here, not you."

I laughed. "No promises."

He waved a hand. "Never. But still, don't forget to call!"

We strode out of the restaurant to shocked murmurs, but also a smattering of applause.

"You have something to tell me, Will Archer?" I asked as we strode out into the foyer.

"Just that I'm putting in my notice this week. As well as my official intention to run for Mayor of Barkley Falls."

"Why give a letter of resignation when you can dramatically storm out?" I said, laughing.

Will helped me into my coat. "Listen, I have teenage daughters, two hopefully-someday adopted school-age daughters, and a future sister-in-law who might just be a little unhinged. What I need is a rock."

My stomach jumped. "What did you say?"

He guided me to the door. "What part?"

"The part about adopted daughters and Reese being your future sister-in-law."

"Oh," Will said. "Just figures of speech."

My jaw fell open. "None that I've ever heard!"

Will pulled me into his arms. "Okay fine. How's this? You're my everything. My sun, my moon, my stars." He bent down, pressing his forehead to mine. "And someday, in the not so distant future, I want to marry you. If you'll have me."

Before I could speak, Will Archer kissed me, sending sparks cartwheeling through me.

"Better?" Will asked.

The man who didn't believe in marriage now talking about us being married? It was what I wanted too. I knew without a trace of doubt. Still, I couldn't let him see that right away. That would ruin the fun.

"Better," I said. "And I'll think about it."

Will laughed, his arm around my shoulder, and we stepped outside together, into the starry night.

∼

Thank you so much for reading All Your Fault! I hope you

loved Michelle and Will's story, and the conclusion to the Jewel Lakes Series.

But wait, it's not over yet!
Get a sneak peak into Will & Michelle's future, a catch-up with all your favorite Jewel Lakes Series characters, and some Bella Eats recipes too, in an exclusive bonus scene available only for my newsletter subscribers.
(Current subscribers: check the bottom of any newsletter for a link). If you're not yet a subscriber, sign up here:
clairewilder.com/extras

Up next: Level With Me
(An enemies-to-lovers romance and the first book in a new series set at the Rolling Hills resort!)
CASSANDRA
The consultant I hired to revive my family's falling-apart resort is the best in the business. He's also a cocky know-it-all I can't decide if I want to strangle or strip down for.
Roll into this all-new Rolling Hills romance now!
https://geni.us/levelwithme

Did you miss it? Jewel Lakes Holiday Special: Finding His Cheer (Standalone Holiday Novella)
After losing my wife, all I care about is raising my daughter and getting through the day in one piece. But when my neighbor comes knocking, suddenly her lights aren't the only thing I want to help turn back on.
Get the single dad romance that will have your Yule log burning any time of year!
clairewilder.com/findinghischeer

You can also read Stella and Dean's story in the standalone romance Speeding Hearts!
This full-length contemporary romance is part of the Blue Collar Romance Series—a multi-author shared world series. **Speed into love here: clairewilder.com/speedinghearts**

Just looking for a quickie? Check out my standalone novella Valentine Veto!
If I hadn't left her, Callie McIntyre wouldn't have ended up mayor of our hometown. She still hasn't forgiven me for breaking her heart. But if she vetoes my new project, she'll never know it was all for her.
Vote yes to this steamy second chance romance today! clairewilder.com/valentineveto

ABOUT THE AUTHOR

Claire Wilder first discovered romance books as a preteen: while staying with family friends, she uncovered a giant stash of old Harlequins languishing in a basement. A ho-hum trip suddenly wasn't long enough! While her tastes have expanded over the years, romance has always been her home. As an author, she writes for both the traditional and indie market. She lives with her husband and three kids on the west coast of Canada.

Claire loves hearing from readers. The easiest way to reach her is through her through her mailing list (clairewilder.com/subscribe).

Made in United States
Orlando, FL
25 May 2022